Secrets

D0610445

Enid Blyton

The Secret Mountain
The Secret of Killimooin

· PARRAGON ·

This edition published in 1995 for
Parragon Book Service Limited
Units 13–17 Avonbridge Industrial Estate
Atlantic Road
Avonmouth, Bristol BS11 9QD
by Diamond Books
77–85 Fulham Palace Road
Hammersmith, London W6 8JB

First edition published 1992 for Parragon
Book Service Limited

All rights reserved

Printed in England

Conditions of Sale
This book is sold subject to the condition
that it shall not, by way of trade or otherwise,
be lent, re-sold, hired out or otherwise circulated
without the publisher's prior consent in any form of
binding or cover other than that in which it is
published and without a similar condition
including this condition being imposed
on the subsequent purchaser.

The Secret Mountain

First published in a single volume in hardback in 1941 by
Basil Blackwell Ltd.
First published in paperback in 1965 in Armada

Copyright reserved Enid Blyton 1941

The author asserts the moral right to be identified as
the author of the work

The Beginning Of The Adventures

One bright sunny morning, very early, four children stood on the rough grass of a big airfield, watching two men busily checking the engines of a gleaming white aeroplane.

The children looked rather forlorn, for they had come to say good-bye to their father and mother, who were to fly themselves to Africa.

"It's fun having a famous father and mother who do all kinds of marvellous flying feats," said Mike. "But it's not such fun when they go away to far-off countries!"

"Well, they'll soon be back," said Nora, Mike's twin sister. "It will only be a week till we see them again."

"I somehow feel it will be longer than that," said Mike gloomily.

"Oh, don't say things like that!" said Peggy. "Make him stop, Jack!"

Jack laughed and slapped Mike on the shoulder. "Cheer up!" he said. "A week from today you'll be here again to welcome them back, and there will be cameramen and newspaper men crowding round to take your picture – son of the most famous air-pilots in the world!"

The children's father and mother came up, dressed in flying suits. They kissed and hugged the children.

"Now, don't worry about us," said their mother. "We shall soon be back. You will be able to follow our flight by reading what the newspapers say every day. We will have a fine party when we come home, and you shall all stay up till eleven o'clock!"

"Gracious!" said Jack. "We shall have to start going to bed early every night to get ready for such a late party!"

It was rather a feeble joke, but everyone was glad to laugh at it. One more hug all round and the two flyers climbed into the cockpit of their tiny aeroplane, whose engines were now roaring in a most business-like way.

Captain Arnold was to pilot the aeroplane for the first part of the flight. He waved to the children. They waved back. The aeroplane engines took on a deeper, stronger note, and the machine began to move gently over the grass, bumping a little as it went.

Then, like a bird rising, the wheels left the ground and the tiny white plane rose into the air. It circled round twice, rose high, and then sped off south with a drone of powerful engines. The great flight had begun!

"Well, I suppose the White Swallow will break another record," said Mike, watching the aeroplane become a tiny speck in the blue sky. "Come on, you others. Let's go and have some lemonade and buns."

Off they went and were soon sitting round a little table in the airfield's restaurant. They were so hungry that they ordered twelve buns.

"It's a bit of luck getting off from school for a couple of days like this," said Mike. "It's a pity we've got to go back today. It would have been fun to go to a cinema or something."

"Our train goes from London in two hours' time," said Peggy. "When does yours go?"

"In three hours," said Jack, munching his bun. "We shall have to go soon. It will take us over an hour to get to London from here, and you girls don't want to miss your train."

"We'll all look in the newspapers each day and see where Mummy and Daddy have got to," said Peggy. "And we'll look forward to meeting you boys here again in about a week's time, to welcome the plane back! Golly, that *will* be exciting!"

"I still feel rather gloomy," said Mike. "I really have got

8

a nasty feeling that we shan't see Dad and Mummy again for a long time."

"You and your nasty feelings!" said Nora laughing. "By the way, how's Prince Paul?"

Prince Paul was a boy at Mike's school. He and the children had had some strange adventures together the year before, when the Prince had been captured and taken from his land of Baronia to be kept prisoner in an old house that had once belonged to smugglers. The children had rescued him – and now Paul had been sent to the same school as his friends, Mike and Jack.

"Oh, Paul's all right," said Mike. "He was furious because the headmaster wouldn't allow him to come with Jack and me to see Dad and Mummy off."

"Well, give him our love and tell him we'll look forward to seeing him in the holidays," said Peggy, who was very fond of the little Prince.

"Come on – we really must go," said Mike. "Where's the taxi? Oh, there it is. Get in, you girls, and we'll be off. Jack and I will have time to come and see you safely into your train."

Before evening came all four children were safely back at their two schools. Prince Paul was watching for his friends, and he rushed to meet Jack and Mike.

"Did you see them off?" he cried. "Did you see the evening papers? There's a picture of Captain and Mrs Arnold in it."

Sure enough the evening papers were full of the big flight that the famous pilots were making. The children read them proudly. It was fun to have such a famous father and mother.

"I'd rather have a famous pilot for a father than a king," said Prince Paul enviously. "Kings aren't much fun, really – but airmen are always doing marvellous things!"

For the next two days the papers were full of the plane's magnificent flight – and then a horrid thing happened.

Mike ran to get the evening paper, and the first thing that met his eye was a great headline that said:

"NO NEWS OF THE ARNOLDS. STRANGE SILENCE. WHAT HAS HAPPENED TO THE WHITE SWALLOW?"

The White Swallow was the name given to the beautiful aeroplane flown by Captain and Mrs Arnold. Mike went pale as he read his headlines. He handed the paper to Jack without a word.

Jack glanced at it in dismay. "What can have happened?" he said. "I say – the girls will be jolly upset."

"Didn't I tell you I felt gloomy when I saw Dad and Mummy off?" said Mike. "I *knew* something was going to happen!"

The girls were just as upset as the boys. Nora cried and Peggy tried to comfort her.

"It's no good telling me they will be all right," wept Nora. "They must have come down in the middle of Africa somewhere, and goodness knows what might happen. They might be eaten by wild animals, or get lost in the forest or—"

"Nora, they've got food and guns," said Peggy. "And if the plane has had an accident, well, heaps of people will be looking and searching day and night. Let's not look on the dark side of things till we know a bit more."

"I wish we could see the boys," said Nora, drying her eyes. "I'd like to know what they say."

"Well, it's half-term holiday the week-end after next," said Peggy. "We shall see them then."

To the children's great disappointment, there was no news of their parents the next day – nor the next day either. Then, as the days slipped by, and the papers forgot about the lost flyers, and printed other fresher news, the children became more and more worried.

Half-term came, and the four of them went to London, where they were to stay for three days at their parents' flat. Miss Dimmy, an old friend of theirs, was to look after them for that short time. Prince Paul was to join them that evening. He had to go and see his own people first, in another part of London.

"What's being done about Dad and Mummy?" asked Mike, feeling glad to see Dimmy, whom they all loved.

"My dear, you mustn't worry – everything is being done that can possibly *be* done," said Dimmy. "Search parties have been sent out all over the district where it is thought that Captain and Mrs Arnold may have come down. They will soon be found."

Dimmy took them all to a cinema, and for a while the children forgot their worries. Prince Paul joined them after tea, looking tremendously excited.

"I say, what do you think?" he cried. "My father has sent me the most wonderful birthday present you can think of – guess what it is!"

"A pink elephant," said Mike at once.

"A blue bed-jacket!" said Nora.

"A clockwork mouse!" said Peggy.

"A nice new rattle!" cried Jack.

"Don't be silly," grinned Paul, who was now quite used to the English children's teasing ways. "You're all wrong – he's given me an aeroplane of my very own!"

The four children stared at Paul in the greatest surprise. They knew that Paul's father was a rich king – but even so, an aeroplane seemed a very extravagant present to give to a small boy.

"An *aeroplane!*" said Mike. "Golly – if you aren't lucky, Paul! But you are too young to fly it. It won't be any use to you."

"Yes, it will," said Paul. "My father has sent me his finest pilot with it. I can fly all over your little country of England and get to know it very well."

A voice came up from the London street below. "Paper! Evening paper! Lost aeroplane found! White Swallow found!"

11

With a yell the four children rushed down the stairs to buy a paper. But what a dreadful disappointment for them! It was true that the White Swallow had been found – but Captain and Mrs Arnold were not with it. They had completely disappeared!

The children read the news in silence. The aeroplane had been seen by one of the searching planes, which had landed nearby. Something had gone wrong with the White Swallow and Captain Arnold had plainly been putting it right – then something had happened to stop him.

"And now they've both disappeared, and, although all the natives round have been questioned about them, nobody knows anything – or they say they don't, which comes to the same thing," said Peggy, almost in tears.

"I wish to goodness *we* could go out to Africa and look for them," said Mike, who hadn't really much idea of how enormous a place Africa was.

Prince Paul slipped a hand through Mike's arm. His eyes shone.

"We *will* go!" he said. "What about my new aeroplane! We can go in that – and Pilescu, my pilot, can take us! He is always ready for an adventure! Don't let's go back to school, Mike – let's go off in my aeroplane!"

The others stared at the little Prince in astonishment. What an idea!

"We couldn't possibly," said Mike.

"Why not?" said Paul. "Are you afraid? Well, I will go by myself then."

"Indeed, you won't!" cried Jack. "Mike – it's an idea! We've had marvellous adventures together – this will be another. Let's go – oh, do let's go!"

In The Middle Of The Night

Not one of the five children thought of the great risk and danger of the adventure they were so light-heartedly planning.

"Shall we tell Dimmy?" said Nora.

"Of course not," said Jack scornfully. "You know what grown-ups are – why, Dimmy would at once telephone Paul's pilot and forbid him to take us anywhere."

"Well, it seems horrid to leave her and not tell her anything," said Nora, who was very fond of Miss Dimmy.

"We'll leave a note for her that she can read when we are well away," said Mike. "But we really mustn't do anything to warn her or anyone else. My word – what a mercy that Paul had that aeroplane for his birthday!"

"When shall we go?" said Paul, his big dark eyes shining brightly. "Now – this very minute?"

"Don't be an idiot, Paul," said Jack. "We've got to get a few things together. We ought to have guns, I think, for one thing."

"I don't like guns," said Nora. "They might go off by themselves."

"Guns don't," said Jack. "You girls don't need to have guns. But where can we get these things – I'm sure I don't know."

"Pilescu, my pilot, can get everything we want," said Prince Paul. "Don't worry."

"But how will he know what to get?" asked Mike. "I hardly know myself what we ought to take."

"I will tell him he must find out," said Paul. "Show me where your telephone is Mike, and I will tell him every-thing."

Soon Paul was holding a most extraordinary talk with his puzzled pilot. In the end Pilescu said he must come round to the flat and talk to his small master. He could not believe that he was really to do what Paul commanded.

"I say – suppose your pilot refuses to do what you tell him?" said Jack. "I'm sure he will just laugh and tell us to go back to school and learn our tables or something!"

"Pilescu is my man," said the little Prince, putting his small chin into the air, and looking very royal all of a sudden. "He has sworn an oath to me to obey me all my life. He has to do what I say."

"Suppose he tells your father?" said Mike.

"Then I will no longer have him as my man," said Paul fiercely. "And that will break his heart, for he loves me and honours me. I am his prince, and one day I will be his king."

"You talk like a history book," said Peggy with a laugh. "All right, Paul – you try to get Pilescu to do what we have planned. He'll soon be here."

In twenty minutes Pilescu arrived. He was a strange-looking person, very tall, very strong, with fierce black eyes and a flaming red beard that seemed on fire when it caught the sun.

He bowed to all the children in turn, for his manners were marvellous. Then he spoke to Paul in a curiously gentle voice.

"Little Prince, I cannot believe that you wish me to do what you said on the telephone. It is not possible. I cannot do it."

Prince Paul flew into a rage, and stamped on the floor, his face bright red, and his dark eyes flashing in anger.

"Pilescu! How dare you talk to me like this? My father, the king, told me that you must do my smallest wish. I will not have you for my man. I will send you back to Baronia to my father and ask him for a better man."

"Little Prince, I held you in my arms when you were

14

born, and I promised then that you should be my lord," said Pilescu, in a troubled voice. "I shall never leave you, now that your father has sent me to be with you. But do not ask me to do what I think may bring danger to you."

"Pilescu! Shall I, the king's son, think of danger!" cried the little Prince. "These are my friends you see here. They are in trouble and I have promised to help them. Do you not remember how they saved me when I was kidnapped from my country of Baronia? Now it is my turn to help them. You will do what I say."

The other four children watched in astonishment. They had not seen Paul acting the prince before. Before ten minutes had gone by the big Baronian had promised to do all that his haughty little master demanded. He bowed himself out and was gone from the flat before Dimmy came to find out who the visitor was.

"Good, Paul!" said Mike. "Now all we've got to do is to wait till Pilescu lets us know how he got on."

Before the night was gone Pilescu telephoned to Prince Paul. The boy came running to the others, his face eager and shining.

"Pilescu has found out everything for us. He has bought all we need, but he says we must pack two bags with all we ourselves would like to have. So we must do that. We must leave the house at midnight, get into the car that will be waiting for us at the corner – and go to the airfield!"

"Golly! How exciting!" said Mike. The girls rubbed their hands, thrilled to think of the adventure starting so soon. Only Jack looked a little doubtful. He was the eldest, and he wondered for the first time if they were wise to go on this new and strange adventure.

But the others would not even let him speak of his doubts. No – they had made up their minds, and everything was ready except for the packing of their two bags. They were going; they were going!

The bags were packed. The five children were so

excited that they really did not know what to pack, and when the bags were full, not one child could possibly have said what was in them! With trembling hands they did up the leather straps, and then Mike wrote out a note for Dimmy.

He stuck the note into the mirror on the girls' dressing-table. It was quite a short note.

"Dimmy Dear,
"Don't worry about us. We've gone to look for Daddy and Mummy. We'll be back safe and sound before long.
"Love from all of us."

Dimmy had been out to see a friend and did not come back until nine o'clock. The children had decided to get into bed fully dressed, so that Dimmy would not have any chance of asking awkward questions.

Dimmy was rather surprised to find all the children so quiet and good in bed. They did not even sit up to talk to her when she came into the bedrooms to kiss them all goodnight. She did not guess that it was because they were not in their night clothes!

"Dear me, you must all be tired out!" she said in surprise. "Well, goodnight, my dears, sleep well. You still have another day's holiday, so we will make the most of it tomorrow."

All the children lay perfectly still until they heard Dimmy go into her bedroom and shut the door. They listened to her movements, and then they heard the click of her bedroom light being turned off.

"Don't get out of bed yet," whispered Jack to Mike. "Give Dimmy time to get to sleep."

So for another half-hour or so the children lay quiet – and Nora fell asleep! Peggy had to wake her up, and the little girl was most astonished to find that she had to get up

16

in the dark, and that she had on her day clothes! But she soon remembered what a big adventure was beginning, and she rubbed her eyes, and went to get a wet sponge to make her wider awake.

"What's the time?" whispered Mike. He flashed his torch on to the bedroom clock – half-past eleven. Nearly time to leave the house.

"Let's go to the dining-room and hunt round for a few biscuits first," said Jack. "I feel hungry. Now for goodness sake be quiet, everyone. Paul, don't trip over anything – and, Nora, take those squeaky shoes off! You sound like a dozen mice when you creep across the bedroom!"

So Nora took off her squeaky shoes and carried them. Jack and Mike took the bags, and the five children made their way quietly down the passage to the dining-room. They found the biscuit tin and began to munch. The noise of the biscuits being crunched in their teeth sounded very loud in the silence of the night.

"Do you think Dimmy will hear us munching?" said Nora anxiously. She swallowed her piece of biscuit too soon and a crumb caught in her throat. She went purple in the face, and tried hard not to cough. Then an enormous cough came, and the others rushed at her.

"Nora! Do be quiet!" whispered Jack fiercely. He caught the cloth off the table and wrapped it round poor Nora's head. Her coughs were smothered in it, but the little girl was very angry with Jack.

She tore off the cloth and glared at the grinning boy. "Jack! You nearly smothered me! You're a horrid mean thing."

"Sh!" said Mike. "This isn't the time to quarrel. Hark – the clock is striking twelve."

Dimmy was peacefully asleep in her bedroom when the five children crept to the front door of the flat. They opened it and closed it very quietly. Then down the stone stairway they went to the street entrance, where another big door had to be quietly opened.

17

"This door makes an awful noise when it is closed," said Mike anxiously. "You have to bang it. It will wake everyone!"

"Well, don't shut it then, silly," said Jack. "Leave it open. No one will bother about it."

So they left the big door open and went down the street, hoping that they would not meet any policemen. They felt sure that a policeman would think it very queer for five children to be out at that time of night!

Luckily they met no one at all. They went down to the end of the street, and Mike caught Jack's arm.

"Look – there's a car over there – do you suppose it is waiting for us?"

"Yes – that's our car," said Jack. "Isn't it, Paul?"

Paul nodded, and they crossed the road to where a big blue and silver car stood waiting, its engine turned off. The children could see the blue and silver in the light of a street lamp. Paul's aeroplane was blue and silver too, as were all the royal aeroplanes of Baronia.

A man slipped out of the car and opened the door silently for the children. His uniform was of blue and silver too, and, like most Baronians, he was enormous. He bowed low to Paul.

Soon the great car was speeding through the night. It went very fast, eating up the miles easily. The children were all tremendously excited. For one thing it was a great thrill to be going off in an aeroplane – and who knew what exciting adventures lay in store for them!

They came to the airfield. It was in darkness, except for lights in the middle of the field, where the beautiful aeroplane belonging to Prince Paul stood ready to start.

"I am to take you right up to the aeroplane in the car," said the driver to Prince Paul, who sat in front with him.

"Good," said Paul. "Then we can all slip into it, and we shall be off before anyone really knows we are here!"

An Exciting Journey

The big blue and silver car drove silently over the bumpy field until it came to the aeroplane. Pilescu was there, his red beard shining in the light of a lamp. With him was another man just as big.

"Hallo, Ranni!" said Prince Paul joyfully. "Are you coming too? I'm so glad to see you!"

Ranni lifted the small Prince off the ground and swung him into the air. His broad face shone with delight.

"My little lord!" he said. "Yes – I come with you and Pilescu. I think it is not right that you should do this – but the lords of Baronia were always mad!"

Paul laughed. It was easy to see that he loved big Ranni, and was glad that the Baronian was coming too.

"Will my aeroplane take seven?" he asked, looking at it.

"Easily," said Pilescu. "But now, come quickly before the mechanics come to see what is happening."

They all climbed up the little ladder to the cockpit. The aeroplane inside was like a big and comfortable room. It was marvellous. Mike and the others cried out in amazement.

"This is a wonderful aeroplane," said Mike. "It's much better than even the White Swallow."

"Baronia has the most marvellous planes in the world," said Pilescu proudly. "It is only a small country, but our inventors are the best."

The children settled down into comfortable armchair seats. Paul, who was tremendously excited, showed everyone how the seats unfolded, when a spring was touched, and became small beds, cosy and soft.

"Golly!" said Jack, making his seat turn into a bed at once, and then changing it back to an armchair, and then into a bed again. "This is like magic. I could do this all night!"

"You must settle down into your seats quickly," ordered Pilescu, climbing into the pilot's seat, with big Ranni just beside him. "We must be off. We have many hundreds of miles to fly before the sun is high."

The children settled down again, Paul chattering nineteen to the dozen! Nobody felt sleepy. It was far too exciting a night to think of sleep.

Pilescu made sure the children had all fastened their seat belts, and started the engines, which made a loud and comfortable noise. Then, with a slight jerk, the aeroplane began to run over the dark field.

It bumped a little – and then, like a big bird, it rose into the air and skimmed over the long line of trees that stood at the far end of the big field. The children hardly knew that it had left the ground.

"Are we still running over the field? asked Mike, trying to see out of the window near him.

"No, of course not," said Ranni laughing. "We are miles away from the airfield already!"

"Goodness!" said Peggy, half-startled to think of the enormous speed at which the plane was flying. The children had to raise their voices when they spoke, because the engine of the plane, although specially silent, made a great noise.

That flight through the dark night was very strange to the children. As soon as the plane left the ground its wheels rose into its body and disappeared. They would descend again when the aeroplane landed. It flew through the darkness as straight as an arrow, with Pilescu piloting it, his eyes on all the various things that told him everything he needed to know about the plane.

"Why did Ranni come?" Prince Paul shouted to Pilescu.

"Because Ranni can take a turn at piloting the plane," answered Pilescu. "Also there must be someone to look after such a crowd of children!"

"We don't need looking after!" cried Mike indignantly. "We can easily look after ourselves! Why, once when we ran away to a secret island, we looked after ourselves for months and months!"

"Yes – I heard that wonderful story," said Pilescu. "But I must have another man with me, and Ranni was the one I could most trust. We may be very glad of his help."

No one knew then how glad they were going to be that big Ranni had come with them – but even so, Ranni was very comforting even in the plane, for he brought the children hot cocoa when they felt cold, and produced cups of hot tomato soup which they thought tasted better than any soup they had ever had before!

"Isn't it exciting to be drinking soup high up in an aeroplane in the middle of the night?" said Peggy. "And I do like these biscuits. Ranni, I'm very glad you came with us!"

Big Ranni grinned. He was like a great bear, yet as gentle as could be. He adored little Paul, and gave him far too much to eat and drink. They all had bars of nut chocolate after the soup, and Pilescu munched as well.

The plane had been flying very steadily indeed – in fact, the children hardly noticed the movement at all – but suddenly there came a curious jerk, and the plane dropped a little. It happened two or three times, and Paul didn't like it.

"What's it doing?" he cried.

Mike laughed. He had been up in aeroplanes before, and he knew what was happening at that moment.

"We are only bumping into air-pockets," he shouted to Paul. "When we get into one we drop a bit – so it feels as if the plane is bumping along. Wait till we get into a big air-pocket – you'll feel funny, young Paul!"

Sure enough, the plane slipped into a very big air-pocket, and down it dropped sharply. Paul nearly fell off his big armchair, and he turned quite green.

"I feel sick," he said. Ranni promptly presented him with a strong paper bag.

"What's this for?" asked Paul, in a weak voice, looking greener than ever. "There's nothing in the bag."

The other four children shouted with laughter. They felt sorry for Paul, but he really did look comical, peering into the paper bag to see if there was anything there.

"It's for you to be sick in, if you want to be," shouted Jack. "Didn't you know that?"

But the paper bag wasn't needed after all, because the plane climbed high, away from the bumpy air-pockets, and Paul felt better. "I shan't eat so much chocolate another time," he said cheerfully.

"I bet you will!" said Jack, who knew that Paul could eat more chocolate than any other boy he had ever met. "I say – isn't this a gorgeous adventure? I hope we see the sun rise!"

But they didn't, because they were all fast asleep! Nora and Peggy began to yawn at two o'clock in the morning, and Ranni saw them.

"You will all go to sleep now," he said. He got up and helped the two girls to turn their big armchairs into comfortable, soft beds. He gave them each a pillow and a very cosy warm rug.

"We don't want to go to sleep," said Nora in dismay. "I shan't close my eyes. I know I shan't."

"Don't then," said Ranni with a grin. He pulled the rugs closely over the children and went back to his seat beside Pilescu.

Nora and Peggy and Paul found that their eyes closed themselves – they simply wouldn't keep open. In three seconds they were all sound asleep. The other two boys did not take much longer, excited though they were.

22

Ranni nudged the pilot and Pilescu's dark eyes twinkled as he looked round at the quiet children.

He and Ranni talked in their own language, as the plane roared through the night. They had travelled hundreds of miles before daylight came. It was marvellous to see the sun rising when dawn came.

The sky became full of a soft light that seemed alive. The light grew and changed colour. Both pilots watched in silence. It was a sight they had often seen and were never tired of.

Golden light filled the aeroplane when the sun showed a golden rim over the far horizon. Ranni switched off the electric lights at once. The world lay below, very beautiful in the dawn.

"Blue and gold," said Ranni to Pilescu, in his own language. "It is a pity the children are not awake to see it."

"Don't wake them, Ranni," said Pilescu. "We may have a harder time in front of us than they know. I am hoping that we shall turn and go back, once the children realise that we cannot possibly find their parents. We shall not stay in Africa very long!"

The children slept on. When they awoke it was about eight o'clock. The sun was high, and below the plane was a billowing mass of snowy whiteness, intensely blue in the shadows.

"Golly! Is it snow?" said Paul, rubbing his eyes in amazement. "Pilescu, I asked you to fly to Africa, not to the North Pole!"

"It's fields and fields of clouds," said Nora, looking with delight on the magnificent sight below them. "We are right above the clouds. Peggy, look – they seem almost solid enough to walk on!"

"Better not try it!" said Mike. "Ranni, you might have waked us up when dawn came. Now we've missed it. I say, I *am* hungry!"

23

Ranni became very busy at the back of the plane, where there was a proper little kitchen. Soon the smell of frying bacon and eggs, toast and coffee stole into the cabin. The children sniffed eagerly, looking down at the fields of cloud all the time, marvelling at their amazing beauty.

Then there came a break in the clouds and the five children gave shouts of joy.

"Look! We are over a desert or something. Isn't it queer?"

The smooth-looking desert gave way to mountains, and then to plains again. It was most exciting to watch.

"Where are we?" asked Mike.

"Over Africa," said Ranni, serving bacon and eggs to everyone, and putting hot coffee into the cups. "Now eat well, for it is a long time to lunch-time!"

It was a gorgeous meal, and most exciting. To think that they had their supper in London – and were having their breakfast over Africa! Marvellous!

"Do you know whereabouts our parents came down, Pilescu?" asked Mike.

"Ranni will show you on the map," said the pilot. "Soon we must go down to get more fuel. We are running short. You children are to stay hidden in the plane when we land on the airfield, for I do not want to be arrested for flying away with you!"

"We'll hide all right!" said Paul, excited. "Where is that map, Ranni? Let us see it. Oh, how I wish I had done better at geography. I don't seem to know anything about Africa at all."

Ranni unfolded a big map, and showed the children where Captain and Mrs Arnold's plane had been found. He showed them exactly where their own plane was too.

"Golly! It doesn't look very far from here to where the White Swallow was found!" cried Paul, running his finger over the map.

Ranni laughed. "Further than you think," he said.

"Now look – we are nearing an airfield and must get fuel. Go to the back of the plane and hide under the pile of rugs there."

So, whilst the plane circled lower to land, the five children snuggled under the rugs and luggage. They did hope they wouldn't be found. It would be too dreadful to be sent back to London after coming so far.

In A Very Strange Country

A number of men came running to meet the plane as it landed beautifully on the runway. Pilescu climbed out of the cockpit and left Ranni on guard inside. The children were all as quiet as mice.

The blue and silver plane was so magnificent that all the groundsmen ran round it, exclaiming. They had never seen such a beauty before. Two of them wanted to climb inside and examine it, but Ranni stood solidly at the entrance, his big body blocking the way. Pilescu spoke to the mechanics and soon the plane was taking in an enormous amount of fuel.

"Pooh! Doesn't it smell horrid?" whispered Paul. "I think I'm going to choke."

"Don't you dare even to sneeze," ordered Jack at once, his voice very low but very fierce.

So Paul swallowed his choking fit and went purple in the face. The girls couldn't bear the smell either, but they buried their faces deeper in the rug and said nothing.

A man's voice floated up to the cockpit, speaking in broken English.

"You have how many passengers, please?" he asked.

"You see me and my companion here," answered Pilescu shortly.

The man seemed satisfied, and walked round the plane admiring it. Pilescu took no notice of him, but began to look carefully into the engines of the plane. He noticed something was wrong and shouted to Ranni.

"Come down here a minute and give me a hand." Ranni stepped down the ladder and went to stand beside Pilescu. As quick as lightning one of the airfield men skipped up the ladder to the cockpit and peered inside the plane.

It so happened that Mike was peeping out to see if all was clear at that moment. He saw the man before the man saw him, and covered his face again, nudging the others to keep perfectly still.

Ranni saw that the man had gone up to the cockpit and he shouted to him. "Come down! No one is allowed inside our plane without permission."

"Then you must give me permission," said the man, whose quick eye had seen the enormous pile of rugs at the back, and who wished to examine it. "We have had news that five children are missing from London, and there is a big reward offered from the King of Baronia if they are found."

Pilescu muttered something under his breath and ran to where the mechanics had just finished refuelling the plane. He pushed them away and made sure nobody was still nearby. Ranni went up the steps in a trice, and tipped the inquisitive man down them. Pilescu leapt into the plane and slipped into the pilot's seat like a fish sliding into water.

There was a good deal of shouting and calling, but Pilescu ignored it. He started the plane and it ran swiftly over the ground. With a crowd of angry men rushing after it, the plane taxied to the end of the field and then rose gently into the air. Pilescu gave a short laugh.

"Now it will be known everywhere that we have the children on board. Get them out, Ranni. They were very good and they must be half smothered under those rugs."

26

The five children were already crawling out, excited to think of their narrow escape.

"Would we have been sent back to London?" cried Paul.

"I peeped out but the man didn't see me!" shouted Mike.

"Are we safe?" said Peggy, sitting down in her comfortable armchair seat again. "They won't send up planes to chase us, will they?"

"It wouldn't be any use," said Ranni, with a grin. "This is the fastest plane on the airfield. No – don't worry. You are all right now. But we must try to find the place where the White Swallow came down, for we do not want to land on any more airfields at the moment."

The day went on, and the children found it very thrilling to look out of the windows and see the mountains, rivers, valleys and plains slipping away below them. They longed to go down and explore them. It was wonderful to be over a strange land, and see it spread out below like a great map.

Towards the late afternoon, as the children were eating sweet biscuits and chocolate, and drinking lemonade, which by some miracle Ranni had iced, Pilescu gave a shout.

Ranni and he put their heads together over the map, and the two men spoke excitedly in their own language. Paul listened, his eyes gleaming.

"What are they saying?" cried Mike impatiently. "Tell us, Paul."

"They say that we are getting near the place where the White Swallow came down," said Paul. "Ranni says he had been in this part of the country before. He was sent to get animals for our Baronian Zoo, and he knows the people. He says they live in tiny villages, far from any towns and they keep to themselves so that few others know them."

27

The plane flew more slowly and went down lower. Ranni searched the ground below them carefully as the plane flew round in big circles.

But it was Mike who first saw what they were all eagerly looking for! He gave such a shout that the girls nearly fell off their seats, and Ranni turned round with a jump, half-expecting to see one of the children falling out of the plane!

"Ranni! Look – there's the White Swallow! Oh, look – oh, we've passed it! Pilescu, Pilesseu go back! I tell you I saw the White Swallow!"

The boy was so excited that he shook big Ranni hard by the shoulder, and would have done the same to the pilot except that he had been warned not to touch Pilescu when he was flying the machine. Ranni looked back, and gave directions to Pilescu.

In a trice the plane circled back and was soon over the exact place where the gleaming white plane stood still and silent. The children gazed at it. To think that they were looking at the very same plane they had waved good-bye to some weeks before – but this time the two famous pilots were not there to wave back.

"I can't land very near to it," said Pilescu. "I don't know how Captain Arnold managed to land there without crashing. He must be a very clever pilot."

"He is," said Peggy proudly. "He is one of the best in the world."

"I shall land on that smooth-looking bit of ground over there," said Pilescu, flying the plane lower. "We may bump a bit, children, because there are rocks there. Get ready for a jolt!"

The plane flew even lower. Then Pilescu found that he could not land with safety, and he rose into the air again. He circled round once more and then went down. This time he let down the wheels of the plane and they touched the ground. One ran over a rock and the plane tilted sideways. For one moment everyone thought that it was going over, and Pilescu turned pale. He did not want to crash in the middle of an unknown country!

But the plane was marvellously built and balanced and it righted itself. All the children had been thrown roughly about in their seats, and everything in the cabin had slid to one side.

But the five children soon sorted themselves out, too excited even to look for bruises. They rushed to the door of the cockpit, each eager to be out first. Ranni shouted to them.

"Stay where you are. I must go out first to see what there is to be seen."

Pilescu stopped the engines, and the big throbbing noise died away. It seemed strange to the children when it stopped. Everything was so quiet, and their voices seemed suddenly loud. It took them a little time to stop shouting at one another, for they always had to raise their voices when they were flying.

Ranni got out of the cockpit, his gun handy. No one appeared to be in sight. They had landed on rough ground, strewn with boulders, and it was really a miracle that they had landed so well. To the left, about two miles away, a range of mountains rose. To the right was a plain, dotted with trees that the children did not know. Small hills lay in the other directions.

"Everything looks very strange, doesn't it?" said Mike. "Look at those funny red-brown daisies over there. And even the grass is different!"

"So are the birds," said Peggy, watching a brilliant red and yellow bird chasing a large fly. A green and orange bird flew round the plane, and a flock of bright blue birds passed overhead. They were not a bit like any of the birds that the children knew so well at home.

"Can we get out, Ranni?" called Mike, who was simply longing to explore. Ranni nodded. He could see no one

29

about at all. All the five children rushed out of the plane and jumped to the ground. It was lovely to feel it beneath their feet again.

"I feel as if the ground ought to bump and sway like the plane," said Nora, with a giggle. "You know – like when we get out of a boat."

"Well, I jolly well hope it doesn't," said Jack. "I don't want an earthquake just at present."

The sun was very hot. Pilescu got out some marvellous sun-hats for the five children and for himself and Ranni too. They had a sort of veil hanging down from the back to protect their spines from the sun. None of them were wearing very many clothes, but even so they felt very hot.

"I'm jolly thirsty," said Mike, mopping his head. "Let's have a drink, Ranni."

They all drank lemonade, sitting in the shade of the plane. The sun was now getting low, and Pilescu looked at the time.

"There's nothing more we can do today," he said. "Tomorrow we will find some local people and see what we can get out of them by questioning them. Ranni thinks he can make them understand, for he picked up some of their language when he was here hunting animals for the Baronian Zoo."

"Well, surely we haven't got to go to bed already?" asked Nora in dismay. "Aren't we going to explore a bit?"

"There won't be time – the sun is setting already," said Ranni. As he spoke the sun disappeared over the horizon, and darkness fell around almost at once. The children were surprised.

"Day went into night, and there was no evening," said Nora, looking round. "The stars are out, look! Oh, Mike – Jack – aren't they enormous?"

So they were. They seemed far bigger and brighter than at home. The children sat and looked at them, feeling almost afraid of their strange beauty.

Ranni kept guard overnight

Then Nora yawned. It was such an enormous yawn that it set everyone else yawning too, even big Ranni! Pilescu laughed.

"You had little sleep last night," he said. "You must have plenty tonight. In this country we must get up very early whilst it is still cool, for we shall have to rest in the shade when the sun climbs high. So you had better go to sleep very soon after Ranni has given you supper."

"Need we sleep inside the plane?" said Jack. "It's so hot there. Can we sleep out here in the cool?"

"Yes," said Ranni. "We will bring out rugs to lie on. Pilescu and I will take it in turns to keep watch."

"What will you watch for?" asked Peggy, in surprise. "Not enemies, surely?"

"Well, Captain and Mrs Arnold disappeared just here, didn't they?" said Pilescu solemnly. "I don't want to wake up in the morning and find that we have disappeared too. I should just hate to go and look for myself!"

Everyone laughed – but the children felt a little queer too. Yes – this wasn't nice, safe old England. This was a strange, unknown country, where queer, unexpected things might happen. They moved a little closer to red-bearded Pilescu. He suddenly seemed very safe and protective as he sat there in the starlight, as firm and solid as one of the big dark rocks around!

Waiting For News

Ranni provided a good meal, and Pilescu built a camp-fire, whose red glow was very comforting. "Wild animals will keep at a safe distance if we keep the fire going well," said Pilescu, putting a pile of brushwood nearby. "Ranni or I will

32

be keeping guard tonight, and we will have a fine fire going."

Rugs were spread around the fire, whose crackling made a very cheerful sound. The five children lay down, happy and excited. They had come to the right place – and now they were going to look for Captain and Mrs Arnold. Adventures lay behind them, and even more exciting ones lay in front.

"I shall never go to sleep," said Nora, sitting up. "Never! What is that funny sound I hear, Ranni?"

"Baboons in the hills," said Ranni. "Never mind them. They won't come near us."

"And now what's *that* noise?" asked Peggy.

"Only a night-bird calling," said Ranni. "It will go on all night long, so you will have to get used to it. Lie down, Nora. If you are not asleep in two minutes I shall put you into the plane to sleep there by yourself."

This was such a terrible threat that Nora lay down at once. It was a marvellous night. The little girl lay on her back looking up at the enormous, brilliant stars that hung like bright lamps in the velvet sky. All around her she heard strange bird and animal sounds. She was warm and comfortable and the fire at her feet crackled most comfortingly. She took a last look at big Ranni, who sat with his back to the plane, gun in hand, and then shut her eyes.

"The children are all asleep," said big Ranni to Pilescu in his own language. "I think we should not have brought them on this adventure, Pilescu. We do not know what will happen. And how shall we find Captain and Mrs Arnold in this strange country? It is like seeking for a nut on an apple tree!"

Pilescu grunted. He was very tired, for he had flown the plane all the way, without letting Ranni help. Ranni was to watch three-quarters of the night, and Pilescu was to sleep – then he would take the rest of the watch.

"We will see what tomorrow brings," he said, his big

red beard spreading over his chest as his head fell forward in sleep. And then another noise was added to the other night-sounds – for Pilescu snored.

He had a wonderful snore that rose and fell with his breathing. Ranni was afraid that he would wake up the children and he nudged him.

But Pilescu did not wake. He was too tired to stir. Jack awoke when he heard the new sound and sat up in alarm. He listened in amazement.

"Ranni! Ranni! Some animal is snorting round our camp!" he called. "Are you awake? Can't you hear him?"

Ranni smothered an enormous laugh. "Lie down, Jack," he said. "It is only our good friend Pilescu. Maybe he snores like that to keep wild animals away. Even a lion might run from that noise!"

Jack grinned and lay down again. Good gracious, Pilescu made a noise as loud as the aeroplane! Well – almost, thought Jack, floating away into sleep again.

Ranni kept watch most of the night. He saw shadowy shapes not far off, and knew them to be some kind of night-hunting animals. He watched the stars move down the sky. He smelt the fragrance of the wood burning on the fire, and sometimes he reached out his hand and threw some more into the heart of the leaping flames.

A little before dawn Ranni awoke Pilescu. The big Baronian yawned loudly and opened his eyes. At once he knew where he was. He spoke to Ranni, and then went for a short walk round the camp to stretch his legs and get wide awake.

Then Ranni slept in his turn, his hand still on his gun. Pilescu watched the dawn come, and saw the whole country turn into silver and gold. When daylight was fully there he awoke everyone, for in such a hot country they must be astir early whilst the air was still cool.

The children were wild with excitement when they awoke and saw their strange surroundings. They ran round the camp, yelling and shouting, whilst Ranni cooked a delicious-smelling meal over the camp fire.

"Hie, look! Here's a kind of little lake!" shouted Jack. "Let's wash in it. Ranni, Pilescu! Could we bathe in this lake, do you think?"

"Not unless you want to be eaten by crocodiles," said Ranni.

Nora gave a scream and tore back to the camp at top speed. Ranni grinned. He went to look at the lake. It was not much more than a pond, really.

"This is all right," he said. "There are no crocodiles here. All the same, you mustn't bathe in it, for there may be slug-like things called leeches, which will fasten on to your legs and hurt you. Please remember to be very careful indeed in this strange country. Animals that you only see at the Zoo in England run wild here all over the place."

This was rather an alarming idea to the two girls. They did a very hasty wash indeed, but the three boys splashed vigorously. The air was cool and delicious, and every one of the children felt as if they could run for miles. But they only ran to the camp beside the plane, for they were so hungry, and breakfast smelt so good. The hot coffee sent its smell out, and the frying bacon sizzled and crackled in the pan.

"What's the plan for today, Pilescu?" asked Jack. "Do we find someone and ask if they know anything of the White Swallow and its pilots?"

"We are in such a remote part of Africa, that the people round here might never have seen a plane before. But Ranni is going to the nearest village to try and get news," said Pilescu, ladling out hot bacon on to the plates.

"But how does he know where the next village is?" asked Mike in wonder, looking round. "I can't see a thing."

"You haven't used your eyes," said Ranni, with a smile. "Look over there."

The children looked in the direction to which he was

35

pointing, where low hills lay. And they all saw at once what Ranni meant.

"A spire of smoke!" said Mike. "Yes – that means a fire – and fire means people. So that's where you are going, Ranni? Be careful, won't you?"

"My gun and I will look after one another," said big Ranni with a grin, and he tapped his pocket. "I shall not be back till nightfall, so be good whilst I am gone!"

Ranni set off soon after breakfast, carrying food with him. He wore his sun-hat, for the sun was now getting hot. The children watched him go.

"I do wish we could have gone with him," said Jack longingly. "I hope he will have some news when he comes back."

"Come, you children can wash these dishes in water from the pool," called Pilescu. "Soon it will be too hot to do anything. Before it is, we must also find some firewood ready for tonight."

Pilescu kept the children busy until the sun rose higher. Then when its rays beat down like fire, he made them get into the shade of the plane. Paul did not want to, for he enjoyed the heat, but Pilescu ordered him to go with the others.

"Pilescu, it is not for you to order me," said the little Prince, sticking his chin into the air.

"Little Paul, I am in command now," said the big Baronian, gently but sternly. "You are my lord, but I am your captain in this adventure. Do as I say."

"Paul, don't be an idiot, or I'll come and get you into the shade by the scruff of your neck," called Mike. "If you get sunstroke, you'll be ill and will have to be flown back to London at once."

Paul trotted into the shade like a lamb. He lay down by the others. Soon they were so thirsty that Pilescu found himself continually getting in and out of the plane with supplies of cool lemonade from the little refrigerator there.

The children slept in the midday heat. Pilescu was sleepy too, but he kept guard on the little company, wondering how big Ranni was getting on. When the sun began to slip down the coppery sky, he mopped his brow and awoke the children.

"There is some tinned fruit in the plane," he told Nora. "Get it, and open the tins. It will be delicious to eat whilst we wait for the day to cool."

Ranni did not come back until the sun had set with the same suddenness as the day before. The children watched and waited impatiently for him, and lighted the bonfire early to guide him.

Pilescu was not worried, for he knew that, although the spire of smoke had looked fairly near, it was really far away – and he knew also that Ranni would not be able to walk far when the midday heat fell on the land like flames from a furnace.

The little company sat round the fire, and above them hung the big bright stars. They all watched for Ranni to return.

"I do wonder if he will have any news," said Nora impatiently. "Oh, Ranni, do hurry! I simply can't wait!"

But she had to wait and so did everyone else. It was late before they heard the big Baronian shouting loudly to them. They all leapt up and trained their eyes to see him.

"There he is!" shouted Jack, who had eyes like a cat's in the dark. "Look – see that moving shadow among those rocks?"

The shadow gave a shout and everyone yelled back in delight.

"Ranni! Hurrah! He's back!"

"What news, Ranni?"

"Hurry, Ranni, do hurry!"

The big Baronian came up to the fire. He was tired and hot. He dropped down to the rugs and wiped his hot forehead. Pilescu gave him a jug of lemonade and he drank it all in one gulp.

"Have you news, Ranni?" asked Pilescu.

"Yes – I have. And strange news it is too," said Ranni. "Give me some more sandwiches or biscuits, Pilescu, and I will tell my tale. Are you all safe and well?"

"Perfectly," said Pilescu. "Now speak, Ranni. What is this strange news you bring?"

Big Ranni Tells A Queer Tale

Ranni lighted his pipe and puffed at it. Everyone waited for him to begin, wondering what he had to tell them.

"I found a small camp," said Ranni. "Not more than four or five men were there. They had been out hunting. When they saw me coming they all hid behind the rocks in terror."

"But why were they so afraid?" asked Nora in wonder.

"Well, I soon found out," said Ranni. "I can speak their language a little, because I have hunted round about this country before, as you know. It seems that they thought I was one of the strange folk from the Secret Mountain."

"From the Secret Mountain!" cried Mike. "What do you mean? What secret mountain?"

"Be patient and listen," said Pilescu, who was listening closely. "Go on, Ranni."

"Somewhere not far from here is a strange mountain," said Ranni. "It is called the Secret Mountain because for years a secret and strange tribe of people have made their home in the centre of it. They are not like the people round about at all."

"What are they like, then?" asked Jack.

"As far as I can make out their skins are a queer creamy-yellow, and their beards and hair are red, like Pilescu's and mine. They are thin and tall, and their eyes are green. No one belonging to any other tribe is allowed to mix with them, and no one has ever found out the entrance into the Secret Mountain."

"Ranni! This is a most wonderful story!" cried Prince Paul, his eyes shining with excitement. "Is it really true? Oh, do let's go and find the secret mountain at once, this very minute!"

"Don't be an idiot, Paul," said Mike, giving him a push. The little Prince was very excitable, and Mike and Jack often had to stop him when he wanted to rush off at once and do something. "Be quiet and listen to Ranni."

"All the people that live anywhere near are afraid of the Folk of the Secret Mountain," said Ranni. "They think that they are very fierce, and they do not come this way if they can possibly help it. When they saw me, with my red hair, they really thought I was a man from the Secret Mountain, and they were too terrified even to run away."

"Did you ask them if they knew anything about Daddy and Mummy?" asked Peggy eagerly.

"Of course," said Ranni. "They knew nothing – but tomorrow a man is coming to our camp here, who saw the White Swallow come down, and who may be able to tell us something. But I think, children, that there is no doubt that Captain and Mrs Arnold were captured by the Folk of the Secret Mountain. We don't know why – but I am sure they are there."

"We cannot search for them, then," said Pilescu. "We must fly to the nearest town and bring a proper search party back here."

"No, no, Pilescu," cried everyone in dismay.

"*We* are going to look for our parents," said Mike proudly. "Pilescu, this is the third great adventure we children have had, and I tell you we are all plucky and daring. We will *not* fly away and leave others to follow this adventure."

All the children vowed and declared that they would

not go with Ranni and Pilescu, and the two men looked at one another over the camp fire.

"They are like a litter of tiger-cubs," said Ranni in his own language to Pilescu.

Prince Paul laughed excitedly. He knew that Ranni wanted to follow the adventure himself, and that this meant that Paul too would be with him, for he would not leave his little master now. Paul turned to the other children.

"It's all right," he said. "We shan't go! Ranni means to help us."

For a long time that night the little camp talked over Ranni's strange tale. Where was the Secret Mountain? Who were the strange red-haired people who lived there? Why had they captured Captain and Mrs Arnold? How in the world were the searchers to find the way into the mountain if not even the people round about know it? For a long time all these questions were discussed again and again.

Then Pilescu looked at his watch. "It is very late!" he exclaimed. "Children, you must sleep. Ranni, I will keep watch tonight, for you must be very tired."

"Very well," said Ranni. "You shall take the first half of the night and I will take the other. We can do nothing but wait until tomorrow, when the man who saw the White Swallow will come to talk to us."

Very soon all the camp was asleep, except Pilescu, who sat with his gun in hand, watching the moving animal-shapes that prowled some distance away, afraid to come nearer because of the fire. Pilescu loved an adventure as much as anyone, and he thought deeply about the Folk of the Secret Mountain, with their creamy-yellow skins, red hair and curious green eyes.

The big Baronian was brave and fierce, as were all the men from the far-off land of Baronia, where Paul's father was king. He was afraid of nothing. The only thing he did not like was taking the five children into danger – but, as Ranni had said, they were like tiger-cubs, fierce and daring, and had already been through some astonishing adventures by themselves.

Morning came, and with it came the native who had seen the White Swallow come down. He was very tall, but with a sly and rather cruel face. Carrying three spears for him came a small, thin boy, with a sharp face and such a merry twinkle in his eyes that all the children liked him at once.

"Who is that boy?" asked Jack, curiously. Ranni asked the man, and he replied, making a scornful face.

"It's his nephew," said Ranni. "He is the naughty boy of the family, and is always running away, exploring the country by himself. Children of this tribe are not allowed to do this – they have to go with the hunters and be properly trained. This little chap is disobedient and wild, so his uncle has taken him in hand, as you see."

"I like the look of the boy," said Jack. "But I don't like the uncle at all. Ask him about the White Swallow, Ranni. See if he knows anything about Captain and Mrs Arnold."

Ranni did not speak the man's language very well, but he could understand it better. The man spoke a lot, waving his arms about, and almost acting the whole thing so that the children could nearly understand his story without understanding his words.

"He says he was hunting not far from here, keeping a good look-out for any of the Secret Mountain Folk, when he heard the sky making a strange noise," said Ranni. "He looked up, and saw a great white bird that said 'r-r-r-r-r-r-r,' as loudly as a thunderstorm."

The children shouted with laughter at this funny description of an aeroplane. Ranni could not help grinning, even though he knew the man had probably never seen a plane before, and went on with his translation.

"He says the big white bird flew lower, and came down

over there. He stayed behind his tree without moving. He thought the big white bird would see him and eat him."

Again everyone laughed. The tribesman grinned too, showing two rows of flashing white teeth. The little boy behind joined in the laughter, but stopped very suddenly when his uncle turned round and hit him hard on the side of the head.

"Oh my goodness!" shouted Jack in surprise. "Why shouldn't he laugh too?"

"Children of this tribe must not laugh if their elders are present," said Ranni. "This man's nephew must often get into serious trouble, I should think! He looks as if he is on the point of giggling every minute!"

The man went on with his story. He told how he had seen two people climb out of the big white bird, which amazed him very much. Then he saw something that frightened him even more than seeing the aeroplane and the pilots. He saw some of the Folk of the Secret Mountain, with their flaming red hair and pale skins!

He had been so interested in the aeroplane that he had stayed watching behind his tree – but the sight of the Secret Mountain Folk had given him such a scare that his legs had come to life and he had run back towards his village.

"So you didn't see what happened to the White Bird people?" asked Ranni, deeply disappointed. The man shook his head. The small boy watching, imitated him so perfectly that all the children laughed, disappointed though they were.

The man looked behind to see what everyone was smiling at and caught his nephew making faces. He strode over to him and knocked him down flat on the ground. The boy gave a yell, sat up and rubbed his head.

"What a horrid fellow this man is," said Pilescu in disgust. "Ranni, ask him if he can tell us the way to the Secret Mountain."

42

Ranni asked him. The man showed signs of fear as he answered.

"He says yes, he knows the way to the mountain, but he does not know the way inside," said Ranni.

"Ask him if he will take us there," said Pilescu. "Tell him we will pay him well if he does."

At first the man shook his head firmly when Ranni asked him. But when Pilescu took a mirror from the cabin of the plane, and showed the man himself in it, making signs to him that he would give it to him as well, the man was tempted.

"He thinks the mirror is wonderful. He is in the mirror as well as outside it," translated Ranni with a grin. "He says it would be a good thing to have it, because then if he is hurt or wounded, it will not matter – the man inside the mirror, which is himself too, will be all right, and he will be him instead."

Everyone smiled to hear this. The man had never seen a mirror before, he had only caught sight of himself in pools. It seemed as if another himself was in the strange gleaming thing that the red-haired man was offering him. He stood in front of the mirror, making awful faces, and laughing.

Ranni asked him again if he would show them the way to the Secret Mountain if he gave him the mirror. The man nodded. The mirror was too much for him. Why, he had never seen anything like it before.

"Tell him we will start tomorrow at dawn," said Pilescu. "I want to make sure that we have everything we need before we set off. Also I want to look at the engines of the White Swallow and our own plane to see that they are all ready to take off, should we find Captain and Mrs Arnold, and want to leave in a hurry!"

The children were in a great state of excitement. They hardly knew how to keep still that day, even when the great heat came down, and they had to lie in the shade, panting and thirsty. It was so exciting to think that they really were to set off the next morning to the strange Secret Mountain.

"I'm jolly glad Ranni and Pilescu are coming with us," said Nora. "I do love adventures – but I can't help feeling a little bit funny in the middle of me when I think of those strange folk that live in the middle of a forgotten mountain.

The Coming Of Mafumu

Pilescu and Ranni tinkered about with the White Swallow, which stood not very far off, and with their own plane most of the day. The children, of course, had thoroughly examined the White Swallow, feeling very sad to think that Captain and Mrs Arnold had had to leave it so mysteriously.

Mike had thought that there might have been a note left to tell what had happened, but the children had found nothing at all.

"That's not to be wondered at," said Pilescu. "If they had had time to write a note, they would have had time also to fly off in the plane! As far as I can see there is nothing wrong with the White Swallow at all – though I can see where some small thing has been cleverly mended. It seems to me that Captain and Mrs Arnold were taken by surprise and had not time to do anything at all."

"Both planes are fit to fly off at a moment's notice," said Ranni, appearing beside Pilescu, very oily and black, his red hair hanging wet and lank over his forehead.

"Ought we to leave anyone on guard?" asked Mike. "Suppose we come back and find that the planes have been damaged?"

Ranni frowned. "We will lock them of course, but I don't

44

think anyone would damage them. I just hope a herd of elephants doesn't come and trample through them! We must just leave the planes and hope for the best."

Pilescu had got ready big packages of food and a few warm clothes and rugs. Paul laughed when he saw the woollen jerseys.

"Good gracious, Pilescu, what are we taking those things for? I'd like to go about in a little pair of shorts and nothing else, like that small boy wears!"

"If we go into the mountains it will be much cooler," said Pilescu. "You may be glad of jerseys then."

The day passed slowly by. The children thought it would never end.

"Why is it that time always goes so slowly when you are looking forward to something lovely in the future?" grumbled Mike. "Honestly, this day seems like a week."

But it passed at last, and the sudden night-time came. Monkeys chattered somewhere around, and big frogs in the washing-pool set up their usual tremendous croaking.

Next day, at dawn, their guide arrived, and behind him, as usual, came the little boy, his nephew, wearing his scanty shorts. The boy wore no hat at all, and the five children wondered why in the world he didn't get sunstroke.

"I suppose he's coming too," said Jack, pleased. "I wonder what his name is. Ask him, Ranni."

The boy grinned and showed all his white teeth when Ranni shouted to him. He answered in a shrill voice:

"Mafumu, Mafumu!"

"His name is Mafumu," said Ranni. "All right, Mafumu, don't shout your name at us any more!"

Mafumu was so overjoyed at being spoken to by the big Ranni that he kept shouting and wouldn't stop.

"Mafumu, Mafumu, Mafumu!"

He was stopped in the usual way by his uncle, who slapped him hard on the head. Mafumu fell over, made a face at his uncle's back, and got up again. The children were very glad he was coming with them. They really couldn't help liking the cheeky little boy, with his twinkling black eyes and his flashing smile.

Ranni closed and locked the entrance door of the cockpit. Then, with a few backward glances at the two gleaming planes, the little company set off on their new adventure. They were silent as they left the camp, for all of them were wondering what might happen in the near future.

Then Mafumu broke the silence by lifting up his shrill voice and singing a strange slow song.

"Sounds a bit like one of the hymns we have in church," said Mike. "Oh no – his uncle is going for him again. Golly, how I wish he'd stop – he is always hitting poor Mafumu."

Mafumu was slapped into silence. He came behind the whole company, sulking, carrying a simply enormous load. His uncle also carried a great many packages, balanced most marvellously on his head. Ranni explained that the natives were used to carrying goods this way and thought nothing of taking heavy loads for many, many miles.

Soon the open space where the planes had landed was left behind. The little company came towards what looked like a wood, but which was really a small forest that reached almost to the foot of the nearest mountain.

It was very dark in the forest after the glare of the sunlight. The trees were so thick, and heavy rope-like creepers hung down from them everywhere. The children could see no path at all to follow, but the tribesman led them steadily on, never once upsetting any of the many packages piled up on his head.

The chattering of monkeys was everywhere. The children saw the little brown creatures peering down at them, and laughed with delight to see a mother monkey

46

holding a tiny baby in her arms. Other wild creatures scuttled away, and once their guide gave a loud shout and flung his spear at a large snake that slid silently away.

"Oooh," said Nora, startled. "I forgot there might be snakes here. I hope I don't tread on one. I say, isn't this an exciting forest? It's like one in a fairy-tale. I feel as if witches and fairies might come out at any moment."

"Well, just make sure you don't wander off looking for fairy castles," said Pilescu. There are probably lots of snakes and insects in the undergrowth, and you can be sure our guide is taking us by the safest path."

Mafumu was enjoying himself. He was a long way behind his uncle, for the guide led the way, and Mafumu came at the tail of the company. Next to him was Jack, and Mafumu was doing his best to make friends with him.

He picked a brilliant scarlet blossom from one of the trees and tried to stick it behind Jack's ear. Jack was most annoyed, and the others laughed till they cried at the sight of Jack with a red flower behind his ear. Mafumu thought that Jack didn't like the colour of the flower, so he picked a bright blue one and tried that.

Jack found himself decorated with this flower, and he took it from his ear crossly, whilst the others giggled again.

"Shut up, Mafumu," he said.

Mafumu was very quick at picking up what he heard the children say, even though he did not understand the words. "Shutup, shutup, shutup," he repeated in delight. He called to Ranni. "Shutup, shutup, shutup!"

Nobody could help laughing at Mafumu. He was so silly, so cheerful, so quick, and even when his uncle was unkind to him he was smiling a moment later.

He still badly wanted to make friends with Jack, and the next present he made to the boy was a large and juicy-looking fruit of some sort. He pressed it into Jack's hand, flashing his white teeth, and saying some thing that sounded like "Ammakeepa-lotti-loo."

47

Jack looked at the fruit. He smelt it. It had a most delicious scent, and smelt as sweet as honey. "Is it safe to eat this, Ranni?" he called.

Ranni looked round and nodded. "Yes – that is a rare fruit, only found in forests like these. Did Mafumu find it for you?"

"Yes," said Jack. "He keeps on giving me things. I wish he wouldn't."

"Well, tell him to give them to me instead," cried Peggy. "I'd love to have those beautiful flowers and that delicious-looking yellow fruit. It looks like a mixture of an extra-large pear and a giant grape!"

Jack tasted it. It was the loveliest fruit he had ever had, so sweet that it seemed to be made of honey. The boy gave a taste to the two girls. They made faces of delight, and Nora called to Mafumu.

"Find some more please, Mafumu; find some more!"

"Shutup, shutup, shutup," replied Mafumu cheerfully, quite understanding what Nora meant, and thinking that his answer was correct. He disappeared into the forest and was gone such a long time that the children began to be alarmed.

"Ranni! Do you think Mafumu is all right?" shouted Jack from the back of the line. "He's been gone for ages. He won't get lost, will he?"

Ranni spoke to the guide in front. The man laughed and made some sort of quick answer.

"He says that Mafumu knows his forest as an ant knows its own anthill," translated Ranni. "He says, too, that he would not care at all if Mafumu were eaten by a crocodile or caught by a leopard. He doesn't seem at all fond of his small nephew, does he?"

"I think he's a horrid man," said Peggy. "My goodness – are there leopards about?"

"Well, you needn't worry even if there are," said Ranni. "Pilescu and I have guns, and our leader has plenty of spears ready."

It was cool and dark in the forest and the little company were able to go for a long way without resting, twisting and turning through the trees. Frogs croaked somewhere, and birds called harshly. Jack spotted some brightly coloured parrots, and there were some rather queer squirrel-like creatures that hopped from branch to branch. The monkeys were most interested in the children, and a little crowd of them swung through the trees, following the company for quite a long way.

At last the forest came to an end. The trees became fewer, and the sun shone between, making golden freckles on the ground that danced and moved as the trees waved their branches.

"Well, that couldn't have been a very big forest if it only took us such a short time to go through," said Mike.

"It is really a very big one," said Pilescu. "But we have only gone through a corner of it. If we went deeper into it we should not be able to get along. We should have to take axes and knives to cut our way through."

The children were still worried about Mafumu, but he suddenly appeared again, bent nearly double under his old load and carrying a new load of the juicy-looking yellow fruit. He gave some to each child, grinning cheerfully.

"Oh, thanks awfully," said Mike. "Golly, this is just what I wanted – I *was* thirsty! This fruit melts in my mouth. Thanks awfully, Mafumu."

"Thanksawfully, shutup," said the little boy in delight.

"I think we'll all have a rest here," said Pilescu. "The sun is still high in the sky and we can't walk any further for it will be too hot once we are out of the forest. We will go on again when the sun is lower."

Nobody felt very hungry, for they were all so hot. Mafumu found some other kind of fruit for everybody, not nearly so nice, but still, very juicy and sweet. His uncle ate no fruit, but took something from a pouch and chewed that.

All the children fell asleep in the noonday sun except

Mafumu. He squatted down beside Jack and watched the boy closely. Jack grinned at him and even when he slept Mafumu stayed by his side.

The grown-ups sat talking quietly together. Ranni looked round at the sleeping company. "The children have done well today," he said to Pilescu. "They must have a good night's rest tonight as well, for tomorrow we must climb high."

"I wish that this adventure was over, and not just beginning," said Pilescu uneasily, fanning Paul's hot face with a spray of leaves. The boy was so sound asleep that he felt nothing.

But not one of the children wished that the adventure was over. No – to be in the middle of one was the most exciting thing in the world!

A Very Long March

For two whole days the company marched valiantly onwards. The children were all good walkers except Paul, and as Ranni carried him on his shoulders when he was very tired, that helped a good deal.

They had now come to the mountains and the guide was leading them steadily upwards. It was tiring to climb always, but the children soon got used to it. Mafumu did not seem to mind anything. He skipped along, and went just as fast uphill as down. He had picked up some more words now, and used them often, much to the children's amusement.

"Goodgracious, shutup, hallo, thanksawfully," he would chant as he skipped along, his load of packages balanced marvellously and never falling. "Hurryup, hurryup, hallo!"

"Isn't he an idiot?" said Jack. But although the children

laughed at his antics, they all liked the cheerful boy enormously. He brought them curious things to eat – toadstools that were marvellous when cooked – strange leaves that tasted of peppermint and were good to chew – fruit of all kinds, some sweet, some bitter, some too queer-tasting to eat, though Mafumu ate everything, and smacked his lips and rubbed his round tummy in delight.

On the second day, when the children were all climbing steadily, Mafumu saw a clump of bushes high up some way in front of them. They were hung with brilliant blue berries, which Mafumu knew were sweet and juicy. He took a short cut away from the path, and climbed to the bushes.

He stripped them of the blue berries and began to jump back to join the company. But on the way his foot caught against a loose stone that rattled down the hillside and fell against his uncle's leg.

In a fury the guide sprang at his nephew and caught hold of him. He beat him hard with his spear, and the little boy cried out in pain, trying his best to wriggle away.

"Oh, stop him, stop him!" yelled Jack, who hated unkindness of any sort. "Mafumu was only getting berries for us. Stop, stop!"

But the guide did not stop, and Jack ran up to him. He wrenched the spear out of the man's hand and threw it down the hillside in anger, his face red with rage.

The spear went clattering down and was lost. The guide turned on Jack, but Ranni was beside him, talking sternly. The man listened, his eyes flashing. He said nothing, but turned to lead the way up the mountain-side once more.

"What did you say to him, Ranni?" asked Mike.

"I told him he would not get paid if he hit anyone again," said Ranni shortly. "He was just about to strike Jack. Don't interfere again, Jack. I'll do the interfering."

"Sorry," said Jack, though he was still boiling with rage. Mafumu had got up from the ground, his face and arms covered with bruises. He ran to Jack and hugged him, speaking excitedly in his own language.

"Stop it, for goodness sake, Mafumu," said Jack uncomfortably. "Oh golly, I wish you wouldn't. Do let go, Mafumu!"

"He says he will be your friend for ever," said Ranni with a grin. "He says he will leave his uncle and his tribe and come and be with the wonderful boy all his life. He says you are a king of boys!"

"King Jack, the king of boys!" shouted Mike, clapping Jack on the shoulder.

"Shut up," growled Jack.

"Shutup, shutup, shutup," echoed Mafumu happily, letting go of Jack and walking as close to his hero as he possibly could.

After that, of course, Mafumu adored Jack even more than before, and Jack got used to seeing the little boy always at his heels, like a shadow. He could not get rid of him, so he put up with it, secretly rather proud that Mafumu should have picked him out to be his friend.

It got steadily cooler as they all climbed higher. The mountains seemed never-ending.

"We shall never, never get to the top," said poor Peggy, who had started a blister on one heel.

"We're not going to the top," said Mike. "All we are doing is climbing to a place where we can pass between two mountains. Ranni says we shall strike off to the east there, by that enormous rock, and make our way to a place where this mountain and the next one meet. There is a pass between them – and from there we can see the Secret Mountain!"

"Golly!" said Paul. "Are we as near as all that?"

"Well – not awfully near," said Mike. "But we'll get there sooner or later. Have you rubbed that stuff that Ranni gave you, all over your heel, Peggy?"

"Yes," said Peggy. "And I've put a wad of cotton-wool over the blister too. I shall be all right."

"Good girl," said Mike. "I don't think things like blisters ought to creep into adventures like ours!"

Everyone laughed. They had put on woollen jerseys now and were glad of them, especially when clouds rolled down the mountain-side and covered them in mist. They were glad of hot drinks, too, heated over a fire of sticks.

Mafumu always knew where water was, and he brought it to the fire in the saucepan that Ranni gave him. It was easy to make hot cocoa with plenty of sugar in it from one of the packages, and how good it tasted!

They slept in a cave that night, stretched out on the rugs. The girls cuddled together for it was very cold. Mafumu slept on nothing at all, and did not seem to feel the cold in the least. He really was a most tough little boy.

Ranni and Pilescu did not both sleep at the same time, but took turns at keeping watch – not only for any mountain leopard that might come into the cave, but also for any of the Folk from the Secret Mountain! They did not know what such strange people might do.

Mafumu was curled up on the rocky ground by Jack. Jack had offered him a share of the rug, but the boy would not take any of Jack's coverings. He even tried to cover Jack up, much to the amusement of everyone else.

"He wants to be your nurse," chuckled Mike.

"Oh, do stop making jokes like that," grumbled poor Jack. "I can't help Mafumu behaving like this, can I? He will keep on doing it."

"Tomorrow we shall see the Secret Mountain," said Nora sleepily. "I'm just longing to get my first glimpse of it. I wonder what it will be like."

"I wonder if Mafumu's unpleasant uncle can possibly tell us any way to get into it," said Mike. "It's not going to be much good gazing at a secret mountain, if we don't know the secret of getting into the middle of it!"

"Do you suppose there are halls and rooms and passages in it?" said Peggy, cuddling closer to Nora to try and get warm. "How I do love secret things!"

Mafumu took hold of Jack's rug and pulled it more closely over the elder boy and for once in a way Jack did not stop him. The boy was almost asleep. He lay there in the cave, his eyes closing.

"Goodnight, Mafumu," said Jack sleepily.

"Hallo, goodnight," answered Mafumu, happy to be with his new friends.

"Tomorrow we shall see the – the – Secret – Mountain," murmured Jack, and then fell fast asleep.

Tomorrow – yes, tomorrow!

The Secret Mountain

The next day dawned very misty. White clouds rolled round about the mountain pass, and it was difficult to see very far ahead. The children were most disappointed.

But as they walked steadily upwards towards the rocky pass between the two mountains, the sun began to shine more strongly through the mists, and soon the last fragments disappeared.

"Isn't everything glorious!" cried Mike, looking round. Below them lay the great hillside they had climbed, and in the distance, stretching for miles, they could see the rolling country of Africa. Above them towered the mountains and overhead was the blazing sky.

"All the colours look so much brighter here," said Peggy, picking a brilliant orange flower and sticking it into her hat. "Oh, Mafumu, for goodness sake!"

Mafumu had darted forward when he saw Peggy picking

the flower, and had plucked a great armful of the orange flowers, which he now presented to her. The little girl laughed and took them. She didn't know what to do with them, but in the end she and Nora stuck them all round their hats.

"I feel like a walking garden now," said Nora. "I wish Mafumu wouldn't be so generous!"

"Soon we shall arrive at the place from which we get our first glimpse of the Secret Mountain," said Ranni.

That made everyone walk forward even more eagerly. For three hours they climbed towards the rocky pass, the guide leading the way, finding a path even when it seemed almost impossible to get by. Sometimes there was hard climbing to be done, and Ranni and Pilescu had to pull and push the children to get them up the hillside or over big rocks. Sometimes they passed through thick little copses of strange trees, where brilliant birds called to one another. It was all unknown country and most exciting.

At last they reached the top of the pass. From here they could see the other side of the range of mountains. Truly it was a marvellous place to stand! From this mountain peep-hole the little company could see both east and west – rolling country behind them for miles, disappearing into purple hills – and in front another range of mountains towering high into the sky, with a narrow valley in between the mountains they were on, and the range opposite.

Everyone stood silent, even the guide. It was surely the most wonderful sight in the world, the children thought. Then Paul spoke eagerly.

"Which is the Secret Mountain? Where is it? Quick, tell us!"

Ranni spoke to the guide, and he raised his spear and pointed with it. He spoke shortly to Ranni.

Ranni turned to the listening children. "Do you see that mountain over there, with clouds rolling round it? Wait till they clear a little, and you will see that the mountain has a curiously flat top. You will also see that it has a yellowish look, because, so this fellow says, a rare yellow bush grows there, which at some season of the year turns a fiery red."

This all sounded rather weird. The children gazed across to the opposite mountains – and each saw the one that had clouds covering it. As they watched, the clouds uncurled themselves, and became thinner and thinner, at last disappearing altogether. And then everyone could see the curious Secret Mountain!

It stood out boldly from the other because of its yellow appearance, and also because of its strange summit. This was almost flat, like a table-top. The guide raised his spear again, and pointed, muttering something to Ranni.

"He says that he has heard that the Folk of the Mountain sometimes appear on the top of it, and that they worship the sun from there," said Ranni. "Though how anyone could see people so far away I can't imagine. However, it is quite possible that there is a way up inside the mountain to the top."

"Isn't it strange to think of a tribe of people taking such a queer home, and living there apart from everyone else?" said Jack in wonder.

"Oh, that has often happened," said Pilescu. "Sometimes there are tribes living apart from others in the middle of dense forests – sometimes on islands – sometimes even in deserts. But a mountain certainly seems one of the strangest places to choose."

"I suppose they come out to hunt, and that is how the other people know about them," said Mike.

"I think you are right," said Ranni. "Well – there's the wonderful Secret Mountain – and here we are. The mountain won't come to us, so we must go to the mountain. Shall we set off again, Pilescu?"

The guide spoke rapidly to Ranni, making faces and waving his arms about.

"He says he doesn't want to come any further," said Ranni. "Is it any good his coming?" He swears he doesn't know any way into the mountain."

"He's going to come with us all the way," said Pilescu firmly. "He may find that he knows the way in after all, once we get there! Anyway, he won't get paid if he doesn't come."

"Where *is* the money?" asked Nora. "It's not being carried along with us, is it?"

"Of course not," said Ranni with a laugh.

"Well, did you put it back into the cabin of the plane?" said Jack. "You locked that."

"No. I wrapped up the money carefully and hid it under the low brances of that big tree by the washing-pool before we left," said Ranni. "I shall tell our guide where it is when he has done his job – but not before!"

"That's a clever idea," said Peggy. Ranni turned to the man and spoke to him again. He shook his head violently. Ranni shrugged his shoulders, and bade the little company set off.

They made their way along a rocky path, leaving the guide and Mafumu behind. But they had not gone very far before loud shouts came from the tribesman, and the children saw him leaping along to catch them up. Mafumu trotted behind, his face was one big smile.

His uncle spoke with Ranni, but Ranni shook his head. The children could quite well guess what was happening – the man was asking to be paid, and Ranni was being determined. In the end the guide agreed to go with them once more, and Ranni promised to tell him where the money was as soon as they reached the Secret Mountain.

It was a good thing that their guide went with them, for the way he led them was one which they would never have found for themselves. It was a hidden way, so that the little company would not be seen by any watchers on the Secret Mountain.

Ranni and Pilescu had had no idea that there was this hidden path to the mountain. They would have tried to lead the party across the valley, over marshy ground, or through such thickly growing bushes that it would have been almost impossible to make their way through.

As it was, the tribesman avoided these, and took them to a narrow river, not much more than a large stream, that flowed along swiftly towards the mountain. This stream was almost completely covered in by bushes and trees that met above the water, making a kind of green tunnel, below which the river gurgled and bubbled.

"Golly! What an exciting river!" cried Jack, thrilled to see the dim green tunnel. "How are we going to get along? Is it shallow enough to wade down the stream?"

"In parts it would be, but I don't fancy doing that," said Pilescu. "What is the fellow doing – and Mafumu too? I believe they are making rough rafts for us!"

"What fun!" cried Paul, and he ran to watch the two workers.

Mafumu was busy bringing armfuls of stuff that looked rather like purple cork to his uncle. He had got it from a marshy piece of ground. It smelt horrible.

"Is it cork?" said Paul.

"No – it looks more like some sort of fungus, or enormous toadstool," said Pilescu. "Look at his uncle binding it together with creeper-ropes!"

In two hours' time four small rafts of the horrible-smelling cork were made. They looked rather queer and they smelt even queerer, but they floated marvellously, bobbing about on the water like strange ducks. The children were delighted. It was going to be splendid fun to float down the hidden river, under a green archway of trees, right up to the Secret Mountain!

"Our guide says that his tribe always use these queer rafts to get quickly down this valley, which they fear because of the Mountain Folk," said Ranni. "The stream goes right round the foot of the Secret Mountain, and joins a river round there. Then it goes into the next valley, which is a fine hunting-ground used by Mafumu's tribe. He says that the rafts don't last long – they gradually fall to bits – but last just long enough to take a man into the next valley with safety!"

Pilescu and Paul got on to one raft. It wobbled dangerously, but sank hardly at all into the water. There was only just room for the two of them to squat. They held on to the creeper-ropes that bound the raft together. Then down the stream they went, bobbing like corks.

Ranni and Nora went next. Mike and Peggy went together, and last of all came the guide, Jack, and, of course, Mafumu, who was determined not to leave Jack for even a minute!

It was a strange journey, a little frightening. The trees met overhead and were so thick that no sunlight pierced through to the swift stream. The only light there was glowed a dim green.

"Your face looks green!" cried Peggy to Mike, as they set off together down the strange river-tunnel.

"So does yours!" said Mike. "Everything looks green. I feel as if we must be under water! It's because we can't see any daylight at all – only the green of the trees and of the stream below."

The stream became swifter as it ran down the valley. In no place did the trees break – the tunnel was complete the whole way. The rafts were really splendid, but towards the end of the journey they began to break up a little. The outside edges fell off, and the rafts began to loosen from the creeper-ropes.

"Hie! We shall soon be in the water!" yelled Ranni. "Where do we land?"

The guide shouted something back. "Well, that's a good thing!" cried Ranni. "We're nearly there, children."

The bobbing rafts spun slowly round and round as they

Paul's raft spun into a pool

went along. It really was a most peculiar journey, but the children loved every minute. They were sad to see their rafts gradually coming to pieces, getting smaller and smaller!

Suddenly the stream ran into a large still pool. It ran out again the other end of the pool, but when the guide gave a loud shout, everyone knew that their journey's end had come. The pool was their stopping place. If they went any further they would go right round the mountain and into the next valley.

Ranni's raft spun into the quiet pool, and by pulling at the branches of a nearby tree he dragged himself and Paul to the bank, on which grew thick bushes. All the others followed, though Mike and Peggy nearly sailed right on, for their raft was right in the very middle of the current! However, they managed to swing it round and joined the others.

"If I don't get off my raft it will disappear from under me," said big Ranni, whose weight had made his raft break up more than those of the others. Everyone jumped off their rafts and stood on the banks of the pool. They had to stand on rotting branches and roots, for the trees and bushes grew so thickly there that the bare ground could not be seen.

"Well – we've arrived," said Pilescu. "And now – where's the mountain? We should be at the foot."

The guide, with a frown on his face, took them through the thick bushes, squeezing his way with difficulty, and came to a tall tree. He climbed it, beckoning the others behind him.

Ranni climbed up, and one by one everyone followed. They all wanted to see what the man had to show them. Monkeys fled chattering from the branches as the little company climbed upwards, helping themselves by using the long creepers which hung down like strong ropes.

Their guide took them almost to the top of the tree. It towered over the bush below, and from its top could be seen, quite close at hand, the Secret Mountain!

Everyone stared in amazement at the Secret Mountain

A Pleasant Surprise

The Secret Mountain towered up steeply. It was covered by the curious yellow bushes, which gave it its strange appearance from a distance. The bushes had yellow leaves and waxy-white flowers over which hovered brilliant butterflies and insects of every kind.

But it was the mountain itself that held the children's eyes. It was so steep. It looked quite impossible to climb. It rose up before their eyes, enormous, seeming to touch the sky. They were very near to it, and Nora was quite frightened by its bigness.

The tribesman frowned as he looked at it and muttered strings of queer-sounding words to himself. He was plainly going no further. Only the money he had been promised had made him come so far. He slid down the tree and spoke rapidly to Ranni.

Ranni told him where he would find his reward, and the man nodded, showing all his white teeth. He called to Mafumu, and the two of them disappeared into the bushes.

"Hie, Mafumu – say good-bye!" yelled Jack, very sorry indeed to see the merry little fellow going. But his uncle had Mafumu firmly by one ear and the boy could do nothing.

"Well, he might at least have said good-bye," said Peggy. "I did like him. I wish he was going with us."

"Did Mafumu's uncle give you any idea at all as to how we might get into the mountain?" Mike asked Ranni. Ranni shook his head.

"All he would say was that we should have to walk through the rock!" he said. "I don't think he really knew what he meant. It was just something he had heard."

"Walk through the rock!" said Jack. "That sounds a bit like Ali Baba and the Forty Thieves. Do you remember – the robbers made their home in a cave inside a hill – and when the robber chief said 'Open Sesame!' a rock slid aside – and they all went in!"

Pilescu and Ranni did not know the tale, and they listened with interest.

"Well, the way in *may* be by means of a moving rock," said Ranni. "But, good gracious, we can't go all round this enormous mountain looking for a moving rock! And if we did find it, I'm sure we should not know the secret of moving it!"

They were all sitting down at the foot of the tree, eating a meal, for they were hungry and tired. It was hot in the valley, even in the shade of the trees. The calls of the birds, the hum of insects and the chattering of monkeys sounded all the time. The sun was sinking low, and Pilescu made up his mind that they must all camp where they were for the night. He glanced up at the enormous branches of the tree they were under, and wondered if, by spreading out the rugs in a big fork halfway up, the children could sleep there safely.

"I don't like letting the children sleep on the ground tonight," he said to Ranni. "I daren't light a fire to keep wild creatures away, because if we do we shall attract the attention of the Mountain Folk – and we don't want to be surrounded and captured in the night. Do you think that tree would hold them all?"

Ranni glanced upwards. "The tree would hold them all right," he said. "But supposing they fall out in their sleep!"

"Oh, we can easily prevent that," said Pilescu. "We can tie them on with those creeper-ropes."

The two men had been talking to one another in their own language, and only Paul understood. He listened with delight.

"We're going to sleep up in a tree!" he told the others, who listened in astonishment. "We daren't light a fire tonight, you see."

"Goly! How exciting!" said Mike. "I really don't think anyone could have had such a lot of thrills in a short time as we've had this week!"

Pilescu made the children climb the tree whilst it was still daylight. Halfway up the branches forked widely, spreading out almost straight, and there was a kind of rough platform. Pilescu stuffed the spaces between the branches with creepers, twigs and some enormous leaves that he pulled from another tree. Then he spread out half the rugs, and told the children to settle down.

They spread themselves on the rugs, joyful to think they were to spend a whole night in a tree. Some monkeys, who had been watching from the next tree, set up a great chattering when they saw the children settling down.

"They think you are their cousins from a far-off land," said Pilescu with a broad grin. "They're not far wrong, either. Now lie still whilst I cover you with these other rugs, and then I'm going to tie you firmly to the branches."

"Oh, Pilescu – we're too hot to be covered!" cried Paul, pushing away the rug.

"It will be very chilly in the early morning," said Pilescu. "Very well – leave the rug half off now, and pull it on again later."

Pilescu and Ranni made a very good job of tying the children to the tree. Now they were safe! The two men slid down the big tree to the ground. The monkeys fled away. The children talked drowsily for a while, and Peggy tried her hardest to keep awake and enjoy the strangeness of a night up a tree.

But her eyes were very heavy, and although she listened for a while to the enormously loud voices of some giant frogs in the nearby marsh, and the curious call of a bird that seemed to say, "Do do it, do do it," over and over again, she was soon as fast asleep as the others.

As usual, Ranni and Pilescu took turn and turn about to watch. They both sat at the foot of the great tree, one at one side, the other at the other. Ranni took first turn, and then Pilescu.

Pilescu was very wide awake. He sat with his gun in his hand watching for any movement or sound nearby that might mean an enemy of some kind. He, too, heard the frogs, and the bird crying "Do do it, do do it." He heard the trumpeting of far-off elephants, the roar of some big forest cat, maybe a leopard, and the stir of the wind in the branches of the trees.

And then, towards dawn, he heard something and saw something that was not bird or animal. Something or someone was creeping between the bushes, very slowly, very carefully. Pilescu stiffened, and took hold of his gun firmly. Could it be any of the Folk of the Secret Mountain?

The Something came nearer, and Pilescu put out a hand and shook Ranni carefully. Ranni awoke at once.

"There's something strange over there," whispered Pilescu. "I can only see a shadow moving. Do you suppose it's a scout sent out by the Mountain Folk?"

Ranni peered between the bushes in the dim light of half-dawn. He, too, could see something moving.

"I'll slip behind that bush and pounce on whatever it is," whispered Ranni. "I can move away from this side of the tree without being seen."

So big Ranni slid away as silently as a cat, and crawled behind the nearest bush. From there he made his way to another bush and waited for the Something to come by.

He pounced on it – and there came a terrified yell, and a shrill voice that cried out something that sounded like "Yakka, longa, yakka, longa!"

Ranni picked up what he had caught and carried it to

66

Pilescu. It was something very small – something that both men knew very well. They cried out in amazement.

"Mafumu!"

Yes – it *was* Mafumu. Poor Mafumu, crawling painfully along the bushes, searching for the friends he had left the day before.

"Mafumu! What has happened?" asked Ranni. The boy told him his story.

"I went back a long way with my uncle, but he was unkind to me, and he told me he would give me to the first crocodile he saw in a river. So I ran away from him to come back to my new friends. And a big thorn went into my foot – see – so I could not walk, I could only crawl."

The poor little boy was so tired, and in such pain that tears fell out of his eyes. As dawn came stealing over the countryside, big Ranni took the poor little fellow into his arms, whilst Pilescu pulled out the great thorn from his foot. He bathed the hurt and bound it up with lint and gauze. He gave the boy something to eat and drink and then told him to sleep.

But comfortable though he was in Ranni's arms, Mafumu would not stay there. He must go to his new friends, and especially Jack!

So up the tree he climbed, and was soon snuggled down beside Jack, who did not even wake when the boy lay almost on top of him.

"Mafumu may be helpful to us," said Pilescu to Ranni. "He knows the language of the tribes around here, he knows where to find fruit and drinking water, and he can guide as well."

In the morning, what loud cries of amazement came from the tree above, when the children awoke and found Mafumu with them!

"Mafumu!"

"How *did* you get here, Mafumu?"

"Mafumu, get off me, I can't move!"

"Mafumu, what have you done to your foot?"

Mafumu sat up on Jack's legs and grinned round happily.

"Me back," he said, proud that he could say some English words with the right meaning. "Me back." Then he went off into his usual gibberish.

"Hallo, goodnight, shutup, what's the matter!"

Everyone laughed. Jack punched him on the back in a friendly manner. "You're an idiot, but an awfully nice idiot," he said. "We're jolly glad to see you again. I shouldn't be surprised if you help us quite a lot!"

And Jack was right, as we shall soon see!

The Wonderful Waterfall

As the little company sat eating their breakfast they talked about what would be the best thing to do. How were they to find a way into the Secret Mountain?

"You know, I believe that Mafumu's uncle knew something," said Ranni. "I rather think there is some sort of secret way in, if only we could find it."

"Ranni! I know how we could find it!" said Mike excitedly. "Couldn't we hide until we see some of the Secret Mountain Folk – and then track them to see how they get inside?"

"Yes – if we could only see some of the folk, without them seeing us!" said Ranni. "We should have to scout round a bit – it is perfectly plain that no one could possibly get into the mountain from *this* side – it's so steep. I don't believe even a goat could get up it!"

"Well – let's explore round the other side," said Mike. "Hurry up and finish your breakfast, girls. I can hardly wait."

"Of course, you realize that we shall all have to be very careful," said Pilescu. "It is quite possible that the folk in the Secret Mountain already know we are here, and are waiting to capture us."

"Oooh," said Nora, not liking the sound of that at all. "I shall keep very near to you and Ranni, Pilescu!"

"I hope you will," said Pilescu, taking the little girl's hand in his. "I would not have come on this mad adventure if I had known what it was to be. But now it is too late to draw back."

"I should think so!" cried Mike indignantly. "Why, Pilescu, things are going very well, I think. We have discovered where our parents are – and we may be able to rescue them at any time now. We've got guns!"

"Yes – but first we have to find where your parents *are!*" said Pilescu. "And how to get to them."

"Well, let's make a start," said Mike. "Come on. It will be too hot soon to explore anywhere! All my clothes are sticking to me already."

The party packed up their things. Ranni and Pilescu carried most of them, but the children had to take some too. Mafumu as usual carried his share balanced on his head. They all set off cautiously, keeping as near to the foot of the queer steep mountain as they could, and yet taking cover as they went, so as not to be seen.

It was difficult going. Mafumu was a great help, for he seemed to know the best paths at once. He went in front, with Ranni and Jack just behind him. Pilescu was at the back, his hand on his gun. He was taking no risks!

As they went round the mountain a strange noise came to their ears.

"What's that?" said Nora, alarmed. They all stood and listened. Mafumu beckoned them on, not knowing why they had stopped.

"Big noise, Mafumu, big noise," said Jack, holding up his hand for Mafumu to listen. The boy laughed.

"Big water," he said. "Big water." He was very proud of himself for being able to answer Jack in his own language. He was as sharp as a needle, and in half an hour was quite able to pick up twenty or more new words.

"Big water" said Jack puzzled. "Does he mean the sea?"

"No – I know what it is – it's a waterfall!" said Mike. "Hark! It sounds like thunder, but it's really water tumbling down the mountain-side not far off. Come on – I bet I'm right."

The little company pressed on, following their new guide. The noise grew louder. It really did sound like thunder, but was more musical. The echoes went rolling round the valley, and now and again the noise seemed to get inside the children's heads in a queer manner. They shook their heads to get it out! It was funny.

And then they suddenly saw the waterfall! It was simply magnificent. It fell almost straight down the steep mountain-side with a tremendous noise. Spray rose high into the air, and hung like a mist over the fall. The children could feel its wetness on their faces now and again from where they stood, awed and silent at the sight of such a wonderful fall of water.

"My goodness!" said Peggy, full of astonishment and delight. "No wonder it makes such a noise! It's a *marvellous* waterfall. It's coming from the inside of the mountain!"

"Yes – it is," said Mike, shading his eyes and looking upwards. "There must be an underground river that wanders through the mountain and comes out at that steep place. Golly! How are we going to get by?"

It was very difficult. They had to go a good way out of their path. The waterfall made a surging, violent river at its foot, that shouted and tumbled its way down the valley, and joined the hidden river down which they had come not long before.

Mafumu was not to be beaten by a waterfall! He made his way alongside the surging water until he came to a shallow part, where big boulders stuck up all the way across.

"Hurryup, hurryup," he said, pointing to the stones. "We go there, hurryup."

"I believe we *could* get across there," said Ranni. "The stones are almost like stepping-stones. I will carry Nora across, and then Peggy – and you take Paul, Pilescu. The boys can manage themselves."

"*I* can manage by *myself*," said the little Prince indignantly. "I'm a boy too, are'nt I?"

"You are not so big as the others," said Pilescu with a grin, and he caught up the angry boy and put him firmly on his shoulder. Paul was red with rage, but he did not dare to struggle in case he sent Pilescu into the water. As it was, Pilescu lost his footing once, and almost fell. He just managed to swing himself back in time, and sat with a bump on a big rock. Paul was almost jerked off his shoulder.

The girls were taken safely across. As Ranni had said, the stones were almost like stepping-stones, although one or two were rather far apart – but fortunately the water there was only waist-deep, so a little wading solved the difficulty. The other three boys got across easily. Mafumu jumped like a goat from one stone to another.

And now they were the other side of the waterfall. The noise of its falling still sounded thunderous, but they liked it.

"The foam is like soap-suds," said Nora, watching some swirling down the river.

The sun was now too high for any of them to go further. Even Mafumu was hot and wanted to rest. Also his foot pained him a little now, in spite of the careful bandaging. Everyone curled up in the cool shade of an enormous tree, where they could occasionally feel the delicious coldness of the misty spray from the waterfall.

"I suppose we ought to have a meal," said Ranni, too lazy to do anything about it.

71

"I'm so hot and tired I couldn't eat even an ant's egg!" said Jack.

"You haven't been offered one," said Peggy. "The only thing *I'd* like would be something sweet to drink."

Mafumu disappeared for a moment. He came back laden with some strange-looking fruit, that looked like half nut, half pomegranate. He slit a hole in the top-end and showed Peggy how to drink from it.

"I suppose it's safe to drink the juice of this funny fruit," said Peggy doubtfully.

Ranni nodded. "Mafumu knows what is good or not," he said. "Taste it and see what it's like. If it's nice I'll have some too!"

Peggy tipped up the queer green fruit. It was full of some thick, fleshy juice that trickled out rather like treacle. At first the taste was bitter, like lemon – but as the little girl sucked hard, a delicious coolness spread over her mouth and down her throat.

"Golly!" said Peggy. "It makes me feel as if I've got ice-cream going down me, but not at all sweet. Do have some, you others!"

Soon everyone was sucking the strange fruit. Nobody liked the bitter taste at first, but they all loved the glorious coolness that came afterwards.

"Mafumu, you are very, very clever," said Jack sleepily to the little boy, who was, as usual, curled up as near to his hero as he could manage. Mafumu grinned in delight. A word of praise from Jack made him very happy.

Soon everyone was sleeping soundly – except Ranni, who was on guard, though he found it very difficult to keep awake in such heat. The heat danced round, and everything shimmered and quivered. If it had not been for the coolness that blew over from the nearby waterfall it would have been quite unbearable.

Even the monkeys were quiet – but when they began to move in the tree and to chatter again Ranni awoke everyone. The great heat of the day was gone. If they were going to do any more exploring they must set off at once.

And soon they had a great surprise – for when they rounded a rocky corner of the yellow mountain they heard voices! They all stopped still at once, hardly daring to breathe. *Voices!* Could they be natives – or folk from the Mountain.

The voices were deep and harsh – like the voices of rooks, Jack thought. Ranni waved Mafumu forward, for he knew that the boy could move as silently as a shadow. Mafumu slid down on to his tummy and wriggled forward like a snake. It was marvellous to watch. The other children could not imagine how he could get along as quickly as he did.

Everyone else sank down quietly behind the bushes and stayed as still as mice. Mafumu wriggled forward into a thick bush. It was prickly, but the boy did not seem to feel the scratches. He parted the bush-twigs carefully and looked through.

Then he looked back towards Ranni, his face full of excitement, and beckoned him forward with a wave of his hand. The children had the amusement of watching big Ranni do his best to wriggle forward on his front, just as Mafumu had done. The enormous Baronian did very well, however, and was soon beside the boy, peering through the prickly bush.

The two of them stayed there for some time. The others waited impatiently, hearing the harsh voices of the strangers, and wondering what Ranni and Mafumu could see.

Suddenly there came a grating sound, a rolling, groaning noise – and the voices stopped. The queer noise came again, such a grating sound that it set everyone's teeth on edge! With the rolling sound of rumbling thunder the noise echoed around – and then stopped. Now only the sharp calls of the birds, the ceaseless hum of thousands

73

of insects and the silly chatter of monkeys could be heard – and behind it all the roaring of the waterfall in the distance.

Ranni and Mafumu crawled back, their faces shining with excitement. They took hold of the other children and hurried them to a safe distance. And in the shade of a great rock Ranni told them what he and Mafumu had seen.

The Way Into The Secret Mountain

"Quick, Ranni, tell us everything!" said Jack.

"We saw some of the Folk of the Secret Mountain!" said Ranni. "They certainly do look queer. It is just as Mafumu's uncle said – they have flaming red hair and beards and their skins are a funny yellow. I couldn't see if their eyes were green. They were dressed in flowing robes of all colours, and they wore turbans that showed their red hair."

"Golly!" said Mike, his eyes wide with excitement. "Go on – what happened?"

"The queerest thing happened," said Ranni. "I hardly know if I believe it or not. Well – let me tell you. As we lay there, watching these people talking together in their funny harsh voices, we noticed that they were near a very curious kind of rock."

"What sort of rock?" asked Pilescu.

"It was an enormous rock," said Ranni. "It was strange because it was much smaller at the bottom than at the top, so that it looked almost as if it must fall over. Well, as we watched, one of the Mountain Folk went up to the rock and pushed hard against it."

"Why, he couldn't surely move an enormous rock!" cried Mike.

"That's what *I* thought," said Ranni. "But that rock must be one of these curious balancing rocks that can be pivoted, or swung round, at a touch, no matter how big they are. There are just a few known in the world, and this is another."

"What happened when the rock swung round?" asked Pilescu.

"It not only swung round, it slid to one side," said Ranni. "Just like the rock in the story of Ali Baba that you told me! And behind it was a great door in the mountain-side studded with shining knobs that glittered in the sun!"

Everyone stared at Ranni in silence, too excited to speak. So that was the way into the mountain! They had stumbled on it quite by accident.

"Go on," whispered Peggy at last.

"I couldn't see how the great doorway was opened," said Ranni. "It seemed to slide to one side, very quietly – but whether it was opened from the outside or the inside I really don't know. Then the rock rolled back into place again, and swung back into position with that terrific roaring, groaning sound you heard."

"And did the people go into the mountain?" asked Mike.

"They did," answered Ranni. "We saw no more of them."

Everyone sat silent for a while, thinking of the queer entrance to the Secret Mountain. So that was what Mafumu's uncle had meant when he said that to get into the mountain one had to walk through rock!

"Well – what are we going to do?" said Jack. "We know the way in – but I wonder how that great studded door is opened! Oh, Ranni – can we try to get in tonight?"

"We'd better," said Ranni. "I will try by myself and see

what happens. You can all find good hiding-places nearby and watch. I'll take my gun, you may be sure!"

The children could hardly wait for the sudden nightfall to come. They found themselves good hiding-places – though Jack and Mafumu found the best. Theirs was up a big tree not far from the mountain entrance. Mafumu found it, of course, and helped Jack up there. The others were behind or in the middle of thick bushes.

When the stars hung brightly, and a crescent moon shone in the sky, Ranni crept forward to the strange rock, whose black shadow was enormous in the night. Everyone watched, hardly daring to breathe in case anything happened to Ranni.

Big Ranni stepped quietly up to the rock. He thought he knew exactly where to heave, for he had seen one of the Mountain Folk move the rock and had noted the exact place. But it was difficult to find it at night.

Ranni shoved and pushed. He pressed against the rock and heaved with all his might. Nothing happened. He stopped and mopped his hot forehead, wondering which was the right place to press against.

He tried again and again – and just as he was giving up something happened. He pushed at the right place quite by accident! With a groaning roar the enormous rock swung slowly round and then slid back. The noise it made was terrific. Ranni sprang back into the shadows, afraid that a hundred Mountain Folk might come rushing out at him.

The studded door shone in the moonlight. It did not open. It stood there, big and solid, strange and silent, barring the way. Nobody came. Nobody shouted to see who had swung back the rock. Only the night-sounds came on the air, and the sound of the distant waterfall.

Everyone waited, trembling with excitement. Jack nearly fell out of his tree, he shivered so much with wonder and expectation. But absolutely nothing

76

happened. The rock remained where it was, the door shone behind.

"Ranni! Maybe the Mountain Folk haven't heard the noise!" whispered Pilescu. "Go and try the door."

Ranni crept forward again, keeping to the deep-black shadows. Once or twice the moonlight glinted on the gun he held in his hand. Ranni was taking no chances!

The others watched him from their hiding-places. He went right up to the door. He felt over it with his hand. He pushed gently against it. He tried to slide it to one side. He tried all the studs and knobs to see if by chance any of them opened the great door. But no matter what he did, the door remained shut.

"Let us come and see," whispered Mike to Pilescu. The boy felt that he could not keep still any longer. Pilescu was also longing to go to the mountain door, so he Mike, Paul, and the two girls crept forward in the shadows.

Jack wanted to come too – and began to climb carefully down the tree, getting caught in a great creeper as he did so. Mafumu tried to untangle him, but the more he tried, the more mixed-up poor Jack got.

And then, just as Jack was almost untangled, there came a grinding, grating roar once more – and the enormous rock slid along in front of the great door and swung round slowly into its place.

Behind it, caught between the rock and the door, was everyone except Mafumu and Jack! The girls, Mike, Paul, Ranni and Pilescu were in the narrow passage between.

Ranni tried to stop the rock from sliding back into place, but once started on its way nothing would stop the enormously heavy rock. No one could escape, either, for there was no time to slip out of the trap.

Jack and Mafumu stared towards the rock in the greatest dismay. Jack leapt down from the tree, almost breaking his ankle, and ran towards the mountain.

"Are you safe, are you safe!" he shouted.

But there was no answer. The swinging rock shut the sound of voices away. Jack beat on the rock, he tried to heave it as he had seen Ranni do, and Mafumu did the same. But neither boy could find the secret balance of the rock, and it stayed where it was, colossal in the moonlight, towering above them as they shouted and hammered on it.

And then, behind the rock, the great door slid back! Jack and Mafumu heard it, and fell silent, listening. What was happening?

What indeed? When the door slid back, the little company in front of it stared with wide eyes into a great hall-like cave. It was lighted by glowing lamps, and a wide flight of steps led downwards for a little way. Up these steps came the Folk of the Secret Mountain, dressed in their flowing robes, and carrying strange yellow wands which glittered from top to bottom.

The leader was a very tall man with a bright red beard and gleaming eyes. He spoke to Ranni in language rather like that used by Mafumu. Ranni understood some of it.

"He wants us to follow him," Ranni said to Pilescu. "Got your gun, Pilescu?"

"Yes," said the big Baronian. "But it's no use using it, Ranni. There are too many of them. Put your gun away for the moment, and we'll see what happens. We are in a nice mess now. Only Jack and Mafumu are safe!"

That was a strange journey into the heart of the mountain. Big carved lamps glowed all the way, lighting up enormous flights of steps, great walls, and high rocky ceilings.

"The mountain is full of hollows which these people have made into halls and rooms," said Ranni in a low voice to Pilescu. "Isn't it amazing? Look at those great pictures drawn in colour on the walls! They are strange but very beautiful."

The children gazed in wonder at the great coloured

pictures on the rocky walls of the mountain-caves. Lamps were set cleverly to light up the pictures so that the men and animals in them seemed almost alive. The Secret Mountain was indeed a marvellous place!

At last the long journey through the heart of the mountain came to an end. The little party found themselves in a queer room, whose rocky ceiling rose too high for them to make out by the light of their lamp. Shining stones were set into the walls, and these glittered like stars in the lamplight.

A rough platform was at one end of the room. On it were piled heaps of wonderful rugs, beautifully woven, and marvellously patterned in all the brightest colours imaginable. The children sat down on them, tired out.

Pitchers of ice-cold water stood on a stone table. Everyone drank deep. Flat cakes lay on a shallow dish beside the pitchers. Mike tasted one. It was sweet and dry, quite pleasant to eat. Everyone made a meal, wondering what was going to happen.

The door to their strange room was made of strong wood and had been fastened on the outside. There was nothing to do but wait. The Mountain Folk had left them quite alone in the heart of their queer home.

"We'd better get some rest," said Ranni, and he covered up the three children with the rugs. "I don't know what to wish about Jack. I'm glad he's not caught – and yet I wish we were all here together."

"Perhaps Jack and Mafumu will find some way of rescuing us," said Peggy hopefully.

Ranni laughed shortly. "It's no good hoping that, Peggy! If he tries to get through the rock entrance, and through that big studded door, he will just find himself a prisoner!"

"Do you suppose we'll see Mummy and Daddy?" asked Nora suddenly. "They must be somewhere in this mountain too."

"Yes – that's quite likely," said Pilescu thoughtfully. "Ranni, I'll keep guard for the first half of the night. You go to sleep with the others now."

In spite of all the tremendous excitement of the day the three children were soon asleep on the soft rugs. Ranni did not sleep at first, but at last he dozed off, sitting half upright in case Pilescu needed him quickly.

But the night passed away silently and no one came to disturb them in their cell-like room. The lamp burned steadily, giving a soft light to the curious, high-roofed room. It burned until the day – and even then it still lit the room, for no daylight, no sunlight ever entered the heart of the Secret Mountain.

Mafumu Makes A Discovery

Jack was almost beside himself with alarm and despair. Mafumu kept close beside him, saying nothing at all, looking at Jack out of his big dark eyes. Both boys beat again and again on the great rock that hid the entrance to the Secret Mountain. They heard the door behind slid back into place once more – and then all was silent.

"Come," said Mafumu at last, and he took Jack's arm. He led him to where everyone had left their packs, and the two sat down together.

"What are we to do?" said Jack at last, burying his head in his hands. "I can't bear to think of everyone captured, and we can't get at them."

Mafumu did not understand. He sat there looking at Jack, muttering something in his own language. Then he made a kind of bed of the packs, and pushed Jack down on them.

"We sleep now. I find way soon," said the younger boy flashing his white teeth in the moonlight. They must wait until the morning.

Jack fell asleep at last. As soon as Mafumu saw that his eyes were closed, and heard his regular breathing he crept away from Jack. He stood upright in the brilliant moonlight and looked at the great mountain. How was he going to find a way inside?

Mafumu was not yet ten years old, but he was the sharpest boy in his tribe. He was mischievous, disobedient and wilful, but he had brains. He had lain thinking and thinking of how he might get into the Secret Mountain without going through the entrance of the sliding rock.

And into his mind had come a picture of the great waterfall. He saw it springing from the mountain-side, a great gushing fall of silvery water. He was going to see if it came from the heart of the Secret Mountain!

The boys slipped away in the moonlight. He ran until he came to the great waterfall. It was magnificent in the light of the moon, and the spray shone like purest silver. The noise was twice as loud at night, and he was half-afraid.

He glanced fearfully all round him. He was not afraid of animals or snakes – but he was afraid of being caught by the Folk of the Mountain. If he should be captured, Jack would be left helpless, for he did not know the countryside as Mafumu did.

Mafumu made his way up the mountain, keeping as close to the waterfall as he could. Several times he was drenched, but he liked that. It was cool! The night was hot, and Mafumu was bathed in perspiration as he climbed upwards. The mountain was very steep indeed. It was only by working his way from rocky ledge to ledge that he could get up at all.

At last he came to where the waterfall began. Mafumu worked his way above the fall, and found that, as he had thought, the water gushed straight out of the mountain

Mafumu crawled along the ledge

itself. There must be an underground river running through the mountain. The great hill towered above him, reaching to the clouds. Just below him the waterfall sprang from the mountain, and the fine spray clung to his skin.

He worked his way down again, almost defeated by the noise of the fall. He came to where the water shot out of the mountain in a great arch. He wriggled his way towards it, and found a rocky ledge, wide and damp, just by the fall itself.

Mafumu stood and shivered with fright, for the noise was tremendous. It flowed all around him like rumbling thunder. He edged his way behind the great arch of water, for the rocky ledge stretched all the way behind.

And there, hidden in the misty spray that hung always around and about the waterfall, Mafumu thought that he had discovered another way into the Secret Mountain! For surely, where the water was able to come out of the mountain, he and Jack would be able to go in!

The moon was now almost gone, and darkness crept across the country. Mafumu shivered. He had a curious charm round his neck, made of crocodile's teeth, and he took it into his hand to bring him good luck. He slid quickly down the mountain-side, grazing himself as he went, and bruising his ankle-bones as he knocked them against rocks and stones. But he did not even feel the hurt, so anxious was he to get back to Jack, and tell him what he had found.

He reached Jack as the dawn was breaking. Jack was awake, and very puzzled because Mafumu was gone. The boy looked white and worried. He simply had no idea at all what would be the best thing to do. He had almost made up his mind that he must try to move the rock somehow and get into the mountain so as to be with the others.

But Mafumu had other plans. In funny, broken English he tried to explain to Jack what his idea was.

"Big, big water," he said, and made a noise like the splashing of the waterfall. "Jack come with Mafumu see big, big water. We go into big water. Come."

Jack thought Mafumu was quite mad, but the other boy was so much in earnest that he nodded his head and said Yes, he would come.

Leaving their packs where they were, covered by boulders and stones, the two boys made their way back to the great waterfall. The noise was so deafening that they had to shout to one another to make themselves heard.

Mafumu remembered the way he had taken in the moonlight. He never forgot any path he had once travelled. He even remembered the bushes and rocks he had passed. So now he found it easy to help Jack up the rocky ledges to where the water gushed out of the mountain-side.

Jack was wet through and almost deaf by the time he reached the place where the water appeared from the mountain. He kept shaking his head to get the noise of the fall out of it – but it was impossible! It went on all the time.

Mafumu was excited. He led Jack behind the great curve of the fall, and showed him how the water thundered out just above their heads. It was a queer feeling to stand immediately under a great waterfall, and see it pouring down overhead and in front, a great blue-green mass of water, powerful enough to sweep the boys off and away if it could have reached them!

"How queer to stand behind a waterfall like this," said Jack. "Mafumu – what's the sense of bringing me here? How do you suppose we're going to crawl through water that's coming out of the mountain at about sixty miles an hour. You must be mad."

But Mafumu was not mad. He took Jack right to the other side of the ledge, and pointed to a narrow rocky path that led into the mountain, where the water ran only two or three inches deep. Nearby, the river had worn a deep channel for itself – but this ledge was just above the level of the river, and had water on it only because of the continual splashing and spray that came from the fall.

"We go in here," grinned Mafumu. "We go in here, yes?"

"Golly, Mafumu – I believe you are right!" said Jack, excited. "I believe we can go in here! Though goodness knows how far we'll get, or where it will take us."

"We go now," said Mafumu. "Hurryup, hurryup."

The boys squeezed themselves on to the rocky ledge. If they had slipped into the great torrent of water that poured out, that would have been the end of them. But they were careful to hold on to bits of jutting-out rock, so as not to fall. The ledge was damp and slippery. The air was full of fine spray. It was queer to be squeezing by a great river that became a waterfall two or three feet away from them!

The rocky ledge ran right into the mountain, keeping a foot or two above the level of the deep hidden river. The boys made their way along it. Soon they had left behind the thunder of the waterfall, and the mountain seemed strangely silent. Just below them, to their left, ran the underground river, silent and swift.

"It's dark, Mafumu," said Jack, shivering. It was not only dark, but cold. No sunshine ever came up the secret river! But soon a queer light showed from the roof and walls of the river tunnel.

It shone green and blue. Mafumu thought it was very odd, but Jack knew that it was only the strange light called phosphorescence. He was glad of its pale gleam, for now they could see more or less where they were going.

We shan't fall down into the river now and be swept out into the waterfall," he thought. "My goodness, Mafumu was clever to think there might be a way into the mountain, where the river came out and made a fall! I should never have thought of that in a hundred years! Wouldn't it be marvellous if we could rescue everyone!"

After a long crawl along the ledge the tunnel opened out into a series of caves, some large, some small. The boys marvelled at some of them, for the walls were agleam with queer bright stones. Mafumu did not like them.

"The walls have eyes that look at Mafumu," he whispered to Jack. Jack laughed – but he soon stopped, for his laugh echoed round and round the caves, and rumbled into the heart of the mountain and came back to him like a hundred giant-laughs, very queer and horrible.

On through the river-caves went the two boys, silent and rather frightened now. Then they came to what seemed a complete stop

"Mafumu! The river is in a tunnel here, and the roof almost touches the top of the water!" said Jack in dismay, "We can't get any further."

Mafumu waded into the river. It was not running very swiftly just there, for it was almost on the level. It was deep, however, and the boy had to swim. He began to make his way up the tunnel to see how far he could go with his head above the water. His head knocked against the roof as he swam – and presently he found that the water touched the roof! So he had to swim under the water, and hoped that before he choked the roof would rise a little and give him air to breathe!

Mafumu was a good swimmer, and was able to hold his breath well – but his lungs were almost bursting by the time that he was able to find a place to stick up his head above the water and breathe again. Even so, the roof fell low again almost at once, and the water bobbed against it. How far would it be before it rose again and Mafumu could breathe?

He had to try. There was nothing else to do, unless he and Jack were to go right back. So he took an enormous breath, dived down and swam vigorously below the water,

86

trying the roof with his hand every now and again to see if he could come above the water and breathe.

He was rewarded. The roof suddenly rose up and the tunnel became a large cave! Mafumu waded out of the water gasping and panting, delighted that he had not given up too soon!

He sat down for a few minutes to get all the breath he could. He had to go back and bring Jack through now! He did not know if the other boy could swim under water as well as he, Mafumu, could!

Back went Mafumu, knowing exactly where to rise and breathe, and where to dive under and swim back to where Jack was anxiously awaiting him, wondering what in the wide world had happened!

Mafumu tried to explain to Jack what he was to do. Jack understood only too well!

"Lead on, Mafumu," said the boy, taking a deep breath. "I'm a good swimmer – but I don't know if I'm as good as you are! Go on!"

So into the river went both boys, swimming below the water where it touched the roof, and coming up, almost bursting, in the place where the roof lifted a little so that they might breathe.

Then into the water they went again, shivering, for it was icy-cold, and once more swam as fast as they could up the low tunnel, their heads bumping the roof till they came thankfully to where the tunnel opened out into the large cave! They crawled out of the water, panting, and sat down to get their breath. Their hearts beat like great pumps, and it was some time before both boys could go on.

"Now which way?" wondered Jack, looking all round at the gleaming cave. "There are three or four archways leading out of this cave, Mafumu, with the river winding silently through the middle. Which way do we go?"

Inside The Mountain

Mafumu was running all round, peering first through one rocky archway and then through another. He stopped at last and beckoned to Jack. Jack went over to him, wondering what the other boy could see, for he was plainly excited.

No wonder Mafumu was excited! Peering through the little archway he had seen an enormous flight of steps leading upwards through the mountain! The steps were cut out of the solid rock, and were polished and shining. At the foot hung a great lamp, very finely made, which gave a curious green light.

The boys stood at the bottom of the rocky stairway, staring upwards. Where could it lead to?

"Shall we go up?" whispered Jack, his whisper starting a rustling echo all around him. Mafumu nodded. In silence the two boys began to climb the great stairway. It went up for a great way, wide and easy to climb. Then it curved sharply to the right and became a curious spiral staircase, still cut into the rock.

"I believe it leads up to the top of the mountain!" said Jack, quite out of breath. "Let's sit down and have a rest. My legs are really tired with all this climbing."

They did not notice that a wooden door opened on to the stairway just behind them. They sat there in silence, resting themselves. And then suddenly they heard the harsh voices of the Folk of the Mountain! The boys looked round quickly and by the light of one of the green lamps hanging at a curve of the stairway they saw the door. It was just opening!

The boys did not know whether the folk would go up

the stairway or down, and they hadn't time to choose! They simply tumbled themselves down the steps, came to a curve and waited there, their hearts thumping, and their legs trembling.

"If they come down the stairway we shall be seen!" thought Jack desperately. "They will touch us as they pass, because the stairway is so narrow."

But the Folk of the Mountain went *up* the stairway, not down! The boys heard their footsteps and their voices disappearing into the distance. They crept back up the stairway to the door – and it was open!

"Golly! What a bit of luck!" Jack whispered to Mafumu, who, although he did not understand the words, knew what Jack meant all right. The boys slipped in through the open door and found themselves in an enormous gallery that ran round the most colossal hall they had ever seen.

"This must be a kind of meeting-hall," thought Jack, gazing down from the rocky gallery to the great floor below. "I bet it's right in the very middle of the mountain! Golly! What a strange place it is!"

Steps led up from the great hall in many directions. They led to fine wooden doors, studded and starred with gleaming metals. The Folk of the Mountain had a strange and mighty home! There was no one at all to be seen and the deep silence seemed very queer. Enormous lamps hung down from the roof, swinging slightly as they burned. Deep shadows moved over the floor as the lamps swung, and Mafumu stared, for he had never seen such a place in all his life.

"Mafumu! Those people will be coming back soon, I expect," said Jack in his ear. "Come on. We must get down into this hall and go up a stairway to see if we can find where the others are. Hurry!"

The boys slipped down into the great hall. They stood there in the shadows, wondering which flight of steps to take. They chose the nearest one, a wide, shallow stretch that led to an open doorway.

Up they went, and through the doorway. A long, dark passage lay before them, with rocky walls and ceiling. They went down it, and turned into another one. They heard the noise of voices and stopped.

No one had heard them, so they crept on again, and came out through a big archway that led into a fine cave. Its walls were hung with the skins of animals and with curtains of shining material. The floor was covered with rich rugs. On them sat the Folk of the Secret Mountain.

How queer they looked in the light of the swinging lamps! The men all had flaming red beards and hair, and their faces looked a sickly yellow. The women were wrapped up to their noses, and showed neither hair nor chins! The boys knew they were the women because they spoke in high-pitched, shrill voices.

All of them were working at something. Some were making rugs. Others were weaving with bright-coloured strands that looked like raffia. Some were hammering at things that the boys could not see.

"We'd better go back," whispered Jack, pushing Mafumu. "Come on. If we're seen here we'd be taken prisoner."

The boys crept back. Mafumu was frightened, for the Folk of the Mountain had looked so strange! The two boys went back until they came to another door. It was shut. They pushed against it and it opened.

The room inside was very odd. It held nothing at all but a rope ladder that went up and up and up into the darkness of the roof!

"There must be a narrow hole that goes up for a long way," whispered Jack. "I wonder where the rope ladder leads to. Sh! Mafumu – there's someone coming!"

Sure enough, voices and footsteps could be heard once more. Mafumu gave a groan of fright, caught hold of the rope ladder, and was up it in a trice, disappearing into the darkness of the high roof at once. Jack thought it was a good idea and he followed as well.

Just in time! Three men came into the little room, shut the door and began to talk in their harsh voices. Jack and Mafumu stayed still on the ladder, for they knew that if they climbed higher the ladder would shake and the men would guess someone was up there.

The men talked for ten minutes, and then went out. The two boys climbed up the ladder at once. They thought they would be safer at the top than at the bottom!

The ladder was fastened to a ledge, and opposite the ledge was another door, strong and heavy. It was bolted on the outside with great heavy bolts that looked impossible to move!

"Somebody's bolted in there," whispered Jack. "Do you suppose it's Peggy and Nora and Mike and the rest of them?"

Mafumu nodded. Yes – he felt sure they had stumbled on the prison of the rest of their little party! He began to pull at the bolts.

Although they were heavy, they were well oiled and ran fairly easily when both boys pulled at them. One by one they slid the back. There was a kind of latch on the door, and Jack slid it up. The door opened.

Not a sound came from the room inside. The boys hardly dared to peep round the door. What would they see? Surely if their friends were in their they would have made some sound, said something or shouted something!

Jack pushed the door wide open and went boldly inside, far more boldly than he felt! And what a surprise he got!

The rest of their party were not there – but Captain and Mrs Arnold were! They lay on piles of rugs in the corner of the dimly lit cave, looking pale and ill. They watched the opening of the door, thinking that someone was bringing them food.

When they saw Jack they sprang to their feet in the greatest amazement! They stared as if they could not believe their eyes. They felt they must be dreaming.

"Jack! Jack! Is it really you?" asked Mrs Arnold at last. "Where are the others – Mike, Peggy and Nora?"

Mike, Peggy and Nora were Mrs Arnold's own children, though she counted Jack as hers too, because he had once helped the others when they were in great trouble. Jack stared at Captain and Mrs Arnold in joy. He flung his arms round Mrs Arnold, for he was very fond of her.

"There isn't time to talk," said Captain Arnold quickly. "Jack has opened our prison door. We'd better get out whilst we have the chance! Follow me. I know where we can go and talk in safety."

He led the way out of the room, taking with him some flat cakes and a pitcher of water. He stopped to fasten the bolts behind him, so that anyone coming that way would not notice anything unusual. Then, instead of going down the rope ladder, Captain Arnold took a little dark passage to the right that led steeply upwards. Before very long, much to the two boy's amazement, they came into a vivid patch of sunlight!

"There are sun-windows cut into the steep sides of this mountain here and there," said Captain Arnold. "The Folk of the Mountain use them for sun-bathing. It is impossible to escape through them because the mountain falls away below them, and anyone squeezing out of a sun-window would roll to the bottom at once! We are safe here. Sometimes my wife and I have been taken here to get a bit of sun, and no one ever comes by."

"Tell us everything, Jack," begged Mrs Arnold. "Quick – what about the others?"

Jack and Mafumu were very glad indeed to curl up in the warm sunshine and feel the light and warmth of the sun once more. They munched the cakes and drank the water whilst Jack quickly told his whole story. Captain and Mrs Arnold listened in the greatest astonishment.

"Well, you have had amazing adventures before – but, really, this is the most extraordinary one you children have yet had!" said Captain Arnold. "And now, let me tell you *our* adventures!"

He told them how he had been forced down to mend something that had gone wrong with the White Swallow. Whilst he was mending it, the Folk of the Mountain had come silently up and captured them. They had been taken off to the secret mountain, and had been kept prisoners ever since.

"We don't exactly know why," said Captain Arnold. "But I'm afraid that the Folk of the Mountain don't mean us any good! They are worshippers of the sun, and I believe they have a great temple-yard up on the top of this mountain where they make sacrifices to the sun. I only hope they don't mean to throw us over the mountain-top to please the sun-god, or something like that!"

"Good gracious!" said Jack, going pale. He had read in history books of ancient tribes who had worshipped strange gods and made sacrifices to them. He had never dreamed it could happen today. "What about the others? Will the Mountain Folk do that sort of thing to them too?"

"Well, we must see that they don't," said Captain Arnold. "The others are in the mountain somewhere – and we must find them! Have you finished your cakes, Jack? Well, we will leave this warm sun-trap now and explore a little. I don't expect anyone will find out that we are gone until the morning, as our guards had already brought us our food for the day. We have a good many hours to hunt for the others!"

At first Mafumu was very shy of the two strange people, but when he saw how Jack chattered to them he soon began grinning and showing his white teeth.

"Me Mafumu," he said. "Me Mafumu. Me Jack's friend!"

"Well, come on, Mafumu. You must keep with us," said Captain Arnold. "Follow me along this passage, and we'll see where it leads us to!"

93

On The Top Of The Mountain

Meanwhile, what had happened to the others? They had slept restlessly in their underground room, with the lamp burning beside them. They only knew when morning came because their watches told them that it was six o'clock.

"I'm hungry," said Mike, yawning. "I hope they give their prisoners plenty to eat in this Secret Mountain!"

No sooner had he spoken than the door was unbolted and two red-haired men came in, the folds of their brightly coloured robes swishing all around them. They carried fresh water and some more of the flat cakes in a big dish. They also brought fruit of all kinds, which the children were delighted to see.

"I do wonder what has happened to Jack and Mafumu," said Mike. "What will they do, do you think, Ranni?"

"I can't imagine," said Ranni, taking some of the fruit. He and Pilescu were far more worried than they would tell the children. They hated the sight of the queer red-haired folk – though both Ranni and Pilescu looked curiously like them sometimes, with their bright red hair and beards. But their eyes were not green, nor was their skin yellow.

Towards the end of the long and boring day, the door was flung open, and one of their guards beckoned the little company out. They followed their guide down long, winding passages, cut out of the mountain rock itself, and at last came to a great door that shone green and blue in the light of the swinging lamps above.

The door slid to one side as they came near it, and behind it the children saw a great flight of steps going up and up. The steps shone with a strange golden colour, and shimmered from orange to yellow as the little company began to climb them.

At every two-hundredth step the stairway, still wide and golden, curved round, and ascended again. The children were soon tired of the endless climb. They sat down to rest.

Behind them came a company of the Folk of the Mountain, chanting a strange and doleful song. Nobody liked it at all. It was horrid.

Many times the company sat down to rest. Ranni and Pilescu felt sure that the stairway led to the summit of the mountain. It was a marvellous piece of work, that stairway, beautiful all the way. Here and there, set at the sides, were glittering lamps in the shape of a rayed sun. These were so bright that the children could hardly bear to look at them.

"I think we must be going to the very top of the mountain," said Ranni. "It's soon sunset – and sunworshippers usually pray to the sun at sunrise or sunset. We shall probably see them at their worship!"

Ranni was right – but he did not guess what an extraordinary place the summit of the mountain was!

Panting and tired, the little party climbed the last of the flight of steps. They came out through a great golden door into a vast corridor, with tall yellow pillars built in two rows.

"Goodness!" said Mike, stopping in amazement. "What a view!"

That was the first thing that struck everyone. The view from the top of the Secret Mountain was simply magnificent. All around rose other mountains, some high, some lower, and in and beyond stretched the green valleys, some with a blue river winding along. It took the children's breath away, and made them feel very small indeed to look on those great mountains.

After they had feasted their eyes on the glorious scenery all around them, they turned to see what the summit of the Secret Mountain was like. It was very strange. For one thing, it had been levelled till it was completely flat. There was an enormous wide space in the centre, floored with some kind of yellow stone that shone yellow and orange like the flight of steps up which they had come. Around this wide space, on three sides, were long pillared corridors – and on the fourth side was a great temple-like building, overlooking the steepness of the eastern side of the mountain.

The children, with Ranni and Pilescu, were taken to the great temple. The wind was very rough and cold on the top of the mountain and everyone shivered. A red-haired man came up and flung shimmering cloaks around their shoulders. These were lined with some kind of wool, and were very warm indeed.

Everyone was taken to the top of the temple, where a tall, rounded tower jutted. From this tower they could see the setting sun, falling over the rim of the western sky. As the sun disappeared, the Folk of the Secret Mountain fell on to their knees and chanted a weird song.

"A sort of prayer to the sun, I suppose," said Ranni grimly. He spoke to Pilescu in his own language. "I don't much like this, do you, Pilescu?"

Prince Paul pricked up his ears. "Why don't you like it, Ranni?" he asked. Ranni would not tell him. All of them watched the sun. It disappeared suddenly over the edge of the world. At once the countryside was plunged into darkness, the valley and mountains disappeared from sight, and only the shimmering of the golden floor lighted the summit of the queer mountain.

A tall, red-haired man went into the centre of the shining courtyard, and spoke loudly and violently. Ranni listened and tried to understand as much as he could.

"What is he saying?" asked Mike.

"As far as I can make out he is asking the sun to stay away and let the rain come," said Ranni. "It seems that the rain is very much overdue, and these people are praying to the sun to dress himself in the thick clouds that will bring the rain they want. I expect they have crops somewhere on the mountain-side and are in danger of losing them if the rains don't come!"

That night the little party slept on rugs in the cold, wind-swept temple. They were all alone on the mountain-top, for their guards disappeared behind the yellow sliding door, slid it back into place again and fastened it with great long bolts. Ranni and Pilescu explored the temple, the courtyards and the corridor by the light of a torch – but there was no other door down into the mountain save the big shining one. It was as impossible to leave the top of the mountain as it had been to leave their underground room the night before.

How everyone wondered where Jack and Mafumu were, and if Captain and Mrs Arnold were anywhere near! They did not know that the four were together! When they had left the sun-trap, they had taken the passage that led inwards, and walking as quietly as they could, had come across a queer collection of store-rooms. No one was there, so they had explored them thoroughly.

In one store-room, cut out of the solid rock, were dyes and paints of all kinds. Captain Arnold examined them closely. "Look," he said, "this explains the red hair of the Folk of the Mountain. This is a very strong red dye, and these people use it for their hair, to scare any strangers they meet. And see – this is the curious yellow pigment they use for their skins!"

Everyone looked at the flat pots he was holding. They were full of the yellow ointment that the Secret Mountain Folk used on their skin! No wonder the Folk looked so very queer! They dyed their hair and painted their skin yellow!

When Jack knew this he no longer felt afraid of the

curious appearance of the mountain people. Golly! If it was only paint and grease there was nothing strange to be afraid of! He took one of the flat pots of yellow grease and put it into his pocket. "It will be interesting to take home!" he said cheerfully.

"If we ever *do* get home," thought Captain Arnold to himself. They left the store-rooms and went on down a curving passage that had a very high roof. Soon they heard a noise – and they came to the banks of the underground river, which swirled along through the mountain, black and swift. It was strange to see it there, running through an enormous cave.

"We shall get lost in this mountain if we are not careful," said Captain Arnold, stopping and looking round. "I wonder if we are getting anywhere near where this river rushed out of the mountainside, Jack."

Jack asked Mafumu, and the boy shook his head. "Long, long, long way," he said mournfully. "Mafumu not know way."

The party of four went across the cave and left the swirling river behind. They were not sure that it was the same one that made the waterfall. Captain Arnold felt certain that the mountain held two or three rivers, that all joined to make one. It was no use to follow the one they had just left.

Soon they came to a curious door, quite round and studded with a strange pattern of suns. Behind it they heard voices! "What are they saying, Mafumu?" whispered Jack.

Mafumu pressed himself as close to the door as he dared. His sharp ears picked up the voices – and as he listened Mafumu grew pale under his dark skin! He crept back to the others.

"They say that the sun-god is angry," whispered Mafumu. "They say that he is burning up the mountains because he has no servant. He needs a servant before he will hide his head in the great clouds and bring rain. And it is from one of us that he asks for a servant!"

Mafumu spoke partly in his own language and partly in Jack's. The other boy understood him and told Captain and Mrs Arnold what he had said. The Captain was silent for a long time.

"It is what I feared," he said. "One of us will be thrown down the mountain-side to lessen the anger of their sun-god! We must try to reach Mike, Peggy, Nora and the others at all costs, as soon as we can. We must warn them!"

A Strange Journey – And A Surprise

As Captain Arnold was speaking the round door was flung open, and a tall, red-bearded man came out. It was dark in the passage, and he did not see the little company pressed against the wall. He was about to step out into the passage when there came the sound of running feet – and someone with flowing robes rushed up from the opposite direction.

There was a sharp talk, and then an excited shouting and calling. Mafumu pressed himself against Captain Arnold and whispered in his ear.

"We run quick, quick!"

Captain Arnold knew at once that their escape had been discovered, and that they must get away from there quickly. But where were they to go?

"Back to the river!" he whispered to Mrs Arnold, and the four of them made their way silently and swiftly down the passages to the dark river. Behind them they felt sure they heard the sound of voices and footsteps.

They went right to the bank of the river. "We could get in and go across to the other side, where that high rock is, and hope that our heads wouldn't show above the water," said Jack.

But just then Mafumu made a curious discovery. He ran to Jack, caught hold of his arm, and whispered something excitedly, pulling at Jack all the time to make him follow him. The boy went – and saw what Mafumu had so unexpectedly found. It was a small boat, of a curious shape, painted in curving stripes.

"Look! Let's get in and go down the river!" said Jack. "I can hear someone coming now, quite plainly!"

There didn't seem anything better they could do. So they all packed themselves into the funny rounded boat and pushed off down the dark river. There were paddle-like oars in the boat, but Captain Arnold did not need to use them because the current took them along strongly.

That was a very strange journey through the heart of the Secret Mountain. Sometimes the river ran through big caves, which gleamed with green phosphorescent light. Sometimes it ran through dank tunnels, and the four in the boat could feel the slimy walls as they floated through. Once the river opened out into an enormous pool, whose sides lapped the walls of a high cave.

Mafumu was terrified. He clung to Jack tightly, and muttered strings of strange-sounding words, fingering his necklace of crocodile teeth. Jack was sorry for the other boy, especially as he felt afraid too!

The river swirled along fast. Sometimes the boat knocked against rocks and nearly upset. Once Mrs Arnold almost fell overboard, and Captain Arnold only just snatched at her in time. Everyone wondered where the journey would end.

It ended in a most astonishing manner. The river suddenly became much less violent, and the current seemed to fall away to nothing. The boat almost stopped and Captain Arnold had to use the paddles to get it forward. They were in a fairly wide tunnel with a low roof, and not far ahead there seemed to be an archway, through which a bright light shone.

"We're arriving somewhere," said Captain Arnold. "Well, we can't go back, so we must go forward! I wonder what that bright light is!"

They soon found out! The boat went slowly forward, passed through the archway – and the four found, to their enormous amazement, that the river flowed through what looked like a big and most magnificent room!

The floor was of great smooth stones, polished till they shone. The walls were covered with brilliant hangings, all the colours of the rainbow, and the ceiling which was domed in glittering stones, rose up high and beautiful. From it hung the great gleaming lamp that gave the bright light the four had seen through the archway.

Stone tables stood here and there, and there were piles of soft rugs on the floor. Great vases and pitchers stood about filled with the brilliant flowers of the countryside. Three parrots screeched in a golden cage and five little monkeys huddled together in a corner.

Through the middle of this strange apartment, hidden right in the heart of the mountain, flowed one of the many underground rivers that gurgled their way towards the openings in the mountain rock through which they could fall down the hillside.

"This reminds me of a fairy-tale!" said Mrs Arnold in the greatest amazement. "What are we going to do? Get out and explore this extraordinary place? It's like a palace or something, built underground!"

No one was in the enormous, beautiful room except the parrots and the monkeys. Captain Arnold wondered whether or not to let his little party get out of the boat, which was still flowing gently along. And then he caught sight of something just ahead of him on the river.

It was a great golden gate stretched across the water! How strange! The boat would certainly be able to get no further, unless they could open the gate. Captain Arnold had a queer feeling that it would be better not to land in the strange room, but to go on, and see if by chance he could open the gate and go on his way.

So the boat went on towards the shining gate – and that was the end of their queer journey! For sitting along the banks of the river beside the gate were about a dozen of the red-haired Folk of the Mountain! As soon as they saw the boat coming they leapt to their feet in amazement and shouted and pointed!

The boat came to a stop by the gate. "It's all up now," said Captain Arnold in disgust. "We can't escape any further! They've got us!"

Sure enough, they were prisoners in about half a minute! The boat was pulled to the bank, and the Mountain Folk dragged the little company from their boat. They seemed astonished to see Jack and Mafumu.

"They don't know that Jack and Mafumu are here, of course," said Captain Arnold. "They know *we've* escaped because our cave is empty, but they didn't know anything about these two boys! Look – they are taking us back to that strange and beautiful room."

They passed through a great doorway into the big apartment they had just floated through. But now it was no longer empty! On a kind of throne at one end sat a tall, red-bearded, yellow-skinned man, whose eyes glinted strangely as he gazed down at the four people before him.

"He must be their chief or king," said Captain Arnold. "I don't like the look of him much."

Behind the chief stood a company of the Mountain Folk, all with flaming red beards. They held curious spears that glittered from end to end, and from their heads rose shining sun-rays that gleamed as they turned

102

to one another. Mafumu was so frightened that he could hardly stand and Jack had to hold him up.

The big chief spoke in a harsh and stony voice. Only Mafumu understood a little of what he said, and what he heard made him tremble, for he knew that these sun-worshippers meant to throw one or more of them down the mountain-side as a kind of sacrifice to the sun. The red-bearded chief gave a sharp order, and at once the men with spears closed round the four and completely surrounded them.

They were marched off through the great room, with the screeching of the three parrots sounding in their ears. And they were taken to the top of the mountain, where the rest of the party were! But the way they went was quite different from the way that the others had taken!

They were marched to a small room in which stood what looked like a cage of gold, beautifully carved and worked. "Look!" said Jack, pointing upwards. "There's a hole going through the roof of this room, up and up and up!"

There was – and it was there for a curious purpose, too. It was to take the cage upwards, just as a lift-shaft holds a rising lift. The golden cage was a kind of simple lift – but the ropes that hauled it up were pulled by men and not by machinery.

The little party were crammed into the cage, with four of the Mountain Folk. The door was shut. One of the men shouted a sharp order – and immediately twenty men began to haul strongly on some massive ropes that hung down from another hole in the roof.

The cage shot upwards like a lift! Mafumu was terrified, he had never even been in a lift before! The others were amazed, but they showed no fear, and Mrs Arnold bent down to comfort the poor little boy.

Up and up they went, sometimes fast, sometimes slow, right to the very top of the mountain. They came to a stop underneath a round and gleaming trap-door, which was bolted underneath. One of the men slid back the bolts, pressed a spring and the door opened upwards, falling back silently on its hinges. The cage rose slowly once again, and when it was level with the ground it stopped.

The door of the golden cage was opened, and everyone stepped out. Captain and Mrs Arnold looked round. They had no idea where they were at first – and then they realized that they were on the very summit of the Secret Mountain! They held their breath as they looked at the magnificent view!

The cage-lift had come up through a hole right in the very middle of the vast courtyard that spread over the top of the mountain. Jack took a quick look round and wondered if any of the others were there, but he could see no one.

They *were* there, of course! They were in the temple, eating some of the fruit that had been brought to them, having wrapped themselves up well in the rugs, for the wind that blew across the mountain at that time of year was strong and cold, despite the hot sun.

It was Prince Paul who saw the strange and surprising sight of the cage-lift coming up in the middle of the courtyard! He was looking out through the open doorway of the temple, and to his very great amazement he saw what seemed to be a big trap-door slowly open and bend itself back. He swallowed his mouthful in surprise, and choked. Mike banged him on the back.

"Don't! Don't! Look! Look!" choked poor Paul, trying to point through the doorway. But everyone thought he was upset because he was choking, and Peggy took a turn at banging him between the shoulders.

Paul saw the golden cage rise up through the trap-door opening. He saw Captain and Mrs Arnold, Jack and Mafumu get out, with their four guards, and his eyes nearly fell out of his head with amazement and delight. He went quite purple in the face, and leapt to his feet.

"*Look!*" he yelled to the others. And at last they looked. When they saw the unexpected appearance of eight people in the middle of the smooth courtyard, and when Mike, Peggy and Nora saw that two of them were their own father and mother, what an excitement there was!

With shouts and shrieks the children rushed down the temple steps and ran towards the little company in the courtyard. In half a minute they were hugging their father and mother, exclaiming over them, thumping Jack on the back, shouting a hundred questions, and hugging little Mafumu, who was quite overjoyed at seeing all his lost friends so suddenly again.

"This *is* a surprise! This *is* a surprise!" everyone kept saying. And, indeed, it was!

The Escape Of Ranni And Pilescu

When everyone had calmd down a little, they lookd round to see what had become of the four guards who had come up in the cage-lift with Jack and the others. But they were gone! They had silently stepped into the golden cage once more, and had disappeared from sight into the heart of the mountain!

Captain Arnold ran to where the trap-door lay smoothly in the floor of the courtyard. He tried to get his fingers between the edges of the door and the stone of the courtyard – but they fitted so exactly that it was impossible.

"In any case it will be locked and bolted the other side," he said. "There's no way of escape there. How did *you* get here, Mike? Through this trap-door?"

Mike told him about the enormous flights of shining steps that led up to the golden door. He showed the newcomers the door itself, but no matter how they tried they could not slide it back.

The children were all so excited at seeing their father and mother again, and at having Jack and Mafumu once more, that they forgot their worries and chatted happily, telling one another their adventures. Only the grown-ups looked grave, and talked solemnly together, apart from the children.

"Somehow we must think of a way to escape," said Pilescu. "These Folk of the Secret Mountain are savage and ignorant. They think that the sun is angry with them, and they want to give him a servant to make their peace with him. Which of us will be chosen for that? I don't like to think."

"None of us is safe," said Captain Arnold. "Is it possible to lie in wait for the guards who come to give you food, Pilescu, overpower them, and escape down the golden stair?"

"We could try," said Ranni doubtfully. "But I fear it would be no use. Still, it seems the only thing to do."

At that moment Jack came up. He had been showing the other children the queer pot of yellow paint that he had taken from the storeroom among the caves in the mountain. He looked very peculiar because he had tried out some of the paint on his own face, and his skin was now as bright yellow as the Folk of the Mountain!

Ranni and Pilescu, who did not know about the pigment, stared at him in horror.

"Jack! What is the matter with you?" cried Pilescu. "Are you ill?"

"Very!" grinned Jack. "I think I must have got yellow fever, Pilescu! Have you got any medicine to make me better?"

The other children crowded round, giggling and

laughing, and Pilescu knew it was a joke. He looked closely at Jack.

"You have got yellow paint on your face," he said. "You look like one of the Folk of the Mountain!"

"And you, Pilescu, would look *exactly* like one if you painted *your* face," said Jack, "because you have a flaming red beard as they have. But yours is a real red beard, not a dyed one!"

No sooner had Jack said these words than the same thought flashed into Pilescu's head and Captain Arnold's at the same moment. Pilescu snatched the pot of pigment from Jack and looked at it. He dipped his finger into it and rubbed it over the back of his hand. At once his skin gleamed the same yellow as the skin of the Mountain Folk.

"I've thought the same thing as you, Pilescu," said Captain Arnold, in excitement. "If you used this paint you would pass for one of the Secret Mountain people! You and Ranni both have the bright red hair and beards of Baronian men – if you paint your skin yellow, you will look very like the Folk of the Mountain – and maybe our way of escape lies through you!"

Immediately all was excitement. Everyone talked at once. Everyone thought it was a simply marvellous idea. In the end Captain Arnold silenced the party and spoke seriously to them all.

"We must lose no further time in talk," he said. "I propose that both Ranni and Pilescu paint their faces with this yellow pigment and try to escape with the guards when they come. If only they can find their way back to where our planes are, they may be able to find some way of rescuing us all. It's the only chance that I can see."

"There are some robes in the temple with the rugs!" cried Mike. "I tried them on this morning. They would fit Ranni and Pilescu. Come and try them!"

In the greatest excitement the little company went to

The chief stood majestically on the tower

the temple. Ranni and Pilescu tried on the coloured robes and they fitted well enough. The flowing garments looked strange on the two big men, and everyone laughed.

Captain Arnold carefully rubbed the curious yellow pigment into the skin of the Baronians' faces, necks and hands. With the flowing robes, yellow skin and flaming beards they looked exactly like the Folk of the Secret Mountain! Poor Mafumu, unused to extraordinary happenings of this sort, could harldy believe that it was still Ranni and Pilescu, and he shrank away from them in fear.

"It is getting near the time when sun-worshippers come to pray to the sun at sunset," said Captain Arnold looking over the mountains to where the sun was swinging down towards the edge of the world. "Maybe many of the Mountain Folk will come, and then you can mix with them easily enough when they go!"

It was decided that Ranni and Pilescu should hide behind two great pillars near the sliding door. If they were not discovered they could mix with the Mountain Folk as they went down the stairs again, and might escape unseen in that way.

The sun swung lower – and suddenly, from behind the great golden door came the sound of chanting. It was the Mountain Folk coming to sing their prayers to the sun! The door slid to one side, and up the shining stairway came scores of the curious Folk, their beards gleaming red in the setting sun.

The leader went to the tower of the temple. All the rest spread themselves out on the flat courtyard, and flung themselves down on their faces when the man in the temple sounded a loud and echoing bell. They chanted a sad and doleful dirge for about ten minutes, whilst Captain Arnold and the rest looked on.

Behind the big pillars Ranni and Pilescu waited their chance. As soon as the sun disappeared over the edge of the world and darkness fell on the mountain the people stood up and ranged themselves in lines. Then still singing, led by their tall leader, they made their way back to the stairway that led down into the dark mountain.

And, slipping to the end of the lines, went two red-bearded folk that did not belong to the mountain! Ranni and Pilescu joined the company, and tried to do exactly as the men in front did. They passed through the shining doorway and down the golden stairs. The door slid back silently into place – and Ranni and Pilescu were gone from sight!

"They've gone!" said Jack, slipping his hand through Mike's arm. "They've gone! Oh, I do wonder how they'll get on. I do hope they won't be caught!"

No one came to disturb them again that evening. The little party went into the temple and tried to find the most sheltered corner. The mountain wind blew without stopping, day and night, and it was difficult to find anywhere that was not full of draughts. The girls cuddled up to Mrs Arnold, and the boys and Captain Arnold found a bigger corner and piled rugs over themselves.

They all slept soundly that night, in spite of the cold. Captain and Mrs Arnold were glad to be with their children again, and hoped against hope that somehow Ranni and Pilescu would find a way to escape from the mountain and bring help to the prisoners.

For two days nothing happened. The Folk of the Mountain came up once at sunrise and once at sunset to chant their strange songs and prayers. Guards came to bring food and water. Curiously enough they did not miss Ranni and Pilescu at all – partly because Captain Arnold had told the party to split up, and be in various places on the summit of the mountain, instead of all together.

"Then when our guards come, they will not be able to count us up, because we shall be all over the place!" said Captain Arnold. "And unless they actually go to look for

110

everyone they will not guess that two of our party are missing!"

But the guards did not think for one minute that anyone *could* be missing! After all, no one could escape down the trap-door for it was bolted underneath – and no one, so they thought, could escape down the golden stairway without being seen. So the little party lived peacefully for two days, with no excitements at all.

Then things began to happen. The golden cage once more came up through the trap-door in the centre of the vast courtyard! Mrs Arnold happened to be standing nearby and she had a great surprise when she saw the trap-door suddenly rise up and the golden cage appear. She ran to tell the others. They came to watch who was coming.

The chief himself walked from the golden lift! He was very tall, and very thin. His beard flamed in the sun, and his clothes swung round him like shimmering water as he walked. His yellow skin was wrinkled and drawn. He was an old, old man, but powerful and with piercing, eagle-like eyes.

He gave a sharp order. Men stepped out from the cage and came behind him. He walked solemnly to the temple, where he chanted several prayers to the sun in a strong harsh voice. Then he turned to his servants rounded up the little company of prisoners, and brought them before the chief. He ran his strange eyes over them and then looked at his servants in surprise. It was quite plain that he thought someone was missing!

He asked a sharp question. The servants hurriedly counted the prisoners and then sent two of their number to search the summit of the mountain thoroughly.

"They've gone to find Ranni and Pilescu," whispered Jack. "Well, they won't find them here!"

And they didn't, of course, though they hunted in every corner and cranny. Ranni and Pilescu had disappeared completely.

The chief was angry. His eyes flamed, and his mouth became hard and straight. He addressed his servants fiercely, and they flung themselves on their faces before him. No one but Mafumu could understand what he was saying, and even Mafumu could not understand everything!

The chief walked majestically over to the company of prisoners and looked into each one's face. No one flinched except poor Mafumu, who was in a state of real terror, partly because he was afraid of the yellow-skinned chief and partly because he knew something that the others didn't know!

The chief was choosing who was to be the servant of the sun! He glared into Jack's face. He stared closely at poor Nora and Peggy. He took Paul's chin in his hand and peered at him. Nobody liked it at all.

Mafumu was very sad. Whom would the chief choose? Somebody must be the sacrifice to the sun. And poor Mafumu would have to break the news, for no one else understood what the yellow-skinned chief was doing!

The Servant Of The Sun

The tall chief took hold of the little prince and called out some strange words to his followers. At once two men stepped forward and took the frightened boy. He did not know what they were going to do with him, but he was determined not to show that he was afraid.

So, rather white, he stood up proudly and looked the chief straight in the face. Mike and the others felt proud of him.

Paul was marched off alone He was taken to the golden

door, which slid back silently. Then he disappeared down the stairway, and the door once more shut like magic. Captain Arnold stepped forward angrily.

"What are you going to do to the boy?" he cried. "Bring him back!"

The chief laughed the turned on his heel. He went up to the tower of the temple and began what seemed like a long prayer to the sun.

It was left to poor trembling Mafumu to break the news to the others. In his few English words he tried to explain that little Paul was to be the servant of the sun. Everyone listened in amazement and horror. Captain and Mrs Arnold who had feared that something like this could happen ever since they had been brought to the temple on top of the mountain, looked despairingly at one another.

"I can't see how we can possibly save him," said Captain Arnold at last. They all sat down in the shade, and Peggy and Nora began to cry. If even grown-up people couldn't do anything, then things were indeed in a bad way!

Mike and Jack and Mafumu talked together. Jack would never give up hope. He was that kind of boy. But Mike was full of dismay, and as for Mafumu, he was simply shivering with worry and fright. He kept as close to Jack as he could, as if he thought that Jack would protect him from everything.

Jack was very edgy, though he didn't show it. "I wish you'd do something instead of shivering all over me," he said to Mafumu, pushing the boy away.

"Give him a pencil or a notebook to play with," said Mike. "He's only a little kid, and you can't blame him for being a bit scared."

Jack put his hand into his pocket and brought out a diary. He had been keeping the tale of their adventures there, day by day. He handed it to Mafumu.

"Here you are. Play with this over in the corner there,"

he said. Mafumu took the notebook eagerly. He turned over each page one by one, rubbing his fingers over the pages in which Jack had written. He could not understand anything, of course, because he could not write or read.

He came to where Jack had written the day before. After that the pages were blank. Mafumu was puzzled. Why was nothing written in one half of the book? He rolled himself over beside Jack and pointed to the blank pages.

Jack tried to explain to Mafumu. "Today I write, tomorrow I write, but not till the day has gone," he said.

"Jack, what's the date today?" asked Mike idly. "I've really lost count of the days, you know! I don't know if it's Sunday, Monday, Tuesday, or what – or if it's the tenth, eleventh, twenty-first, or thirtieth of the month!"

"Well, I can tell you, because I've written down our adventures every day," said Jack. "It's Wednesday – and it's the sixteenth. Look."

Mike took the diary. He glanced at the next day, and gave an exclamation.

"Oh, Jack! Look what it says for tomorrow!"

"What?" asked Jack, surprised.

"It says there will be an eclipse of the sun," said Mike. "I do wonder if we'll see it here?"

"Let's ask your father," said Jack. So the two boys went across to Captain Arnold, with the faithful Mafumu following at their heels.

"Dad! It says in Jack's diary that there is an eclipse of the sun tomorrow!" said Mike. "Do you think there is any chance at all of seeing it here?"

"What's an eclipse of the sun?" asked Peggy. "I know we've learnt about it in school, but I've quite forgotten what happens."

"It's quite simple," said Mike. "All that happens is that the moon on its way through the sky passes in front of the sun, and blocks out the sun's light for a little while. It

114

eclipses the sun's light, and for a time the world looks queer and strange because there is no sunlight in the daytime!"

Captain Arnold sprang to his feet. To Mike's enormous surprise he snatched Jack's diary from him and looked at what was printed there in the space for the next day.

"Eclipse of the sun, 11.43 a.m.," he read. "Is this this year's diary? Yes! My word! Eclipse of the sun *tomorrow!* It's unbelievable!"

He spoke in such an excited voice that everyone came round him at once.

"What's the matter? Why are you so excited?" cried Mike. Only Mrs Arnold guessed. Her eyes were bright and hopeful.

"I'll tell you. Listen carefully," said Captain Arnold. He lowered his voice, for although he did not think that any of the Mountain Folk were listening anywhere, or could understand a word he said, he was not taking any chances.

"Mike has told you what an eclipse of the sun means. It means that the moon passes exactly in front of the sun, and it only happens rarely. If we were in England the sun would not be competely hidden by the moon – but here in Africa it will, and the whole countryside will become as dark as night!"

The children listened in excitement. What a strange happening it would be!

"Now these Mountain Folk are sun-worshippers," said Captain Arnold. "It is quite plain that they have the custom of throwing unfortunate people over the mountain-side to sacrifice to the sun, when they want to please him, or ask him to grant a prayer. I am afraid that our little Paul has been chosen, and will be beyond our help tomorrow unless we do something. And now I see what we can do!"

"What?" cried everyone.

"Well, we will get Mafumu to explain to these people,

when they next come up here, that I will kill the sun tomorrow, unless they set Paul free!" said Captain Arnold.

"How do you mean – kill the sun?" asked Nora in wonder.

"Well, to them, when the eclipse happens, it will seem as if the sun is being killed!" said Captain Arnold, smiling. "They won't know that it is only the moon passing in front of the sun that is blocking out the light – they will really think I have done something to the sun they worship!"

"Oh, Captain Arnold – it sounds too good to be true!" cried Jack. "Won't they be amazed? I wonder if they will set us all free if we do this."

"Probably," said Captain Arnold. "We can do our best, anyway. Now, I wonder if the Mountain Folk will come up at sunset tonight, and sing their mournful prayers!"

But, to everyone's great disappointment, not a single person came. No word was heard of the little Prince. Nothing happened at all. Captain and Mrs Arnold felt uneasy about Paul, but they did not tell the others.

"Probably there is a great hunt going on in the mountain for Ranni and Pilescu!" said Captain Arnold. "I do wonder what has happened to them. If only they have managed to slip out of the rock-entrance, and find help somewhere."

The night passed. It was cold up on the mountain-top and everyone slept as usual muffled up in the soft warm rugs. The children missed Prince Paul and were sad when they thought of him. They knew he must be feeling very lonely and frightened all by himself, no matter how brave a face he put on when the Mountain Folk were there.

The dawn came, and the whole sky around was full of dancing silvery light.

"You can see such an enormous lot of sky from the top of a mountain," said Mike, gazing all round. "Look – there comes the sun!"

The golden sun rose slowly into the sky and the children watched it. It was so beautiful that each child was filled with awe.

"It's certainly the king of the sky!" said Mike. "I really am not surprised that these strange wild tribes worship the sun! Oh dear – I do miss Paul. I wonder where he is."

They soon saw him again. Mike spied the trap-door slowly open in the middle of the big courtyard, and he called out to the others.

"Someone's coming. Look!"

They all looked. The golden cage rose slowly through the space left by the trap-door, and in it the children could see the tall chief with his flaming red beard, two servants – and a small figure dressed in the most wonderful shimmering robes they had ever seen.

"Why – it's Paul dressed like that!" cried Mike in amazement. "And look what he's got on his head!"

Paul was certainly dressed in a very queer manner. He wore the shimmering golden garments down to his feet, and the flowing sleeves even covered his hands. On his head was a great head-dress made in the likeness of a glittering sun, with golden rays springing upwards.

The boy looked magnificent, and he walked very proudly. He had guessed that he was to be the servant of the sun, and he was afraid – but he was going to show Mike and the others that he was brave and courageous. He walked behind the chief, and sent a cheerful though rather quivery smile at his friends.

"Dear Paul. Good little Paul," said Nora.

"I do feel proud of him," said Mike, with a funny little break in his voice.

And then Captain Arnold stepped forward and shouted in such a tremendous voice that everyone jumped.

"*Stop!* I command you to *stop!*"

The tall chief stopped in his walk and glared round at Captain Arnold. He did not understand the words that the

117

captain said – but he understood their meaning. There was no mistaking that at all!

"Come here Mafumu," commanded Captain Arnold. The little boy came to him, trembling. "Tell the chief that I will kill the sun if he does anything to Paul," said the Captain. Mafumu did not understand, so Jack explained as best he could in simple words.

Mafumu nodded. He knelt down before the chief, and banged his forehead on the ground before him.

Mafumu cried out some strange words to the chief, and then banged his forehead on the ground again. The chief frowned and looked at Captain Arnold. He said something sharp to Mafumu.

"Chief say no, Captain will not kill sun," said the little boy. "He say that when the sun is high, high, high, Paul will go to the sun."

"When the sun is high," repeated Captain Arnold. "That means noon – twelve o'clock – and the eclipse is due at about a quarter to. Well – that will just about do it! Tell the chief I *will* kill the sun unless he sets us all free, Mafumu."

But the chief laughed in their faces. He set off towards the tower of the temple, Paul following behind in his shimmering robes. Everyone watched them go – and how the children hoped that the eclipse of the sun would actually happen. It seemed too strange a thing to be really true.

The Sun Disappears!

The little company of prisoners were not allowed to go into the temple that morning. The two servants stood at the door and prevented anyone from entering. Mike could see the figure of Paul up on the tower with the tall chief, who was muttering and chanting all kinds of weird words to the sun. Paul waved to Mike once, and Mike waved back.

"It's all right, Paul. You needn't be afraid," shouted Mike. "We're going to save you!"

But the wind took away his words and Paul did not hear. He stood there bravely, the wonderful head-dress he was wearing shining and glinting in the sun.

As the sun rose higher and the day gew hotter, Captain Arnold and the rest of his party found what shade they could. There was always a big wind blowing on the summit of the high mountain, but even so the rays of the sun as it rose high were flaming hot.

At about eleven o'clock the great golden door slid open, and an enormous company of Mountain Folk came singing up the shining stairway. They were dressed in shimmering robes rather like Paul's, and looked marvellous as they trooped out on to the great courtyard. Their faces were yellower than ever, and the men's beards had been freshly dyed and flamed like fire.

They ranged themselves over the courtyard and then began to dance a strange dance. Their feet stamped, their robes swung and shimmered, their voices rose and fell in a queer chant.

"A sort of sun dance," said Captain Arnold. Everyone was worried and anxious, but they could not help marvelling as they watched the curious sun-worhippers performing their extraordinary dance.

Captain Arnold glanced at his watch. It was half-past eleven. He looked anxiously up at the sun, which was almost at its highest point. No moon could be seen, of course, for the sun was so bright. But it was there all right, travelling through the sky.

An enormous gong boomed out from the temple. One of the servants of the chief was sounding it. The children had seen it there, but there had been nothing to bang it with – and now it was sounding over the mountain-top, booming its great solemn note all around. The valleys below took up the note and threw it back – and soon, from everywhere around, the echoes came back until it seemed as if the whole earth and sky were filled with the booming of the gong.

At once all the sun-worshippers fell on their knees. The chief waited until the sound of the gong had died away and then he spoke in a loud voice. He brought Prince Paul forward, and the boy stood there on the temple tower, his robes blowing and shining in the wind.

"Captain Arnold, will the eclipse start soon?" asked Jack nervously. He was terribly afraid that something would happen to Paul before they could prevent it. Captain Arnold glanced at his watch.

"It will begin in two minutes," he said. "Now, *I* am going to take a hand in this game! Watch me!"

He ran with quick, light steps to the tower. The servants at the entrance were taken by surprise, and he slipped through easily. He raced up the stone steps and in a moment or two was standing beside the chief and Paul.

And then things began to happen! Captain Arnold turned to the great sun and shook his fist at it. He shouted at it! He snatched a knife from his belt and threw it high into the air at the sun! The knife made a great curve in the air and disappeared over the mountainside!

The great chief knelt before Captain Arnold

"He kills the sun, he kills the sun!" shouted Mafumu, who suddenly understood what Captain Arnold was pretending to do. The Mountain Folk understood Mafumu's shout and rose to their feet in alarm and confusion. The servants of the chief ran to capture Captain Arnold – and then a strange thing happened.

A tiny piece seemed suddenly to be bitten out of the sun! A small black shadow appeared at one side! The moon was beginning to pass in front of it, and was hiding a very small piece.

Mafumu saw it and was astonished. He pointed at the sun, and shouted in alarm. "The sun is being eaten! See, see!"

A great silence fell on the mountain-top. Everyone was watching the sun in the sky, covering their faces with their hands, and looking through their fingers to avoid the brilliance. The servants who had come to capture Captain Arnold watched, too, trembling.

The moon passed further in front of the sun and a bigger piece became completely dark. A moan of fear came from the watching Mountain Folk. They did not understand what an eclipse of the sun was, and they really thought that their precious sun was being killed!

Not one of them guessed that it was merely the moon passing in front of the sun and blocking out its light for a while. They fell on their faces and muttered all kinds of strange prayers. And when they looked up again they saw that half of the sun was gone!

And now the world began to look queer and unearthly. The sunlight dwindled and died. A queer half-light came over the whole countryside. Birds stopped singing. The monkeys in the trees huddled together, frightened. The frogs thought that night was coming and began to croak.

The children were afraid too, although they knew quite well that it was only an eclipse they were watching. They had never seen one before, and this was a complete eclipse, with every bit of daylight and sunlight gradually going from the world they looked upon. As for poor Mafumu he had never in his life been so frightened. He crouched on the ground shivering like a jelly, and Jack did his best to comfort him.

The chief up on the tower was watching the dying sun with fear and amazement. He too was trembling. Could it be that this man was really killing their wonderful sun-god who shone so brightly in the sky each day? He could not understand it. He threw out his arms to the sun, and shouted to it, trying to comfort the failing sun, and to make it shine brightly again! Captain Arnold folded his arms, looked very stern, and it really seemed for all the world as if he were the conjurer who had worked the trick!

And now even stranger things happened! The sky became as black as night and the stars came out. They shone brilliantly, and starlight lighted the earth instead of sunlight.

"Don't be afraid," Mrs Arnold said to the scared children, who had not expected this. "The sun is gone now, lost behind the moon – so, of course, it is like night-time, and the stars shine out. You must remember that the stars are always in the sky, all through the day – but we don't see them because daylight is so bright. But now that the daylight has gone, we can see the stars shining.

It all seemed simple enough when Mrs Arnold explained it – but the terrified Mountain Folk had no idea of what was really happening, and they were quite mad with fear and terror. They shouted and moaned, and beat their foreheads and dropped to their knees.

Up on the tower it was quite dark. Captain Arnold caught hold of the astonished little prince and whispered in his ear.

"Go down the stone steps and join the others, Paul. No one will stop you now. You are safe."

Paul made his way to the steps and went down them

123

thankfully. He felt his way to the children, and clasped Mike's hand in joy. Mike put his arms round him, and the others clustered round Paul, who felt strange in his flowing garments.

"The eclipse came just at the right moment to save you, Paul, old boy," said Jack in his ear. "You're safe now. You *were* brave. We were awfully proud of you."

Paul's heart glowed. He had often been laughed at because he was rather a baby – and now he felt a hero! He kept close to the children and watched the rest of the eclipse.

As soon as Captain Arnold saw that the sun was completely gone, he began to shout, pretending that he was threatening the lost sun. The chief went down on his knees and begged for mercy, quite certain that Captain Arnold was the most powerful magician in the whole world!

Then gradually the moon passed right across the sun, and a little bit of one side began to show again. The stars slowly disappeared as the moon passed from the sun, and the strange half-light appeared once more. This was too much for the Mountain Folk. It was bad enough to have seen the sun die, as they thought – but now something else was happening, and they could not bear it.

Shouting and groaning, they rushed to the golden stairway and poured down it, slipping and falling as they went. The two servants who had been on the tower went too, deserting their chief in their fear. He was left on the tower, kneeling down before Captain Arnold.

Gradually the sun became itself again as the moon passed right across it, and the black shadow fled. The glorious daylight flooded the mountains, and the golden sun poured its rays down once more. Birds sang again. The monkeys chattered in delight. The brief and unexpected night was gone, and the world was itself again.

Captain Arnold took the frightened chief by the shoulder and led him firmly down the steps. He called to Mafumu.

"Mafumu, tell the chief he must let us all go now, or I will

124

kill his sun again," commanded the Captain. Mafumu understood. He was feeling better now that the sun had come back, and he thought that Captain Arnold must be the most powerful man in all the world. No matter how often the others explained what had really happened, Mafumu would never, never believe anything but that Captain Arnold had done something to the sun!

Mafumu, feeling important and grand, said something to the chief. The man was angry that such a small boy should speak in that way to him, and he took no notice at all. He strode away from Captain Arnold and went towards the trap-door, which was still lying open, flat on the ground. The golden cage was there awaiting him.

"Mafumu, tell him that we are going down the golden stairway, and that his servants must let us out of the rock-entrance," said Captain Arnold. Mafumu shouted at the chief. The man nodded, and entered the cage. In a trice he was gone, and the trap-door still lay flat on the ground, for he had not troubled to bolt it.

"Well, *he's* gone, and so has everyone else," said Mike, with a laugh. "My word – what an adventure! I don't mind saying that I felt very queer myself when the sun began to disappear and the stars shone out. I could do with something to eat. Let's go and get some of those flat cakes from the temple before we go down the stairs."

"Well, hurry then," said Captain Arnold. "I want to go whilst the going is good!"

The boys ran to get the cakes and some fruit. They brought it out in the flat dishes, and joined Captain and Mrs Arnold and the girls, who were walking towards the golden door.

But as they came near, the door began to slide silently shut! Captain Arnold gave a shout and ran towards it.

"Hurry! They are shutting us out!"

He got there just as the door completely closed. There it rose above him, a tall, shining door, as wide as a great gate – fast shut.

"They've tricked us!" shouted the Captain angrily, and he hammered on the door. But there was no handle, no latch, nothing to get hold of or to loosen. There was no getting through that enormous door it was plain!

Big, Big Bird That Sings R-r-r-r-r-r!

"The trap-door!" shouted Mike. "We can escape through that. The chief has left it open!"

The boys ran helter-skelter across the vast courtyard to where the opening was. They were half-afraid that the trap-door would close before they got there. But it didn't.

The four boys stood by the lift-opening and looked down. The lift-shaft ran straight down below their feet, cut out of solid rock. The golden cage was not to be seen, of course. The opening looked dark and narrow as it disappeared into the darkness of the heart of the mountain.

"I don't see how we could escape down there," said Mike. "We would need a tremendous long rope to begin with – which we haven't got – and also, just suppose the lift came up as we went down!"

"That golden cage was pulled up and down by ropes, wasn't it?" said Mrs Arnold. "Well, surely those must still be running down one side of the opening."

"Of course they must," said Captain Arnold. "We'll look for those."

But the ropes that sent the lift up and down had been cut! Captain Arnold found them easily enough, running in a cleverly cut groove at one side of the lift-opening. But when he pulled at them they came up in his hand, not more than ten feet long! Somehow they had been cut and were of no use at all!

"We may as well shut the trap-door," said Captain Arnold, in disgust and disappointment. "It is dangerous to leave it open in case one of you goes and tumbles down the hole. Well – we really are in a fix now!"

"How all the Mountain Folk must be laughing at us!" said Mike. "We are nicely caught! Can't get down, and can't get up – here we are stuck on the top of a mountain for the rest of our lives!"

Captain Arnold did not like the look of things at all. He was afraid that the Folk of the Secret Mountain would open the sliding door and spring on them during the night. But he said this only to Mrs Arnold, for he did not want to frighten the children.

"Well, we've all had a great deal of excitement today," he said. "Let's go into the cool temple, have a good meal, and a rest."

So into the temple they went, and were soon munching away at the flat cakes and the sweet juicy fruit. Then the children and Mrs Arnold settled themselves down for a rest whilst Captain Arnold kept watch. It was arranged that either the Captain, Jack or Mike should keep guard, so that at any rate the little party would not be taken unawares.

The night came as suddenly as usual. The stars flashed out brightly, and the world of mountains lay peacefully under the beautiful starlight. Captain Arnold went to examine the trap-door to make sure that no one could come upon them from there, and then he went to look at the sliding door. But it was still fast shut and there seemed to be no sound from the other side at all.

The night passed peacefully. First the Captain kept watch and then the two boys. But nothing happened. The dawn came, and the sun rose. The children awoke and stretched themselves. They were hungry – but, alas, except for a few of the flat cakes, there was no food left at all.

"I hope they are not going to starve us out," said Mike hungrily, as Captain Arnold shared out the few cakes between the party. "I shouldn't like that at all."

"This adventure is exciting, but awfully uncomfortable," said Nora.

At about ten o'clock the great golden door slid back again. Up the stairs came the Folk of the Mountain – but this time they carried shining spears! They were on the warpath, that was plain!

Captain Arnold had half-expected this. He made the children go into a corner, and he went to meet the tall chief, with Mafumu close beside him to talk for him.

But the chief was in no mood for talking. He too carried a spear, and he looked very fiercely at Captain Arnold.

"Tell him I will kill his sun again, Mafumu," said the Captain desperately.

"Chief say he kill you first," said poor Mafumu, his teeth chattering. And, indeed, it certainly looked as if this was what the chief meant to do, for he lowered his spear and pointed it threateningly at Captain Arnold.

The Captain had a revolver. He did not want to shoot the chief, but thought he might as well frighten him. He drew his revolver and fired it into the air. The noise of the shot echoed round the mountains in a most terrifying manner. The chief jumped with fright. All the Mountain Folk began to jabber and shout.

But one, cleverer than the others, aimed his spear at Captain Arnold. The shining weapon flew through the air, struck the gun in the Captain's hand, and sent it flying to ground with a clang. None of the Mountain Folk dared to pick it up, and Captain Arnold did not dare to either – for a different reason! He was not afraid of the revolver – but he *was* afraid of the spears around him!

128

The chief shouted out a harsh order, and twelve men ran up with spears. They took hold of all the little company, and before ten minutes had gone by, each grown-up and child was bound with thin, strong ropes!

"What will they do with us?" said Nora, who was very angry because her wrists had been bound too tightly.

Nobody knew. But it was plain that the little party were to be taken below into the heart of the mountain. They were not to be left on the summit.

"I expect the chief is afraid we will do something to his beloved sun if he leaves us up here," said Jack. "I wish another eclipse would happen! What a shock it would give them all!"

The chief gave orders for the captives to be taken down the shining stairway – but just as they were about to go, there came a most extraordinary noise!

At first it was far away and quiet – a little humming – but soon it grew louder and louder, and the mountain-side echoed with the sound of throbbing.

"R-r-r-r-r-r-r!" went the noise. "R-r-r-r-r-r! R-r-r-r-r-r-r!"

The Folk of the Secret Mountain stopped and listened, their eyes wide with amazement. This was a strange noise. What could it be?

The children were puzzled at first too – but almost at once Jack knew what the noise was, and he lifted up his voice in a shout.

"It's an aeroplane! An aeroplane! Can't you hear it? It's coming nearer!"

Captain Arnold was amazed. He knew that it was the noise made by the throbbing of aeroplane engines – but what aeroplane? Surely – surely – it could not be the White Swallow?

The noise came nearer – and then a black speck could be seen flying towards the mountain-side. It really *was* an aeroplane – no doubt about that at all!

The Mountain Folk saw it too. They cried out in surprise and pointed to it. "What are they saying, Mafumu?" shouted Jack.

"They say, 'Big, big bird, big, big bird that sings r-r-r-r-r-r!'" said Mafumu, his eyes shining and his teeth flashing. The children laughed, excited and eager. Something was going to happen – they were sure of it!

The aeroplane came nearer and nearer, growing bigger as it came. "It *is* the White Swallow!" shouted Captain Arnold. "I'd know the sound of her engines anywhere, the beauty! Ranni and Pilescu must have somehow got back to the planes, made the White Swallow ready for taking off – and flown up in her."

"Can they land here?" cried Paul.

"Of course!" said Mike. "Look at this great smooth courtyard – an ideal landing-ground if ever there was one! Oh, if only Ranni and Pilescu know this mountain when they see it, and they come here!"

The aeroplane came nearer, rising high as it flew, as if it were going to fly right over the summit of the mountain. The Mountain Folk were terrified, and crouched to the ground. The aeroplane, gleaming as white as a gull, circled overhead as if it were looking for something.

"It's going to land, it's going to land!" yelled Jack, jumping about even though his hands and legs were bound. "Golly, what a shock for the red-beards!"

The white aeroplane circled lower – and even as it made to land there came another noise echoing around the mountains.

"R-r-r-r-r-r! R-r-r-r-r-r!"

"That's *my* aeroplane; I bet it is, I bet it is!" yelled Prince Paul, his face red with excitement as he tried his hardest to get rid of the ropes that bound him, "I'd know the sound of *my* aeroplane anywhere too!"

Whilst the White Swallow made a perfect landing,

running gracefully on her big wheels over the enormous flat courtyard, the second aeroplane could be seen rising slowly up the mountain-side.

"It's Paul's blue and silver plane," cried Peggy. "Oh, my goodness – this is too thrilling for anything! Look who's in the White Swallow! Ranni, Ranni, Ranni!"

A Thrilling Rescue!

The chief and his servants were full of amazement and fear when they heard the noise of the aeroplanes and saw them coming. When the White Swallow zoomed immediately overhead all the Mountain Folk fell down in fear and moaned as if they were in pain.

"Look out! You'll be hurt by the plane!" yelled Mike, when the White Swallow made to land. The terrified people leapt to their feet and ran helter-skelter to the sides of the courtyard. The plane missed everyone, and it was good to see Ranni's smiling face as he jumped down from the cockpit. He glanced at the Mountain Folk but none were near, and ran across the courtyard to the prisoners. He pulled a fierce-looking knife from his belt and cut them all free.

The children crowded round him, hugging him and raining questions. "You should have seen me yesterday!" yelled Paul, who was now very proud of his narrow escape. "I wore clothes of gold and sun-rays on my head!"

Captain and Mrs Arnold were delighted too, though the Captain kept a stern eye on the Mountain Folk, who were crowded together, trembling, watching the aeroplane.

"They look as if they expect it to jump on them, or bark at them or something," grinned Jack.

131

'I think it would be a good thing if we took off at once," said Ranni. "You never know when these people will find their senses and start making things unpleasant for us! They've only got to damage our plane and we are done for!"

"Here comes Pilescu with *my* plane!" cried Paul in delight, as the big blue and silver aeroplane circled overhead, making a tremendous noise. The mountains around threw the echoes back, and the aeroplane sounded like a rumbling thunderstorm! Round and round it circled, and the Mountain Folk gave groans of terror and threw themselves on their faces again.

The little prince's plane made just as good a landing as the White Swallow. It let down its wheels and lightly touched the ground, running along smoothly over the enormous courtyard.

"Really, it is a perfect landing-ground!" said Captain Arnold, watching. "Smooth, big, and with plenty of wind!"

The blue and silver plane came to a stop. The door of the cockpit opened as the engines stopped. Pilescu looked out, his eyes hidden by sun-glasses. Ranni had not worn them, and the sight of Pilescu gave the Mountain Folk an even bigger fright!

Half of them rushed to the big stairway and disappeared down it, shouting. The other half, with the chief, knelt on the ground, the chief muttering something.

"He say, 'Big chief want mercy!'" grinned Mafumu, who was now enjoying himself immensely.

"Well, if he thinks I'm going to throw him down the mountain-side or take him off in the planes, he's mistaken," said Captain Arnold. "I shan't take any notice of him at all. Come along – we really ought to get off at once. It is a miraculous escape from great danger."

"The two planes will easily take us all," said Mike joyfully. "Who's going in-which ?"

"Ranni, Pilescu, Paul, Jack and the girls can go in Paul's big plane," said Captain Arnold. "I'd like Mike with us – and Mafumu had better come with me too. We can't leave him here."

They all began to climb up into the two cockpits. It didn't take long. Pilescu took the controls of his plane and looked round.

"All ready?" he asked. Then he looked again. "Where's Paul? I thought he was to come in this plane."

"He's not here," said Jack. "I expect he climbed into the White Swallow. I know he always wanted to fly in her."

"Right," said Pilescu, and pulled at a handle. But Ranni stopped him.

"We *must* see if Paul is in the other plane!" he said. "We don't want to arrive in England and find that Paul isn't in either plane!"

Ranni opened the door of the cockpit again and leaned out. He yelled to the White Swallow. "Hallo there! Have you got Paul all right?"

"What?" yelled Captain Arnold, who was just about to take off.

"Is PAUL with you?" shouted Ranni.

"No," shouted back Captain Arnold, after a quick look round his own plane. "I said he was to go with you. The White Swallow isn't big enough for more than four."

Ranni went white. He loved the little Prince better than anyone else in the world – and here they were, about to take off from the mountain-top without Paul! Whatever in the world had become of him?

Ranni leapt out of the plane. Nora called to him. "Look. Isn't that Paul over there in the temple?"

Ranni rushed towards the temple, imagining that all kinds of dreadful things were happening to the little prince. He took out his gun, quite determined to give the whole of the Mountain Folk the worst shock of their lives if they were taking little Paul a prisoner again!

oody but Paul was in the temple. He was in a corner
iggling with something. Ranni gave a roar.

"Paul! What is it? We nearly went without you!"

Paul stood up. In his arms was the beautiful shimmering robe of golden cloth that he had worn the day before, and over his shouder he had slung his sun-ray headress. Young Paul was determined to take those back to school with him, to show his admiring friends. How else would they believe him when he told them of his great adventure?

He had slipped away from his party when no one was looking, for he had felt certain that Captain Arnold would say no, if he asked if he might go and get the garments. The clothes had been difficult to gather up and carry, and Paul did not realise that the planes were starting off so soon!

"Hallo, Ranni! I just went to get these sun-clothes of mine," said Paul. "You haven't seen them, Ranni. Look, you must. . . ."

But to Paul's enormous astonishment Ranni gave him a resounding slap, picked up the boy, clothes and all, and ran back to the big blue and silver plane with him. The Mountain Folk, seeing Ranni run, began to jabber, and one or two picked up their spears.

A gleaming spear flew past Ranni's big head. He dodged to one side, sprang up the ladder of the cockpit and threw Paul on to a seat.

"The little idiot had gone into the temple to get his sun-clothes!" said Ranni, angry and alarmed because they had so nearly gone without Paul.

Paul was angry too. He sat up on the seat. "How dare you hit me?" he shouted to Ranni. "I'll tell the King, my father. He'll, he'll, he'll . . ."

"Shut up, Paul," said Jack. "I'll slap you myself if you say any more! You might have stopped us escaping. The Mountain Folk are looking rather nasty now."

Sure enough some of them were creeping towards the planes, spears in hand. Both planes started up their engines. The throbbing noise arose on the air again. The Mountain Folk shrank back in alarm.

The White Swallow took off first. Gracefully she rose into the air, circled round twice, and then made off over the mountains. Then the blue and silver plane rose up and she was off too.

Jack looked downwards. Already the Secret Mountain looked far off and small. He could just see the folk there running about like ants. How angry they must be because their prisoners had escaped in such an extraordinary way!

"Well, we're off again," said Jack to the girls. "And glad as I was to see the Secret Mountain, I am even gladder to leave it behind! Cheer up, Paul, don't look so blue! We're safe now, even though you nearly messed things up!"

Prince Paul was feeling very foolish. "Sorry," he said. "I didn't think. Anyway, thank goodness I've got the sunclothes. Won't the boys at school think I'm lucky! I shall dress up in them and show the Head."

Eveyrone laughed. It was exciting to be in the plane again. Jack called to Ranni.

"Ranni! You haven't told us your adventures yet. How did you escape from the Secret Mountain?"

"It was unexpectedly easy," shouted back Ranni, who was sitting beside Pilescu. "No one suspected that Pilescu and I were anything but ordinary Mountain Folk when we went down the golden stairway with them. We went down and down for ages and at last came to a big cave where most of them seem to live."

"Oh yes, Mafumu and I once saw that," said Jack. "Go on, Ranni."

"We didn't like to go and sit in the cave in case somebody spoke to us and we couldn't answer in their language," said Ranni. "So we waited about in a passage

135

we saw a little party of the Mountain Folk going
g with spears. We thought they must be going hunting
we joined them, walking behind them."

"How exciting!" said Nora. "Didn't they guess who you
were?"

"Not once," said Ranni. "We followed them down all
kinds of dark passages until we came into the big hall-like
place whose steps lead up to the rock-entrance. They
worked a lever and the big door slid open. Then they set
that great rock turning and sliding, and the way was open
to us!"

"You *were* lucky," said Jack. "I wish I had shared that
adventure."

"It wasn't quite so good after that," said Ranni. "We
had to find our way back to the planes and we got competely lost up in the mountain-pass. We found our way at
last by a great stroke of luck – and arrived at the planes,
very tired indeed, but safe!"

"It didn't take you long to get them going," shouted
Peggy. "Did you find it difficult to spot the Secret
Mountain?"

"No. Very easy," said Ranni. "It looks so yellow from
the air – and besides, it's the only one with a flat top."

"I say! What's the White Swallow doing?" cried Jack
suddenly. "It's going down! Is it going to land, Ranni?"

"It looks like it," said Ranni. "I wonder what's the
matter! My word, I hope nothing has gone wrong. This
plane is large but it won't take everyone."

The White Swallow flew lower still. Below was a fine
flat stretch of grass, and the plane was making for that. It
landed easily and came to a stop.

"We must land too, and see what's up," said Ranni,
looking worried. So the blue and silver plane circled
round too, and flew slowly towards the flat piece of grass.
It let down its wheels and landed gently and smoothly,
running along for a little way and then stopping.

Captain Arnold was already out of his plane and was helping little Mafumu down.

"What's the matter? Anything wrong?" yelled Ranni, climbing from his cockpit. "Let me come and help!"

Goodbye To Mafumu – And Home At Last!

Captain Arnold looked round and shook his head. "No – there's nothing wrong," he said. "But we can't take Mafumu to England with us! He would be miserable away from his own people. His own folk live near here – look, you can see the village over there – and I am taking him home.

"The children will want to say good-bye to him," said Ranni at once. "Little Mafumu has been a good friend to us. We couldn't have rescued you without his help. Hie, Jack – bring Paul and the girls to say good-bye to Mafumu. We're leaving him here."

Everyone climbed from the two aeroplanes. The children were sad to say good-bye to their small friend. They had grown very fond of cheeky Mafumu, and they did not want to leave him behind at all.

"Can't we possibly take Mafumu home with us?" asked Paul. "Do let's. He could live with us – and he could come to school with Mike and Jack and me!"

"Mafumu wouldn't be happy," said Ranni. "One day we will all pay a visit to him again, and see how he is getting on. I shouldn't be surprised if some day he is made chief of his tribe – he is brave and intelligent, and has all the makings of a fine leader."

"I hope that uncle of his won't hit him too much," said

Jack. "Golly, look – all the people are running out from the village. Have they seen Mafumu, do you think?"

Sure enough, from the little native village nearby came many men, women and children. They had seen Mafumu, and although they had been unsure about the aeroplanes, they felt that the "big roaring birds" as they called them could not be very dangerous if Mafumu was in one of them!

Mafumu's uncle was with the people. Jack wondered if he would take hold of the little boy and give him a shaking for having run away from him back to his friends. He glanced at Mafumu to see if he was afraid. But the boy held himself proudly. Was he not friends with these people? Had he not helped them? He felt a real king that day.

"Mafumu, take this for a parting present," said Prince Paul, and he gave Mafumu his best pocket-knife, a marvellous thing with a bright gold handle. Mafumu was overjoyed. He had often seen Paul using it, and had not even dared to ask if he might borrow it. Now it was his own! Mafumu could hardly believe his good luck.

And then, of course, everyone wanted to give little Mafumu something. Nora gave him a bead necklace, and Peggy gave him her little silver brooch with P on. Mafumu pinned it onto his shorts!

"P doesn't stand for Mafumu, but as he doesn't know his letters it doesn't matter," said Peggy. "What are you giving Mafumu, Mike?"

Mike had three fine glass marbles which he always carried about with him in his pocket. He gave them to Mafumu, whose eyes grew wider and wider as these presents were given to him! His teeth flashed white as he grinned round at everyone.

Jack gave him a pencil. It was a silver one, whose point went up or down when the bottom end was screwed round. Mafumu thought this was very clever and he was

138

overjoyed to have the wonderful pencil for his own. He threw his arms round Jack and gave him a big hug.

"Shut up, Mafumu," said Jack uncomfortably, for the others were giggling. But Mafumu hadn't finished he hugged Jack again and again, so tightly that Jack nearly fell over.

"Shut *up*, Mafumu," said Jack again. Mafumu at last let go. His eyes swimming in tears, for it nearly broke his little heart to part from Jack. He had nothing of his own to give Jack – except his very precious necklace of crocodile teeth! He took it off, muttered a few words over it, and then pressed it into Jack's hand.

"No, Mafumu," said Jack. "No. I know quite well that you think these crocodile teeth are your special good luck charm and keep you from danger. I don't want them."

But Mafumu would not take no for an answer, and in the end Jack put the crocodile necklace into his pocket, feeling a funny lump in his throat. Dear old Mafumu – it wasn't easy to part from him.

Ranni gave the boy a little mirror for himself. Pilescu gave him a notebook to scribble in with his new pencil. Captain Arnold gave him an odd pair of sunglasses, which were in a locker at the back of the White Swallow. These nearly sent Mafumu mad with joy. He at once put them on, and looked so peculiar that everyone shrieked with laughter.

And then Mrs Arnold gave the boy a photograph of all the children. It was one that she always took about with her, and was in a brown leather folding frame. Mafumu was so pleased that he did a kind of war-dance, holding all his gifts above his head, and wearing his sunglasses over his eyes. Everyone laughed till their sides ached.

The folk from the village had come nearer and nearer, full of amazement to see Mafumu receiving gifts from his friends. Mafumu took off his sunglasses and beamed round at the children.

"Goodbye," he said, in English. "Goodbye. Come again. Mafumu is your friend."

Everyone hugged Mafumu and then they got back into the planes. The villagers came right up to Mafumu when they saw that the others were safely in the "big roaring birds." Mafumu's uncle was jealous. He wanted the necklace that Nora had given to little Mafumu. The boy glared at his uncle. Then, with a quick movement, he put on his sunglasses and shouted in a most warlike manner.

With shrieks the whole of the villagers ran away, Mafumu's uncle running the fastest. Then Mafumu, with slow and stately steps, stalked after them, feeling himself a very chief of chiefs! That was the last sight the children had of their small friend, for the two planes took off. Mafumu turned for a moment and waved. Then, too proud to feel sad just then, he went on his way to his village, feeling quite certain that his cruel uncle would not try many more tricks on him!

"I do hate leaving Mafumu behind," sighed Peggy. "I really do hate it. He's quite one of us."

"Jack's lucky to have those crocodile teeth," said Paul.

"And you're lucky to have that glorious, shimmering robe and sun-ray head-dress," said Peggy. "I wish I had it!"

"I'll lend it to you whenever you want it," said Paul generously. "I truly will."

The aeroplanes were flying well and fast. Nora looked down to see if they were still over mountains and she gave a cry.

"We're over the Secret Mountain again! Look, everybody! We must have gone out of our way to take Mafumu back – and now we're flying the opposite way home."

Everyone looked down. Yes – there was the Secret Mountain, with its curious yellow colouring. And there was the flat top, with the vast smooth courtyard on which had happened their most exciting adventures.

"Wasn't the eclipse fun?" said Nora.

"And didn't Paul look marvellous when he came up that stairway dressed in those wonderful robes?" said Peggy.

"And wasn't it glorious when we stood on the top of the mountain and suddenly heard the roar of the White Swallow's engines?" said Jack.

"I wish we could have this adventure all over again," said Paul. "It was a bit too exciting at times, but I like exciting things."

"Well, let's hope the adventure is finished as far as excitement and danger are concerned," said Ranni. "I've had quite enough, I can tell you! All I want now is to get back to England safely, and see you all safe and sound at school again!"

"School! Fancy going back to school after all this!" cried Paul. "I don't want to. I want to go off flying in my plane again, Ranni."

"You can want all you like, but school is the best and safest place for *you*," said Ranni. "And, anyway, you have plenty to tell the boys. My word, they'll think you a hero, you may be sure!"

"Will they really?" asked the little prince, his eyes shining. "I'm not really a hero – but I wouldn't a bit mind people thinking me one."

The planes flew on steadily. At last they came to a big airport, where they landed. They took in fuel and the children had a good meal. Captain Arnold sent a message to England to say that they were all safe and sound. Then off they set again.

The children slept the night through peacefully. Adventures were lovely – but it *was* nice to feel safe again. They began to look forward to seeing England and Dimmy, and to telling their tremendous story.

And at last they were home! They landed at the big airport, and what a crowd was there to welcome them! Photographers ran up to take their picture, people crowded up to clap them on the backs and to shake hands, and Captain Arnold had to speak a few words into a microphone to say they were safely back at last!

Then they all squeezed into two cars and off they went to London and to Dimmy. They chattered and laughed, excited and proud. It was grand to be back home again, and to be welcomed in such a lovely way.

Dimmy was standing on the steps to welcome them herself. The children tumbled out of the cars and rushed to her, shouting their news.

"We've been to Africa!"

"We found a Secret Mountain!"

"Paul was nearly made a sacrifice to the sun!"

"An eclipse came, and the people thought we had killed the sun!"

"Well, you'll certainly kill *me* if you hug me like this!" said Dimmy, her eyes full of happy tears, because she was so thankful to see them again. She had been terribly worried and anxious when all the children had left her so suddenly – but now everything was all right!

That evening Captain Arnold had to go off to broadcast his story. It was to be at a quarter past nine, after the news. The children switched on the radio and listened in. It was fun to hear Captain Arnold's deep voice booming into the room as he began the tale of their adventures.

Dimmy listened in amazement. She had already heard bits and pieces from the children, but here was the tale told in full, just as it might be written in a book. It was marvellous!

For half an hour the tale went on – and then it was over. Dimmy switched off the radio.

"Well, well," she said, "we've been through some adventures together, children – but this one is the most exciting of all. Did it really happen? Could such things happen to ordinary children like you?"

"Well, they *did!*" said Jack, and he showed Dimmy his

142

necklace of crocodile teeth. "Look here – these are teeth from a crocodile that nearly ate Mafumu one day. His father and uncles killed it, and gave Mafumu some of the teeth. And he gave them to me."

"I wonder what Mafumu is doing now," said Mike. "Wasn't he a fine friend? We wouldn't be here now if it wasn't for old Mafumu."

"And you're not going to be *here* much longer," said Dimmy, getting up. "It's long past your bedtime!"

"*Bed*time! Is there such a thing as *bed*time?" said Peggy. "I'd forgotten all about it! We haven't been properly to bed for weeks. I don't think I shall really bother about bedtime any more."

"Well, *you* may not – but I shall!" said Dimmy. "Come along, all of you. *Bedtime!* There are biscuits and lemonade for those who come now – and none for those who dawdle!"

So biscuits and lemonade it was, and a long, long talk in the bedrooms! And then Dimmy firmly switched off the lights, tucked everybody up, said, "No more talking," in a very stern voice – and left them.

We must leave them, too, dreaming of their adventures – dreaming of the strange, far-away Secret Mountain!

The Secret of Killimooin

First published in a single volume in hardback in 1943 by
Basil Blackwell Ltd.
First published in paperback in 1965 in Armada

Copyright reserved Enid Blyton 1943

The author asserts the moral right to be identified as
the author of the work

A Fine Surprise

Three excited boys stood on a station platform, waiting for a train to come in.

"The train's late," said Mike, impatiently. "Five minutes late already."

"I'm going to tell the girls the news," said Jack.

"*I'm* going to tell them!" said Prince Paul, his big dark eyes glowing. "It's *my* news, not yours."

"All right, all right," said Mike. "You tell Nora and Peggy then, but don't be too long about it or I shall simply have to burst in!"

The three boys were waiting for Nora and Peggy to come back from their boarding-school for the summer holidays. Mike, Jack and Prince Paul all went to the same boys' boarding-school, and they had broken up the day before. Mike was the twin brother of Nora, and Peggy was his other sister, a year older than Mike and Nora.

Jack was their adopted brother. He had no father or mother of his own, so Captain and Mrs Arnold, the children's father and mother, had taken him into their family, and treated him like another son. He went to boarding-school with Mike, and was very happy.

Prince Paul went to the same school too. He was a great friend of theirs, for a year or two back the children had rescued him when he was kidnapped. His father was the King of Baronia, and the little prince spent his term-time at an English boarding-school, and his holidays in his own distant land of Baronia. He was the youngest of the five.

"Here comes the train, hurrah!" yelled Mike, as he heard the sound of the train in the distance.

"The girls will be sure to be looking out of the window," said Jack.

147

The train came nearer and nearer, and the engine chuffed more and more loudly. It ran alongside the platform, slowed down and stopped. Doors swung open.

Prince Paul gave a yell. "There they are! Look! In the middle of the train!"

Sure enough, there were the laughing faces of Peggy and Nora, leaning out of the window. Then their door swung open and out leapt the two girls. Nora was dark and curly-haired like Mike. Peggy's golden hair shone in the sun. She had grown taller, but she was still the same old Peggy.

"Peggy! Nora! Welcome back!" yelled Mike. He hugged his twin-sister, and gave Peggy a squeeze too. All five children were delighted to be together again. They had had such adventures, they had shared so many difficulties, dangers and excitements. It was good to be together once more, and say, "Do you remember this, do you remember that?"

Prince Paul was always a little shy at first when he met the two girls. He held out his hand politely to shake hands, but Peggy gave a squeal and put her arms round him.

"Paul! Don't be such an idiot! Give me a hug!"

"Paul's got some news," said Mike, suddenly remembering. "Buck up and tell it, Paul."

"What is it?" asked Nora.

"I've got an invitation for you all," said the little prince. "Will you come to my land of Baronia with me for the holidays?"

There was a shriek of delight from the two girls.

"PAUL! Go to Baronia with you! Oh, I say!"

"Oh! What a marvellous surprise!"

Paul beamed. "Yes, it *is* a fine surprise, isn't it?" he said. "I thought you'd be pleased. Mike and Jack are thrilled too."

"It will be a real adventure to go to Baronia," said Mike. "A country hidden in the heart of mountains – with

148

a few beautiful towns, hundreds of hidden villages, great forests – golly, it will be grand."

"Oh, Paul, how decent of your father to ask us!" said Nora, putting her arm through the little prince's. "How long will it take us to get there?"

"We shall fly in my aeroplane," said Paul. "Ranni and Pilescu, my two men, will fetch us tomorrow."

"This is just too good to be true!" said Nora, dancing round in joy. She bumped into a porter wheeling a barrow. "Oh – Sorry, I didn't see you. I say, Mike, we'd better get our luggage. Can you see a porter with an empty barrow?"

All the porters had been engaged, so the five children had to wait. They didn't mind. They didn't mind anything! It was so marvellous to be going off to Paul's country the next day.

"We thought we were going to the seaside with Daddy and Mummy," said Nora.

"So we were," said Jack. "But when Paul's father cabled yesterday, saying he was sending the aeroplane to fetch Paul, he said we were all to come too, if we were allowed to."

"And you know how Daddy and Mummy like us to travel and see all we can!" said Mike. "They were just as pleased about it as we were – though they were sorry not to have us for the holidays, of course."

"We are not to take many clothes," said Jack. "Paul says we can dress up in Baronian things – they are much more exciting than ours! I shall feel I'm wearing fancy dress all the time!"

The girls sighed with delight. They imagined themselves dressed in pretty, swinging skirts and bright bodices – lovely! They would be real Baronians.

"Look here, we really *must* get a porter and stop talking," said Nora. "The platform is almost empty. Hi, porter!"

A porter came up, wheeling an empty barrow. He lifted

the girls' two trunks on to it and wheeled them down to the barrier. He got a taxi for the children and they all crowded into it. They were to go to their parents' flat for the night.

It was a very happy family party that sat down to a big tea at the flat. Captain and Mrs Arnold smiled round at the five excited faces. To come home for holidays was thrilling enough – but to come home and be told they were all off to Baronia the next day was almost too exciting for words!

Usually the children poured out all the doings of the term – how well they had played tennis, how exciting cricket had been, how fine the new swimming-pool was, and how awful the exams were. But today not a word was said about the term that had just passed. No – it was all Baronia, Baronia, Baronia! Paul was delighted to see their excitement, for he was very proud of his country.

"Of course, it is not a very big country," he said, "but it is a beautiful one, and a very wild one. Ah, our grand mountains, our great forests, our beautiful villages! The stern rough men, the laughing women, the good food!"

"You sound like a poet, Paul," said Peggy. "Go on!"

"No," said the little prince, going red. "You will laugh at me. You English people are strange. You love your country but you hardly ever praise her. Now I could tell you of Baronia's beauties for an hour. And not only beauties. I could tell you of wild robbers . . ."

"Oooh," said Peggy, thrilled.

"And of fierce animals in the mountains," said Paul.

"We'll hunt them!" Mike chimed in.

"And of hidden ways in the hills, deep forests where no foot has ever trodden, and . . ."

"Oh, let's go this very minute!" said Nora. "I can't wait! We might have adventures there – thrilling ones, like those we've had before."

The little prince shook his head. "No," he said. "We shall have no exciting adventures in Baronia. We shall live in my father's palace, and wherever we go there will be guards with us. You see, since that time I was kidnapped, I am never allowed to go about alone in Baronia."

The other children looked disappointed. "Well, it sounds grand to have a bodyguard, I must say, but it does cramp our style a bit," said Mike. "Are we allowed to climb trees and things like that?"

"Well, I have never been allowed to in my own country," said Paul. "But, you see, I am a prince there, and I have to behave always with much dignity. I behave differently here."

"I should just think you do!" said Mike, staring at him. "Who waded through the duck-pond to get his ball, and came out covered with mud?"

"And who tore his coat to rags squeezing through a hawthorn hedge, trying to get away from an angry cow?" asked Jack.

"I did," said Paul. "But then, here, I am like you. I learn to behave differently. When you go to Baronia you, too, will have different manners. You must kiss my mother's hand, for instance."

Mike and Jack looked at him in alarm. "I say! I'm not much good at that sort of thing!" said Jack.

"And you must learn to bow – like this," said the little prince, thoroughly enjoying himself. He bowed politely from his waist downwards, stood up and brought his heels together with a smart little click. The girls giggled.

"It will be fun to see Mike and Jack doing things like that," said Nora. "You'd better start practising now, Mike. Come on – bow to me. And, Jack, you kiss my hand!"

The boys scowled. "Don't be an idiot," said Mike, gruffly. "If I've got to do it, I will do it – but not to you or Peggy."

"I don't expect it will be as bad as Paul makes out," said his mother, smiling. "He is just pulling your leg. Look at him grinning!"

"You can behave how you like," said Paul, with a chuckle. "But don't be surprised at Baronian manners. They are much better than yours!"

"Have you all finished tea?" asked Captain Arnold. "I can't imagine that any of you could possibly eat any more, but I may be wrong."

"I'll just have one more piece of cake," said Mike. "We don't get chocolate cake like this at school!"

"You've had four pieces already," said his mother. "I am glad I don't have to feed you all the year round! There you are – eat it up."

There was very little packing to be done that evening – only night-clothes and tooth-brushes, flannels and things like that. All the children were looking forward to wearing the colourful Baronian clothes. They had seen photographs of the Baronian people, and had very much liked the children's clothes. They were all so thrilled that it was very difficult to settle down and do anything. They talked to Captain and Mrs Arnold, played a game or two and then went off to bed.

Not one of them could go to sleep. They lay in their different bedrooms, calling to one another until Mrs Arnold came up and spoke sternly.

"One more shout – and you don't go to Baronia!" After that there was silence, and the five children lay quietly in their beds, thinking of the exciting day tomorrow was going to be.

Off To Baronia

It was wonderful to wake up the next morning and remember everything. Jack sat up and gave a yell to wake
the others. It was not long before everyone was dressed
and down to breakfast. They were to go to the airport to
meet Ranni and Pilescu, the big Baronians, at ten o'clock.
All the things they were taking with them went into one
small bag.

"Mummy, I'm sorry I won't see much of you these
hols." said Peggy.

"Well, Daddy and I may fly over to Baronia to fetch
you back," said her mother. "We could come a week or
two before it's time for you to return to school, so we
should see quite a bit of you!"

"Oh – that would be lovely!" said Nora and Peggy
together, and the boys beamed in delight. "Will you come
in the White Swallow?"

The White Swallow was the name given to Captain
Arnold's famous aeroplane. In it he and Mrs Arnold had
flown many thousands of miles, for they were both excel-
lent pilots. They had had many adventures, and this was
partly why they liked their children to go off on their own
and have their own adventures too.

"It doesn't do to coddle children too much and shelter
them," said Captain Arnold many a time to his wife. "We
don't want children like that – we want boys and girls of
spirit and courage, who can stand on their feet and are not
afraid of what may happen to them. We want them to
grow up adventurous and strong, of some real use in the
world! So we must not say no when a chance comes along
to help them to be plucky and independent!"

"If we can grow up like you and Mummy, we shall be all

153

right!" said Peggy. "You tried to fly all the way to Australia by yourselves in that tiny plane – and you've set up ever so many flying records. We ought to be adventurous children!"

"I think you are," said her mother, with a laugh. "You've certainly had some marvellous adventures already – more than most children have all their lives long!"

When the car drew up at the door to take the children to the airport, they all clattered down the steps at once. "It's a good thing it's a big car!" said Mike. "Seven of us is quite a crowd!"

Everyone got in. The car set off at a good speed, and soon came to the big airport. It swept in through the gates. Mike, who was looking out of the window, gave a loud shout.

"There's your aeroplane, Paul! I can see it. It's the smartest one on the air-field."

"And the loveliest," said Nora, looking in delight at the beautiful plane towards which they were racing. It was bright blue with silver edges, and it shone brilliantly in the sun. The car stopped a little way from it. Everyone got out. Paul gave a yell.

"There's Pilescu! And Ranni! Look, over there, behind the plane!"

The two big Baronians had heard the engine of the car and they had come to see if it was the children arriving. Pilescu gave a deep-throated shout.

"Paul! My little lord!"

Paul raced over the grass to Pilescu. The big red-bearded man bowed low and then lifted the boy up in his strong arms.

"Pilescu! How are you? It's grand to see you again," said Paul, in the Baronian language that always sounded so strange to the other children.

Pilescu was devoted to the little prince. He had held him in his arms when he was only a few minutes old, and had vowed to be his man as long as he lived. His arms pressed so tightly round the small boy that Paul gasped for breath.

"Pilescu! I can't breathe! Let me down," he squealed. Pilescue grinned and set him down. Paul turned to Ranni, who bowed low and then gave him a hug like a bear, almost as tight as Pilescu's.

"Ranni! Have you got any of the chocolate I like so much?" asked Paul. Ranni put his hand into his pocket and brought out a big packet of thick chocolate, wrapped in colourful paper. It had a Baronian name on it. Paul liked it better than any other chocolate, and had often shared it with Mike and Jack, when a parcel had arrived for him from Baronia.

Ranni and Pilescu welcomed the other children, beaming in delight to see them all, and Captain and Mrs Arnold too. They had all shared a strange adventure in Africa, hidden in a Secret Mountain, and it was pleasant to be together again.

"Look after all these rascals, Pilescu," said Mrs Arnold, as she said goodbye to the excited children. "You know what monkeys they can be!"

"Madam, they are safe with me and with Ranni," said Pilescu, his red beard flaming in the sun. He bowed from his waist, and took Mrs Arnold's small hand into his big one. He kissed it with much dignity. Mike felt perfectly certain he would never be able to kiss anyone's hand like that.

"Is the plane ready?" asked Captain Arnold, climbing into the cockpit to have a look round. "My word, she is a marvellous machine! I'll say this for Baronia – you have some mighty fine designers of aircraft! You beat us hollow, and we are pretty good at it, too."

All the children were now munching chocolate, talking to Ranni. The big bear-like man was happy to see them all again. Nora and Peggy hung on to him, remembering the thrilling, dangerous days when they had all been inside the Secret Mountain in Africa.

A mechanic came up and did a few last things to the

155

engine of the great aeroplane. In a minute or two the engines started up and a loud throbbing filled the air.

"Doesn't it sound lovely?" said Mike. "We're really going!"

"Get in, children," said Pilescu. "Say your goodbyes – then we must go."

The children hugged their parents, and Paul bowed, and kissed Mrs Arnold's hand. She laughed and gave him a squeeze. "Goodbye, little Paul. Mind you don't lead my four into trouble! Jack, look after everyone. Mike, take care of your sisters. Nora and Peggy, see that the boys don't get up to mischief!"

"Goodbye, Mummy! Goodbye, Daddy! Write to us. Come and fetch us when the hols are nearly over!"

"Goodbye, Captain Arnold! Goodbye, Mrs Arnold!"

The roar of the aeroplane drowned everything. Pilescu was at the controls. Ranni was beside him. The children were sitting behind in comfortable armchairs. The engine roared more loudly.

"R-r-r-r-r-r-r! R-r-r-r-r-r—!" The big machine taxied slowly over the runway – faster – faster – and then, light as a bird, it left the ground, skimmed over the hedges and the trees, and was up in the sky in two minutes.

"Off to Baronia!" said Mike, thrilled.

"Adventuring again," said Jack. "Isn't this fun?"

"The runway looks about one inch long!" said Nora, peering out of the window.

"In half an hour we shall be over the sea," said Paul. "Let's look out for it."

It was grand to be in the big aeroplane once more. All the children were used to flying, and loved the feeling of being high up in the sky. Sometimes clouds rolled below them, looking like vast snow-fields. The sun shone down on the whiteness, and the clouds below the plane became almost too dazzling to look at.

Suddenly there was a break in the clouds, and Mike gave a yell.

"The sea! Look – through the clouds. Hi, Ranni, Ranni, isn't that the sea already?"

Ranni turned and nodded. "We are going very fast," he shouted. "We want to be in Baronia by lunch time."

"I'm so happy," said Nora, her eyes shining. "I've always wanted to go to Baronia, Paul. And now we're really going."

"I am happy too," said Paul. "I like your country, and I like you, too. But I like Baronia better. Maybe you also will like Baronia better."

"Rubbish!" said Mike. "As if any country could be nicer than our own!"

"You will see," said the little prince. "Have some more chocolate?"

The children helped themselves from Paul's packet. "Well, I certainly think your chocolate is better than ours," said Mike, munching contentedly. "Look, there's the sea again. "Doesn't it look smooth and flat?"

It was fun watching for the sea to appear and reappear between the gaps in the clouds. Then the plane flew over land·again. The clouds cleared away, and the children could see the country below, spread out like an enormous, coloured map.

They flew over great towns, wreathed in misty smoke. They flew over stretches of green countryside, where farms and houses looked like toys. They watched the rivers, curling along like blue and silver snakes. They flew over tall mountains, and on some of them was snow.

"Funny to see that in the middle of summer," said Mike. "How's the time getting on? I say – twelve o'clock already! We shall be there in another hour or so."

The plane roared along steadily. Ranni took Pilescu's place after two hours had gone by. He sat and talked to the children for a while, gazing devotedly at the little prince. Mike thought he was like a big dog, worshipping his master! He thought Paul was very lucky to have such friends as Ranni and Pilescu.

157

A palace that almost seemed to have come straight from a fairy tale!

"Soon we shall see the palace," he said, looking down. "Now we are over the borders of Baronia, Paul! Look, there is the river Jollu! And there is the town of Kikibora."

Paul began to look excited. It was three months since he had been home, and he was longing to see his father and mother, and his little brothers and sisters.

Mike and Jack fell silent. They wondered if Paul's mother would be at the airfield to greet them. Would they have to kiss her hand? "I shall really feel an awful idiot," thought Mike, uncomfortably.

"There is the palace!" cried Paul, suddenly. The children saw a palace standing on a hillside – a palace that almost seemed to have come straight from a fairytale! It was a beautiful place, with shining towers and minarets,

158

and below it was a blue lake in which the reflection of the palace shone.

"Oh! It's beautiful!" said Nora. "Oh, Paul – I feel rather grand. Fancy living in a palace! It may seem ordinary to you – but it's wonderful to me!"

The aeroplane circled round and flew lower. Beside the palace was a great runway, on which the royal planes landed. Ranni's plane swooped low like a bird, its great wheels skimmed the ground, the plane slowed down and came to a halt not far from a little crowd of people.

"Welcome to Baronia!" said Paul, his eyes shining. "Welcome to Baronia!"

The Palace In Baronia

Ranni and Pilescu helped the five children down from the plane. Paul ran straight to a very lovely lady smiling nearby. He bowed low, kissed her hand, and then flung himself on her, chattering quickly in Baronian. It was his mother, the queen. She laughed and cried at the same time, fondling the little prince's hair, and kissing his cheeks.

Paul's father was there, too, a handsome man, straight and tall, dressed in uniform. Paul saluted him smartly and then leapt into his arms. Then he turned to four smaller children standing nearby, his brothers and sisters. Paul kissed the hands of his little sisters and saluted his brothers. Then they kissed, all talking at once.

Soon it was the other children's turn to say how-do-you-do. They had already met Paul's father and liked him, but they had never seen the little prince's mother. Nora and Peggy thought she looked a real queen, lovely enough to be in a fairy tale. She wore the Baronian dress beautifully, and her full red and blue skirt swung gracefully as she walked.

She kissed Nora and Peggy and spoke to them in English. "Welcome, little girls!" she said. "I am so glad to see Paul's friends. You have been so good to him in England. I hope you will be very happy here."

Then it was the boys' turn to be welcomed. Both of them felt hot and bothered about kissing the Queen's hand, but after all, it was quite easy! Mike stepped forward first, and the Queen held out her hand to him. Mike found himself bending down and kissing it quite naturally! Jack followed, and then they saluted Paul's father.

"Come along to the palace now," said the Queen. "You

must be very hungry after your long journey. We have all Paul's favourite dishes – and I hope you will like them too."

The children were glad that Paul's mother could speak English. They had been trying to learn the Baronian language from Paul, but he was not a good teacher. He would go off into peals of laughter at the comical way they pronounced the difficult words of the Baronian language, and it was difficult to get any sense out of him when he was in one of his giggling fits.

The children stared in awe at the palace. They had never seen one like it before, outside of books. It was really magnificent, though not enormous. With the great mountain behind it, and the shining blue lake below, it looked like a dream palace. They walked through a garden full of strange and sweet-smelling flowers and came to a long flight of steps. They climbed these and entered the palace through a wide-open door at which stood six footmen in a line, dressed in the Baronian livery of blue and silver.

After them clattered the little brothers and sisters of Paul, with their nurses. Peggy and Nora thought the small children were sweet. They were all very like Paul, and had big dark eyes.

"We shan't be bothered much with these babies," said Paul, in rather a lordly voice. "Of course, they wanted to welcome me. But they live in the nurseries. We shall have our own rooms, and Pilescu will wait on us."

This was rather a relief to hear. Although the children liked the look of Paul's father and mother very much, they had felt it might be rather embarrassing to live with a king and queen and have meals with them. It was good to hear that they were to be on their own.

Paul took them to their rooms. The girls had a wonderful bedroom overlooking the lake. It was all blue and silver. The ceiling was painted blue with silver stars shining there. The girls thought it was wonderful. The bedspread was the same beautiful blue, embroidered with shining silver stars.

"I shall never dare to sleep in this bed," said Peggy, in an awed voice. "It's a four-poster bed – like you see in old pictures – and big enough to take six of us, not two! Oh, Nora – isn't this marvellous fun?"

The boys had two bedrooms between them – one big one for Mike and Jack, with separate beds. "About half a mile apart!" said Jack, with a laugh, when he saw the enormous bedroom with its two beds, one each end. Paul had a bedroom to himself, leading out of the other one, even bigger!

"However do you manage to put up with living in a dormitory with twelve other boys, when you have a bedroom like this at home?" said Mike to the little prince. "I say – what a wonderful view!"

Mike's room had two sets of windows. One set looked out over the blue lake and the other looked up the hillside on which the palace was built. It was a grand country.

"It's wild and rugged and rough and beautiful," said Paul. "Not like your country. Yours is quite tame. It is like a tame cat, sitting by the fire. Mine is like a wild tiger roaming the hills."

"He's gone all poetic again!" said Mike, with a laugh. But he knew what Paul meant, all the same. There was something very wild and exciting about Baronia. It looked so beautiful, smiling under the summer sun – but it might not be all it seemed to be on the surface. It was not "tamed" like their own country – it was still wild, and parts of it quite unknown.

The children washed in basins that seemed to be made of silver. They dried their hands on towels embroidered with the Baronian arms. Everything was perfect. It seemed almost a shame to dirty the towels or make the clear water in the basins dirty and soapy!

They went with Paul to have lunch. They were to have it with the King and Queen, although after that they would have meals in their own play-room, a big room near their bedrooms, which Paul had already shown them. The toys there had made them gasp. An electric railway ran down one side of the room, on which Paul's trains could run. A Meccano set, bigger than any the children had ever seen, was in another corner, with a beautiful bridge made from the pieces, left by Paul from the last holidays. Everything a boy could want was there! It would be great fun to explore that play-room!

The lunch was marvellous. The children did not know any of the dishes, but they all tasted equally delicious. If this was Baronian food they could eat plenty! Paul's mother talked to them in English, and Paul's father made one or two jokes. Paul chattered away to his parents, sometimes in Baronian and sometimes in English. He told them all about the things he did at school.

Jack nudged Mike. "You'd think Paul was head-boy to hear him talk!" he said, in a low tone. "We'll tease him about this afterwards!"

It was a happy meal. The children were very hungry, but by the time lunch was nearing an end they could not eat another scrap. Jack looked longingly at a kind of pink ice-cream with what looked like purple cherries in it. But no – he could not even manage another ice.

Ranni and Pilescu did not eat with the others. They stood quietly, one behind the King's chair and one behind Paul's. A line of soldiers, in the blue and silver uniform, stood at the end of the room. The four English children couldn't help feeling rather grand, eating their lunch with a king, a queen, and a prince, with soldiers on guard at the back. Baronia was going to be fun!

Paul took them all over the palace afterwards. It was a magnificent place, strongly built, with every room flooded with the summer sunshine. The nurseries were full of Paul's younger brothers and sisters. There was a baby in a carved cradle too, covered by a blue and silver rug. It opened big dark eyes when the two girls bent over it.

The nurseries were as lovely as the big play-room that belonged to Paul. The children stared in wonder at the amount of toys.

"It's like the biggest toy-shop I've ever seen!" said Jack. "And yet, when Paul's at school, the thing he likes best of all is that little old ship I once carved out of a bit of wood!"

Paul was pleased that the others liked his home. He did not boast or show off. It was natural to him to live in a palace and have everything he wanted. He was a warm-hearted, friendly little boy who loved to share everything with his friends. Before he had gone to England he had had no friends of his own – but now that he had Mike, Jack, Peggy and Nora, he was very happy. It was marvellous to him to have them with him in Baronia.

"We'll bathe in the lake, and we'll sail to the other side, and we'll go driving in the mountains," said Paul. "We'll have a perfectly gorgeous time. I only hope it won't get too hot. If it does, we'll have to go to the mountains where it's cooler."

The children were very tired by the time that first day came to an end. They seemed to have walked miles in and around the palace, exploring countless rooms, and looking out of countless turrets. They had gone all round the glorious gardens, and had been saluted by numbers of gardeners. Everyone seemed very pleased to see them.

They had tea and supper on the terrace outside the play-room. Big, colourful umbrellas sheltered the table from the sun. The blue lake shimmered below.

"I wish I hadn't eaten so much lunch," groaned Mike, as he looked at the exciting array of cakes and biscuits and sandwiches before him. "I simply don't know what to do. I know I shan't want any supper if I eat this tea – and if supper is anything like lunch, I shall just break my heart if I'm not hungry for it."

"Oh, you'll be hungry all right," said Paul. "Go on – have what you want."

Before supper the children went for a sail on the lake in

164

Prince Paul's own sailing boat. Ranni went with them. It was lovely and cool on the water. Jack looked at the girls' burnt faces.

"We shall be brown as berries in a day or two," he said. "We're all brown now – but we shall get another layer very quickly. My arms are burning! I shan't put them in water tonight! They will sting too much."

"You'll have to hold your arms above your head when you have your bath, then," said Mike. "You will look funny!"

The children were almost too tired to undress and bath themselves that night. Yawning widely they took off their clothes, cleaned their teeth and washed. A bath was sunk into the floor of each bedroom. Steps led down to it. It seemed funny to the children to go down into a bath, instead of just hopping over the side of one. But it was all fun.

The girls got into their big four-poster, giggling. It seemed so big to them after the narrow beds they had at school.

"I shall lose you in the night!" said Nora to Peggy.

The boys jumped into their beds, too. Paul left the door open between his bedroom and that of Mike's and Jack's, so that he might shout to them. But there was very little shouting that night. The children's eyes were heavy and they could not keep them open. The day had been almost too exciting.

"Now we're living in Baronia," whispered Peggy to herself. "We're in Baronia, in . . ." And then she was fast asleep, whilst outside the little waves at the edge of the lake lapped quietly all night long.

An Exciting Trip

The first week glided by, golden with sunshine. The children enjoyed themselves thoroughly, though Nora often complained of the heat. All of them now wore the Baronian dress, and fancied themselves very much in it.

The girls wore tight bodices of white and blue, with big silver buttons, and full skirts of red and blue. They wore no stockings, but curious little half-boots, laced up with red. The boys wore embroidered trousers, with cool shirts open at the neck, and a broad belt. They, too, wore the half-boots, and found them very comfortable.

At first they all felt as if they were in fancy dress, but they soon got used to it. "I shan't like going back to ordinary clothes," said Nora, looking at herself in the long mirror. "I do so love the way this skirt swings out round me. Look, Mike – there are yards of material in it."

Mike was fastening his belt round him. He stuck his scout knife into it. He looked at himself in the mirror, too. "I look a bit like a pirate or something," he said. "Golly, I wish the boys at school could see me now! Wouldn't they be green with envy!"

"They'd laugh at you," said Nora. "You wouldn't dare to wear those clothes in England. I hope the Queen will let me take mine back with me. I could wear them at a fancy-dress party. I bet I'd win the prize!"

That first week was glorious. The children were allowed to do anything they wanted to, providing that Ranni or Pilescu was with them. They rode little mountain ponies through the hills. They bathed at least five times a day in the warm waters of the lake. They sailed every evening. They went by car to the nearest big town, and rode in the buses there. They were quaint buses, fat and squat, painted blue and silver. Everything was different, every thing was strange.

"England must have seemed very queer to you at first, Paul," said Mike to the little prince, realizing for the first time how difficult the boy must have found living in a strange country.

Paul nodded. He was very happy to show his friends everything. Now, when he was back at school again in England, and wanted to talk about his home and his country, Jack and Mike would understand all he said, and would listen gladly.

Towards the end of the first week Pilescu made a suggestion. "Why do you not take your friends in the aeroplane, and show them how big your country is?" he asked Paul. "I will take you all."

"Oh *yes*, Pilescu – let's do that!" cried Mike. "Let's fly over the mountains and the forests, and see everything!"

"I will show you the Secret Forest," said Prince Paul, unexpectedly.

The others stared at him. "What's the Secret Forest?" asked Jack. "What's secret about it?"

"It's a queer place," said Paul. "Nobody has ever been there!"

"Well, how do you know it's there, then?" asked Mike.

"We've seen it from aeroplanes," said Paul. "We've flown over it."

"Why hasn't anyone ever been into this forest?" asked Peggy. "Someone *must* have, Paul. I don't believe there is anywhere in the whole world that people haven't explored now."

"I tell you no one has ever been in the Secret Forest," said Paul, obstinately. "And I'll tell you why. Look – get me that map over there, Mike."

Mike threw him over a rolled-up map. Paul unrolled it and spread it flat on a table. He found the place he wanted and pointed to it.

"This is a map of Baronia," he said. "You can see what

167

a rugged, mountainous country it is. Now look – do you see these mountains here?"

The children bent over to look. The mountains were coloured brown and had a queer name – Killimooin. Paul's brown finger pointed to them. "These mountains are a queer shape," said the little prince. "Killimooin mountains form an almost unbroken circle – and in the midst of them, in a big valley, is the Secret Forest."

His finger pointed to a tiny speck of green shown in the middle of Killimooin mountains. "There you are," he said. "That dot of green is supposed to be the Secret Forest. It is an enormous forest, really, simply enormous, and goodness knows what wild animals there are there."

"Yes, but Paul, *why* hasn't anyone been to see?" asked Mike, impatiently. "Why can't they just climb the mountains and go down the other side to explore the forest?"

"For a very good reason!" said Paul. "No one has ever found a way over Killimooin mountains!"

"Why? Are they so steep?" asked Nora, astonished.

"Terribly steep, and terribly dangerous," said Paul.

"Does anyone live on the mountain-sides?" asked Peggy.

"Only goatherds," said Paul. "But they don't climb very high because the mountains are so rocky and so steep. Maybe the goats get to the top – but the goatherds don't!"

"Well!" said Mike, fascinated by the idea of a secret forest that no one had ever explored. "This really is exciting, I must say. Do, do let's fly over it in your aeroplane, Paul. Wouldn't I just love to see what that forest is like!"

"You can't see much," said Paul, rolling up the map. "It just looks a thick mass of green that's all, from the plane. All right – we'll go tomorrow!"

This was thrilling. It would be grand to go flying again, and really exciting to roar over the Killimooin mountains and peer down at the Secret Forest. What animals lived

168

there? What would it be like there? Had anyone ever trodden its dim green paths? Mike and Jack wished a hundred times they could explore that great hidden forest!

The next day all five children went to the runway beside the hangar where Paul's aeroplane was kept. They watched the mechanics run it out on to the grass. They greeted Ranni and Pilescu as the two men came along.

"Ranni! Do you know the way to fly to Killimooin mountains? We want to go there!"

"And when we get there, fly as low down as you can, so that we can get as near to the Secret Forest as possible," begged Nora.

Ranni and Pilescu smiled. They climbed up into the aeroplane. "We will go all round Baronia," said Pilescu, "and you will see, we shall fly over Killimooin country. It is wild, very wild. Not far from it is the little palace the King built last year, on a mountain-side where the winds blow cool. The summers have been very hot of late years in Baronia, and it is not healthy for children. Maybe you will all go there if the sun becomes much hotter!"

"I hope we do!" said Paul, his eyes shining. "I've never been there, Pilescu. We should have fun there, shouldn't we?"

"Not the same kind of fun as you have in the big palace," said Pilescu. "It is wild and rough around the little palace. It is more like a small castle. There are no proper roads. You can have no car, no aeroplane. Mountain ponies are all you would have to get about on."

"I'd like that," said Jack. He took his seat in the big plane, and watched the mechanics finishing their final checks on the plane. They moved out of the way. The engine started up with a roar. Nobody could hear a word.

Then off went the big plane, as smoothly as a car, taxiing over the grass. The children hardly knew when it rose in the air. But when they looked from the windows, they saw the earth far below them. The palace seemed no bigger than a doll's house.

"We're off!" said Jack, with a sigh. "Where is the map? You said you'd bring one, Paul, so that we could see exactly where we are each minute."

It really was interesting to spread out the map, and try to find exactly where they were. "Here we are!" said Jack, pointing to a blue lake on the map. "See? There's the lake down below us now – we're right over it – and look, there's the river flowing into it, shown on the map. Golly, this is geography really come alive! I wish we could learn this sort of geography at school! I wouldn't mind having geography every morning of the week, if we could fly over the places we're learning about!"

The children read out the names of the towns they flew over. "Ortanu, Tarribon, Lookinon, Brutinlin – what funny names!"

"Look – there are mountains marked here. We ought to reach them soon."

"The plane is going up. We must be going over them. Yes – we are. Look down and see. Golly, that's a big one over there!"

"Aren't the valleys green? And look at that river. It's like a silvery snake."

"Are we coming near the Secret Forest? Are we near Killimooin? Blow, I've lost it again on the map. I had it a minute ago."

"Your hand's over it, silly! Move it, Jack – yes, there, look! Killimooin. We're coming to the mountains!"

Ranni yelled back to the children. "Look out for the Secret Forest! We are coming to the Killimooin range now. Paul, you know it. Look out now, and tell the others."

In the greatest excitement the five children pressed their faces against the windows of the big plane. It was rising over steep mountains. The children could see how wild and rugged they were. They could not see anyone on them at all, nor could they even see a house.

"Now you can see how the Killimooin mountains run all

170

round in a circle!" cried Paul. "See – they make a rough ring, with their rugged heads jagged against the sky! There is no valley between, no pass! No one can get over them into the Secret Forest that lies in the middle of their mighty ring!"

The children could easily see how the range of mountains ran round in a very rough circle. Shoulder to shoulder stood the rearing mountains, tall, steep and wild.

The aeroplane roared over the edge of the circle, and the children gazed down into the valley below.

"That's the Secret Forest!" shouted Paul. "See, there it is. Isn't it thick and dark? It fills the valley almost from end to end."

The Secret Forest lay below the roaring, throbbing plane. It was enormous. The tops of the great trees stood

The aeroplane roared over the edge of the circle

close together, and not a gap could be seen. The plane roared low down over the trees.

"It's mysterious!" said Nora, and she shivered. "It's really mysterious. It looks so quiet – and dark – and lonely. Just as if really and truly nobody ever has set foot there, and never will!"

Hot Weather!

The aeroplane rose high again to clear the other side of the mountain ring. The forest dwindled smaller and smaller. "Go back again over the forest, Ranni, please do!" begged Jack. "It's weird. So thick and silent and gloomy. It gives me a funny feeling!"

Ranni obligingly swung the big plane round and swooped down over the forest again. The trees seemed to rise up, and it almost looked as if the aeroplane was going to dive down into the thick green!

"Wouldn't it be awful if our plane came down in the forest, and we were lost there, and could never, never find our way out and over the Killimooin mountains?" said Nora.

"What a horrid thought!" said Peggy. "Don't say things like that! Ranni, let's get over the mountains quickly! I'm afraid we might get lost here!"

Ranni laughed. He swooped upwards again, just as Jack spotted something that made him flatten his nose against the window and stare hard.

"What is it?" asked Nora.

"I don't quite know," said Jack. "It couldn't be what I thought it was, of course."

"What did you think it was?" asked Paul, as they flew high over the other side of the mountain ring.

"I thought it was a spiral of smoke," said Jack. "It couldn't have been, of course – because where there is smoke, there is a fire, and where there is a fire, there are men! And there are no men down there in the Secret Forest!"

"*I* didn't see any smoke," said Mike.

"Nor did I," said Paul. "It must have been a wisp of low-lying cloud, Jack."

"Yes – it must have been," said Jack. "But it *did* look like smoke. You know how sometimes on a still day the smoke from a camp fire rises almost straight into the air and stays there for ages. Well, it was like that."

"I think the Secret Forest is very, very strange and mysterious," said Peggy. "And I never want to go there!"

"I would, if I got the chance!" said Mike. "Think of walking where nobody else had ever put their foot! I would feel a real explorer."

"This is Jonnalongay," called Ranni from the front. "It is one of our biggest towns, set all round a beautiful lake."

The children began to take an interest in the map again. It was such fun to see a place on the big map, and then to watch it coming into view below, as the aeroplane flew towards it. But soon after that they flew into thick cloud and could see nothing.

"Never mind," said Ranni. "We have turned back now, and are flying along the other border of Baronia. It is not so interesting here. The clouds will probably clear just about Tirriwutu, and you will see the railway lines there. Watch out for them."

Sure enough, the clouds cleared about Tirriwutu, and the children saw the gleaming silver lines, as Pilescu took the great plane down low over the flat countryside. It was fun to watch the lines spreading out here and there, going to different little villages, then joining all together again as they went towards the big towns.

"Oh – there's the big palace by the lake!" said Nora, half-disappointed. "We're home again. That was simply lovely, Paul."

"But the nicest part was Killimooin and the Secret Forest," said Jack. "I don't know why, but I just can't get that mysterious forest out of my head. Just suppose that *was* smoke I saw! It would mean that people live there – people no one knows about – people who can't get out and never could! What are they like, I wonder?"

"Don't be silly, Jack," said Mike. "It wasn't smoke, so there aren't people. Anyway, if people are living there

174

now, they must have got over the mountains at some time or other, mustn't they? So they could get out again if they wanted to! Your smoke was just a bit of cloud. You know what funny bits of cloud we see when we're flying."

"Yes, I know," said Jack. "You're quite right, it couldn't have been real smoke. But I rather like to think it was, just for fun. It makes it all the more mysterious!"

The aeroplane flew down to the runway, and came to a stop. The mechanics came running up.

"You have had the best of it today!" one called to Ranni, in the Baronian language, which the children were now beginning to understand. "We have almost melted in the heat! This sun – it is like a blazing furnace!"

The heat from the parched ground came to meet the children as they stepped out of the plane. Everything shimmered and shook in the hot sun.

"Gracious!" said Nora. "I shall melt! Oh for an ice-cream!"

They walked to the palace and lay down on sunbeds on the terrace, under the big colourful umbrellas. Usually there was a little wind from the lake on the terrace – but today there was not a breath of air.

"Shall we bathe?" said Jack.

"No good," said Mike. "The water was too warm to be pleasant yesterday – and I bet it's really hot today. It gets like a hot bath after a day like this."

A big gong boomed through the palace. It was time for lunch – a late one for the children. Nora groaned.

"It's too hot to eat! I can't move. I don't believe I could even swallow an ice-cream!"

"Lunch is indoors for you today," announced Ranni, coming out on to the terrace. "It is cooler indoors. The electric fans are all going in the play-room. Come and eat."

None of the children could eat very much, although the dishes were just as delicious as ever. Ranni and Pilescu, who always served the children at meal-times, looked quite worried.

175

"You must eat, little Prince," Ranni said to Paul.

"It's too hot," said Paul. "Where's my mother? I'm going to ask her if I need wear any clothes except shorts. That's all they wear in England in the summer, when it's holiday-time and hot."

"But you are a prince!" said Ranni. "You cannot run about with hardly anything on."

Prince Paul went to find his mother. She was lying down in her beautiful bedroom, a scented handkerchief lying over her eyes.

"Mother! Are you ill?" asked Paul.

"No, little Paul – only tired with this heat," said his mother. "But listen, we will go to the mountains to the little castle your father built there last year. I fear that this heat will kill us all! Your father says he will send us tomorrow. How we shall get there with all the children and the nurses I cannot imagine! But go we must! I don't know what has happened this last few years in Baronia! The winters are so cold and the summers are so hot!"

Paul forgot that he had come to ask if he could take off his clothes. He stared at his mother, thrilled and excited. To go to the mountains to the new little castle! That would be fine. The children could explore the country on mountain ponies. They would have a great time. The winds blew cool on the mountain-side, and they would not feel as if they wanted to lie about and do nothing all day long. "Oh, mother! Shall we really go tomorrow?" said Paul. "I'll go and tell the others."

He sped off, forgetting how hot he was. He burst into the play-room, and the others looked at him in amazement.

"However can you possibly race about like that in this heat?" asked Jack. "You must be mad! I'm dripping wet just lying here and doing nothing. It's hotter than it was in Africa – and it was hot enough there!"

"We're going to the new little castle in the mountains tomorrow!" cried Paul. "There's news for you! It will be

176

cool there, and we can each have a pony and go riding up and down the mountains. We can talk to the goatherds, and have all kinds of fun!"

Jack sat up. "I say!" he said. "Did you hear Pilescu say that your new little palace was near Killimooin? Golly, what fun! We might be able to find out something about the Secret Forest!"

"We shan't!" said Paul. "There's nothing to find out. You can ask the goatherds there and see. Won't it be fun to go and stay in the wild mountains? I *am* glad!"

All the children were pleased. It really was too hot to enjoy anything in the big palace now. The idea of scampering about the mountains on sturdy little ponies was very delightful. Jack lay back on the couch and wondered if it would be possible to find out anything about the Secret Forest. He would ask every goatherd he saw whether he could tell anything about that mysterious forest, hidden deep in the heart of Killimooin.

"If anyone knows anything, the goatherds should know," thought the boy. Then he spoke aloud. "Paul, how do we go to the mountains where the little castle is? Do we ride on ponies?"

"No – we drive most of the way," said Paul. "But as there is no proper road within twenty miles, we shall have to go on ponies for the rest of the way. I don't know how the younger children will manage."

"This is a lovely holiday!" said Nora, dreamily. "Living in a palace – flying about in aeroplanes – peering down at the Secret Forest – and now going to live in a castle built in the wild mountains, to which there is not even a proper road. We *are* lucky!"

"It's getting hotter," said Mike, with a groan. "Even the draught from the electric fan seems hot! I hope it will get a bit cooler by the time the evening comes."

But it didn't. It seemed to get hotter than ever. Not one of the five children could sleep, though the fans in their big bedrooms went all night long. They flung off the sheets. They turned their pillows to find a cool place. They got out of bed and stood by the open windows to find a breath of air.

By the time the morning came they were a heavy-eyed, cross batch of children, ready to quarrel and squabble over anything. Paul flew into a temper with Ranni, and the big man laughed.

"Ah, my little lord, this heat is bad for you all! Now do not lose your temper with me. That is foolish, for if you become hot-tempered, you will feel hotter than ever! Go and get ready. The cars will be here in half an hour."

The boys went to have cool baths. It was too hot to swim in the lake, which was just like a warm bath now. They came out of the cold water feeling better. Mike heard the noise of car engines, and went to the window. A perfect fleet of cars was outside, ready to take the whole family, with the exception of Paul's father. The five older children, the five younger ones, Paul's mother, three nurses, and Ranni and Pilescu were all going.

"Come on!" yelled Paul. "We're going. Nora, you'll be left behind. Hurry up!"

And into the cars climbed all the royal household, delighted to be going into the cool mountains at last.

Killimooin Castle

It took quite a time to pack in all the five younger children. One of the nurses had the baby in a big basket beside her. The other nursery children chattered and laughed. They looked pale with the heat, but they were happy at the thought of going to a new place.

Ranni and Pilescu travelled with the four English children and Prince Paul. There was plenty of room in the enormous blue and silver car. Nora was glad when at last they all set off, and a cool draught came in at the open windows. The little girl felt ill with the blazing summer heat of Baronia.

"The new castle is called Killimooin Castle," announced Paul. "I've never even seen it myself, because it was built when I was away. It's actually on one of the slopes of Killimooin. We can do a bit of exploring."

"You will not go by yourselves," said Ranni. "There may be robbers and wild men there."

"Oh, Ranni – we must go off by ourselves sometimes!" cried Jack. "We can't have you always hanging round us like a nursemaid."

"You will not go by yourselves," repeated Ranni, a little sternly, and Pilescu nodded in agreement.

"Killimooin is about two hundred miles away," said Paul. "We ought to get there in four or five hours – as near there as the roads go, anyway."

The great cars purred steadily along at a good speed. There were five of them, for servants had been taken as well. Behind followed a small van with a powerful engine. In the van were all the things necessary for the family in the way of clothes, prams and so on.

The countryside flew by. The children leaned out of the

windows to get the air. Ranni produced some of the famous Baronian chocolate, that tasted as much of honey and cream as of chocolate. The children munched it and watched the rivers, hills and valleys they passed. Sometimes the road wound around a mountain-side, and Nora turned her head away so that she would not see down into the valley, so many hundreds of feet below. She said it made her feel giddy.

"I don't know what we would do if we met another car on these curving roads that wind up and up the mountain-side," said Peggy.

"Oh, the roads have been cleared for us," said Paul. "We shan't meet any cars on the mountain roads, anyway, so you needn't worry."

They didn't. The cars roared along, stopping for nothing – nothing except lunch! At half-past twelve, when everyone was feeling very hungry, the signal was given to stop. They all got out to stretch their legs and have a run round. They were on a hillside, and below them ran a shining river, curving down the valley. It was a lovely place for a picnic.

As usual the food was delicious. Ranni and Pilescu unpacked hampers and the children spread a snow-white cloth on the grass and set out plates and dishes.

"Chicken sandwiches! Good!" said Mike.

"Ice-cream pudding! My favourite!" said Nora.

"About thirty different kinds of sandwiches!" said Jack. "I am glad I feel so terribly hungry."

It was a good meal, sitting out there on the hillside, where a little breeze blew.

"It's cooler already," said Nora, thankfully.

"It will be much cooler in Killimooin Castle," said Ranni. "It is built in a cunning place, where two winds meet round a gully! It is always cool there on the hottest day. You will soon get back your rosy cheeks."

Everyone climbed back into the cars when lunch was finished, and off they went again. "Only about an hour

The little sturdy animals trotted away up the rough mountain path

more and the road ends for us," said Pilescu, looking at his watch. "It goes on round the mountains, but leaves Killimooin behind. I hope the ponies will be there, ready for us."

"How is the baby going to ride a pony?" asked Nora. "Won't she fall off?"

"Oh, no," said Pilescu. "You will see what happens to the little ones."

After about an hour, all the cars slowed down and stopped. The children looked out in excitement, for there was quite a gathering in front of them. Men with ponies stood there, saluting the cars. It was time to mount and ride, instead of sitting in a car!

It took a long time to get everyone on to the sturdy, shaggy little ponies. Nora soon saw how the little children

181

were taken! The bigger ponies had a big, comfortable basket strapped each side of them – and into these the younger children were put! Then with a man leading each pony, the small ones were quite safe, and could not possibly fall!

"I'm not going in a basket," said Nora, half afraid she might be told to. But all the other children could ride and were expected to do so. Each child sprang on to the pony brought beside him or her and held the reins. The ponies were stout and steady, very easy to ride, though Nora complained that hers bumped her.

"Ah no, Nora – it is you who are bumping the pony!" said Pilescu, with a laugh.

The little company set off. The nurses, who had all been country girls, thought nothing of taking their children on ponies to the castle. The smaller boys and girls chattered in high voices and laughed in delight at the excitement.

The men leading the ponies that carried baskets or panniers leapt on to ponies also, and all the little sturdy animals trotted away up the rough mountain path that led to the new castle. The people who had come to watch the royal family's arrival waved goodbye and shouted good wishes after them. Their cottages were here and there in the distance.

The little company turned a bend in the path, and then the children saw the towering mountains very clearly, steep and forbidding, but very grand. Up and up they had to go, climbing higher little by little towards the castle Paul's father had built the year before. No houses, no cottages were to be seen. It was very desolate indeed.

"Look at those goats!" said Peggy, pointing to a flock of goats leaping up the rocky slopes. "What a lot of them! Where's the goatherd?"

"Up there," said Paul. "Look – by that crooked tree."

The goatherd stared down at the company. He had the flaming red beard that most Baronians had, and he wore ragged trousers of goat-skin, and nothing else.

"He looks awfully wild and fierce," said Nora. "I don't think I want to talk to goatherds if they look like that!"

"Oh, they are quite harmless!" said Ranni, laughing at Nora's scared face. "They would be more frightened of you than you would be of them!"

It was fun at first to jog along on the ponies for the first few miles, but when the road grew steeper, and wound round and round, the children began to wish the long journey was over.

"There's one thing, it's lovely and cool," said Jack.

"It will be quite cold at nights," said Ranni. "You will have to sleep with thick covers over you."

"Well, that will be a change," said Jack, thinking of how he had thrown off everything the night before and had yet been far too hot. "I say – I say – is that Killimooin Castle?"

It was. It stood up there on the mountain-side, over-looking a steep gully, built of stones quarried from the mountain itself. It did not look new, and it did not look old. It looked exactly right, Nora thought. It was small, with rounded towers, and roughly hewn steps, cut out of the mountain rock, led up to it.

"I shall feel as if I'm living two or three hundred years ago, when I'm in that castle," said Peggy. "It's a proper little castle, not an old ruin, or a new make-believe one. I do like it. Killimooin Castle – it just suits it, doesn't it?"

"Exactly," said Jack. "It's about half-way up the mountain, isn't it? We're pretty high already."

So they were. Although the mountains still towered above them, the valley below looked a very long way down. The wind blew again and Nora shivered.

"Golly, I believe I shall be too cold now!" she said, with a laugh.

"Oh, no – it's only the sudden change from tremendous heat to the coolness of the mountains that you feel," said Ranni. "Are you tired? You will want a good rest before tea!"

"Oh, isn't it nearly tea-time?" said Mike, in disappointment. "I feel so hungry. Look – we're nearly at that fine flight of steps. I'm going to get off my pony."

The caretakers of the castle had been looking out for the royal arrivals. They stood at the top of the flight of steps, the big, iron-studded door open behind them. The children liked them at once.

"That is Tooku, with Yamen his wife," said Pilescu. "They are people from the mountains here. You will like to talk to them sometime, for they know many legends and stories of these old hills."

Tooku and Yamen greeted the children with cries of delight and joy. They were cheerful mountain-folk, not scared at the thought of princes and princesses arriving, but full of joy to see so many little children.

It seemed no time at all before the whole company were in their new quarters. These were not nearly so grand and luxurious as those the children had had in the big palace, but not one of them cared about that. The castle rooms were small, but with high ceilings. The walls were hung with old embroidered tapestries. There were no curtains at the narrow windows – but, oh, the view from those windows!

Mountains upon mountains could be seen, some wreathed in clouds, most of them with snow on the top. The trees on them looked like grass. The valley below seemed miles away.

"Killimooin Castle has quite a different feel about it," said Jack, with enjoyment. "The palace was big and modern and everything was up to date. Killimooin is grim and strong and wild, and I like it. There's no hot water running in the bedrooms. I haven't seen a bathroom yet – and our beds are more like rough couches with rugs and pillows than beds. I do like it."

It was great fun settling down in the castle. The children could go anywhere they liked, into the kitchens, the towers, the cellars. Tooku and Yamen welcomed them anywhere and any time.

It was deliciously cool at Killimooin after the tremendous

heat of the palace. The children slept well that first night, enjoying the coolness of the air that blew in at the narrow windows. It was good mountain air, clean and scented with pine.

Next morning Ranni spoke to the five children. "You have each a pony to ride, and you may ride when and where you will, if Pilescu or I are with you."

"Why can't we go alone?" said Paul, rather sulkily. "We shan't come to any harm."

"You might lose your way in the mountains," said Ranni. "It is an easy thing to do. You must promise never to wander off without one of us."

Nobody wanted to promise. It wasn't nearly so much fun to go about with a grown-up, as by themselves. But Ranni was firm.

"You must promise," he repeated. "No promise, no ponies. That is certain!"

"I suppose we must promise, then," said Jack. "All right – I promise not to go wandering off without a nursemaid!"

"I promise too," said Mike. The girls promised as well.

"And you, little lord?" said big Ranni, turning to the still-sulky boy.

"Well – I promise too," said Paul. "But there isn't any real danger, I'm sure!"

Paul was wrong. There *was* danger – but not the kind that anyone guessed.

Blind Beowald, The Goatherd

Two days later a great mist came over Killimooin and not even Ranni and Pilescu dared to ride out on their ponies, although they had said that they would take the children exploring round about.

"No one can see his way in such a mist," said Ranni, looking out of the window. "The clouds lie heavy over the valley below us. Up here the mist is so thick that we might easily leave the mountain path and go crashing down the mountain-side."

"It's so disappointing," sighed Paul. "What can we do instead?"

Yamen put her head in at the door as she passed. "You can come down to tea with Tooku and me," she invited. "We will have something nice for you, and you shall ask us all the things you want to know."

"Oh, good," said Jack. "We'll ask all about the Secret Forest. Maybe they know tales about that! That will be exciting."

Tea-time down in the big kitchen of the castle was great fun. An enormous fire glowed on the big hearth, and over it hung a black pot in which the soup for the evening meal was slowly simmering. A grand tea was spread on the wooden table, and the children enjoyed it. There were no thin sandwiches, no dainty buns and biscuits, no cream cakes – but, instead, there were hunks of new-made bread, baked by Yamen that morning, crisp rusks with golden butter, honey from the wild bees, and a queer, rich cake with a bitter-sweet taste that was delicious.

"Yamen, tell us all you know about the Secret Forest," begged Nora, as she buttered a rusk. "We have seen it when we flew over in an aeroplane. It was so big and so mysterious."

"The Secret Forest!" said Yamen. "Ah, no one knows anything of that. It is lost in the mountains, a hidden place unknown to man."

"Doesn't anyone live there at all?" asked Jack, remembering the spire of smoke he thought he had seen.

"How could they?" asked Tooku, in his deep, hoarse voice, from the end of the table. "There is no way over Killimooin mountains."

"Hasn't anyone *ever* found a way?" asked Jack.

Tooku shook his head. "No. There is no way. I have heard it said, however, that there is a steep way to the top, whence one can see this great forest – but there is no way down the other side – no, not even for a goat!"

The children listened in silence. It was disappointing to hear that there really was no way at all. Tooku ought to know, for he had lived among the mountains for years.

"Ranni won't let us go about alone," complained Paul. "It makes us feel so babyish, Tooku. Can't you tell him the mountains are safe?"

"They are not safe," said Tooku, slowly. "There are robbers. I have seen them from this very castle. Ah, when this place was built last year, the robbers must have hoped for travellers to come to and fro!"

"What robbers?" asked Jack. "Where do they live? Are there many of them?"

"Yes, there are many," said Tooku, nodding his shaggy head. "Sometimes they rob the poor people of the countryside, coming in the night, and taking their goats and their hens. Sometimes they rob the travellers on the far-off road.'

"Why aren't they caught and punished?" demanded the little prince indignantly. "I won't have robbers in my country!"

"No one knows where these robbers live," said Yamen. "Aie-aie – they are a terrible band of men. It is my belief that they have a stronghold far up the mountains."

"Perhaps they live in the Secret Forest!" said Jack.

"Oh, you and your Secret Forest!" said Nora. "Don't keep asking about it, Jack. You've been told ever so many times there's no way for people to get to it."

"Are there any wild animals about the mountains?" asked Mike.

"There are wolves," said Yamen. "We hear them howling in the cold wintertime, when they can find no food. Yes, they came even to this castle, for I saw them myself."

"How frightening!" said Nora, shivering. "Well, I'm jolly glad I promised Ranni I wouldn't go out without him or Pilescu! I don't want to be captured by robbers or caught by wolves."

"You don't want to believe all their stories," said Peggy, in a low voice.

Yamen heard her, and although she did not understand what the little girl said, she guessed.

"Ah!" she said, "you think these are but tales, little one? If you want to know more, go to the goatherd, Beowald, and he will tell you many more strange tales of the mountain-side!"

Beowald sounded rather exciting, the children thought. They asked where he could be found.

"Take the path that winds high above the castle," said Tooku. "When you come to a crooked pine, struck by lightning, take the goat-track that forks to the left. It is a rocky way, but your ponies will manage it well. Follow this track until you come to a spring gushing out beside a big rock. Shout for Beowald, and he will hear you, for his ears are like that of a mountain hare, and he can hear the growing of the grass in spring, and the flash of a shooting star in November!"

The next day was fine and clear. The children reminded Ranni of his promise and he grinned at them, his eyes shining in the brilliant sunlight.

"Yes, we will go," he said. "I will get the ponies. We will take our lunch with us and explore."

"We want to find Beowald the goatherd," said Paul. "Have you heard of him, Ranni?"

Ranni shook his head. He went to get the ponies, whilst Nora and Peggy ran off to ask Yamen to pack them up some lunch.

Soon they were all ready. Ranni made them take thick Baronian cloaks, lined with fur, for he said that if a mist suddenly came down they would feel very cold indeed.

They set off up the steep mountain-way that wound high above the castle. The ponies were sure-footed on the rocky path, though they sent hundreds of little pebbles clattering down the mountain-side as they went. They were nice little beasts, friendly and eager, and the children were already very fond of them.

Ranni led the way, Pilescu rode last of all. It was a merry little company that went up the steep mountain that sunny morning.

"We've got to look out for a crooked pine tree, struck by lightning," said Jack to Ranni, who was just in front of him. "Then we take the goat-track to the left."

"There's an eagle!" said Nora, suddenly, as she saw a great bird rising into the air, its wings spreading out against the sun. "Are eagles dangerous, Pilescu?"

"They will not attack us," said Ranni. "They like to swoop down on the little kids that belong to the goats and take them to feed their young ones, if they are nesting."

"I wonder if we shall see a wolf," said Peggy, hoping that they wouldn't. "I say, isn't it fun riding up and up like this! I do like it."

"There's the crooked pine tree!" shouted Paul. "Look – over there. We shall soon come up to it. Isn't it ugly? You don't often see a pine tree that is not tall and straight."

The crooked pine tree seemed to point to the left,

'There's an eagle!" said Nora, suddenly

where the path forked into two. To the left was a narrow goat-track, and the ponies took that way, their steady little hooves clattering along merrily.

It was lovely up there in the cool clear air, with the valley far below, swimming in summer sunshine. Sometimes a little wispy cloud floated below the children, and once one floated right into them. But it was nothing but a mist when the children found themselves in it!

"Clouds are only mists," said Nora. "They look so solid when you see them sailing across the sky, especially those mountainous, piled-up clouds that race across in March and April – but they're nothing but mist!"

"What's that noise?" said Jack, his sharp ears hearing something.

"Water bubbling somewhere," said Nora, stopping her pony. "It must be the spring gushing out, that Tooku and

Yamen told us about. We must be getting near where Beowald should be."

"Look at the goats all about," said Peggy, and she pointed up the mountain-side. There were scores of goats there, some staring at the children in surprise, some leaping from rock to rock in a hair-raising manner.

"Goats have plenty of circus-tricks," said Mike, laughing as he watched a goat take a flying leap from a rocky ledge, and land with all four feet bunched together on a small rock not more than six inches square. "Off he goes again! I wonder they don't break their legs."

"They must be Beowald's goats," said Peggy. "Ranni, call Beowald."

But before Ranni could shout, another noise came to the children's ears. It was a strange, plaintive noise, like a peculiar melody with neither beginning nor end. It was odd, and the children listened, feeling a little uncomfortable.

"Whatever's that?" asked Peggy.

They rode on a little way and came to a big rock beside which gushed a clear spring, running from a rocky hole in the mountain-side. On the other side, in the shelter of the rock, lay a youth, dressed only in rough trousers of goat-skin. Round his neck, tied by a leather cord, was a kind of flute, and on this the goatherd was playing his strange, unending melodies.

He sat up when the children dismounted. The children saw that his strange dark eyes were blind. There was no light in them. They could see nothing. But it was a happy face they looked on, and the goatherd spoke to them in a deep, musical voice.

"You are come!" he said. "I heard you down the mountain two hours since. I have been waiting for you."

"How did you know we were coming to see you?" asked Paul in astonishment.

Beowald smiled. It was a strange smile, for although his mouth curved upwards, his eyes remained empty and dark.

191

"I knew," said Beowald. "I know all that goes on in my mountains. I know the eagles that soar above my head. I know the wolves that howl in the night. I know the small flowers that grow beneath my feet, and the big trees that give me shade. I know Killimooin as no one else does."

"Well, Beowald, do you know anything about the Secret Forest then?" asked Paul, eagerly. The other children could now understand what was said in the Baronian language, though they were not able to speak it very well as yet. They listened eagerly for Beowald's answer.

Beowald shook his head. "I could take you where you can see it," he said. "But there is no way to it. My feet have followed my goats everywhere in these mountains, even to the summits – but never have they leapt down the other side. Not even for goats is there any path."

The children were disappointed. "Are there robbers here?" asked Jack, trying to speak in Baronian. Beowald understood him.

"Sometimes I hear strange men at night," he said. "They creep down the mountain path, and they call to one another as the owls do. Then I am afraid and I hide in my cave, for these robbers are fierce and wild. They are like the wolves that roam in the winter, and they seek men to rob and slay."

"Where do the robbers live?" asked Paul, puzzled.

Beowald shook his head, gazing at the little prince with his dark blind eyes. "That is a thing I have never known," he said. "They are men without a home. Men without a dwelling-place. That is why I fear them. They cannot be human, these men, for all men have a dwelling-place."

"That's silly," said Jack, in English. "All men have to live somewhere, even robbers! Paul, ask Beowald if they could live somewhere in a mountain cave, as he does."

Paul asked the goatherd, but he shook his head. "I know every cave in the mountains," he said. "They are my caves, for only I set foot in them. I live up here all the summer, and only in the cold winter do I go down to the valley to be with my mother. In the good weather I am happy here, with my goats and my music."

"Play to us again," begged Peggy. The goatherd put his wooden flute to his lips and began to play a strange little tune. The goats around lifted their heads and listened. The little kids came quite near. A great old goat, with enormous curling horns, stepped proudly up to Beowald and put his face close to the goatherd's.

Beowald changed the tune. Now it was no longer like the spring that ran down the mountain-side, bubbling to itself. It was like the gusty wind that blew down the hills and swept up the valleys, that danced and capered and shouted over the pine trees and the graceful birches.

The children wanted to dance and caper too. The goats felt the change in the music and began to leap about madly. It was an odd sight to see. Jack looked at the blind youth's face. It was completely happy. Goats, mountains – and music. Beowald wanted nothing more in his quiet, lonely life!

A Day In The Mountains

"Can't we have lunch here with Beowald?" asked Paul, suddenly. "I feel very hungry, Ranni. It would be lovely to sit here in the wind and the sun and eat our food, listening to Beowald."

"I expect the goatherd would rather eat with you than play whilst you gobble up all the food!" said Ranni with a laugh. "Ask him if he will eat with you."

The goatherd smiled when he heard what Ranni said. He nodded his head, gave an order that scattered his goats, and sat quite still, gazing out over the valleys below as if he could see everything there.

"Where do you sleep at night?" asked paul. "Where is your cave?"

"Not far from here," answered Beowald. "But often I sleep in the daytime and walk at night."

"But how can you find your way then?" said Peggy, thinking of the darkness of the mountain-side and its dangerous ledges and precipices.

"It is always dark for me," said Beowald. "My ears see for me, and my feet see for me. I can wander in these mountains for hours and yet know exactly where I am. The pebbles beneath my feet, the rocks, the grass, the flowers, they all tell me where I am. The smell of the pine trees, the scent of the wild thyme that grows nearby, the feel of the wind, they tell me too. I can go more safely over this steep mountain with my blind eyes than you could go, seeing all there is to be seen!"

The children listened to the blind goatherd, as Ranni and Pilescu set out the lunch. There were sandwiches for everyone, and hard, sweet little biscuits to eat with cheese made from goats' milk. Beowald ate with them, his face happy and contented. This was a great day in his life!

"Beowald, take us up to where we can see the Secret Forest," begged Paul. "Is it very far?"

"It will be two hours before we get there," said the goatherd. He pointed with his hand, and it seemed to the children as if he must surely see, if he knew where to point. "The way lies up there. It is steep and dangerous. But your ponies will take you safely."

The children felt thrilled at the idea of seeing the Secret Forest from the summit of the mountain. They were very high up now, though the summit still seemed miles away. The air was cold and clear, and when the wind blew, the children wrapped their fur-lined cloaks around them. They could not imagine how Beowald could wear nothing but trousers.

When they had eaten all they could, they stood up. Ranni fetched the little ponies, who had been nibbling at the short grass growing where the mountain-side was least rocky. The children sprang into the saddles and the ponies jerked their heads joyfully. Now, they thought, they were going back home!

But they were mistaken. Beowald led the way up a steep, rocky track that even goats might find difficult to tread.

"I can't think how Beowald knows the way," called Peggy to Nora. "There isn't a sign of any path, so far as I can see."

"It's probably one that only the goats know," said Ranni. "See, that old goat with the great curling horns is before us. It almost looks as if he is leading the way!"

"Ah, my old one knows when I need him," said the goatherd, and he put his flute to his mouth. He played a few merry little notes and the big goat came leaping lightly down to him. "Stay by me, old one," said Beowald.

The goat understood. He trotted in front of Beowald, and waited for him when he leapt up on to a rock.

195

Beowald was as nimble as a goat himself, and it was amazing to the children to think that a blind youth should be so sure-footed. But then Beowald knew every inch of the mountain-side.

Up they went and up. Sometimes the way was so steep that the ponies almost fell as they scrambled along, and sent crowds of stones rumbling down the mountain-side. Ranni and Pilescu began to be doubtful about going farther. Ranni reined in his fat little pony.

"Beowald! Is the way much steeper?" he asked. "This is dangerous for the children."

"Ranni! It isn't!" cried Paul indignantly. "I won't go back without seeing over the top. I won't!"

"We shall soon be there," said Beowald, turning his dark eyes to Ranni. "I can smell the forest already!"

The children all sniffed the air eagerly, but they could smell nothing. They wished they had ears and nose like Beowald's. He could not see, but he could sense many things that they could not.

They came to a narrow ledge and one by one the ponies went round it, pressing their bodies close against the rocky side of the mountain, for a steep precipice, with a fall of many hundreds of feet, was the other side! Nora and Peggy would not look, but the boys did not mind. It was exciting to be so high.

The old goat rounded the ledge first, and Beowald followed. "We are here!" he called.

The ledge widened out round the bed – and the children saw that they were on the other side of Killimooin mountains! They were not right at the top of the mountain they were on, but had rounded a bend on the shoulder, and were now looking down on the thing they wanted so much to see – the Secret Forest!

"The Secret Forest!" cried Paul, and Jack echoed his words.

"The Secret Forest! How big it is! How thick and dark! How high we are above it!"

All eight of them stared down into the valley that lay hidden and lost between the big ring of mountains. Only Beowald could not see the miles upon miles of dark green forest below, but his eyes seemed to rest on the valley below, just as the others' did.

"Isn't it mysterious?" said Jack. "It seems so still and quiet here. Even the wind makes no sound. I wish I could see that spire of smoke I thought I saw when we flew down low over the forest in the aeroplane."

But there was no smoke to be seen, and no sound to be heard. The forest might have been dead for a thousand years, it was so still and lifeless.

"It's funny to stand here and look at the Secret Forest, and know you can't ever get to it," said Mike. He looked down from the ledge he was standing on. There was a sheer drop down to the valley below, or so it seemed to the boy. It was quite plain that not even a goat could leap down.

"Now you can see why it is impossible to cross these mountains," said Ranni. "There is no way down the other side at all. All of them are steep and dangerous like this one. No man would dare to try his luck down that precipice, not even with ropes!"

The girls did not like looking down such a strange, steep precipice. They had climbed mountains in Africa but none had been so steep as this one.

"I want to go back now," said Nora. "I'm feeling quite giddy."

"It is time we all went," said Ranni, looking at his watch. "We must hurry too, or we shall be very late."

"I can take you another way back," said Beowald. "It will be shorter for you to go to the castle. Follow me."

With his goats around him, the blind youth began to leap down the mountain-side. He was as sure-footed as the goats, and it was extraordinary to watch him. The ponies followed, slipping a little in the steep places. They were tired now, and were glad to be going home.

Down they all went and down. Nora gave a sudden shout that made the others jump. "I can see Killimooin Castle. Hurrah! Another hour and we'll be home!"

They rounded a bend and then suddenly saw a strange place built into the rocky mountain-side. They stopped and stared at it.

"What's that?" asked Paul. Ranni shook his head. He did not know and neither did Pilescu.

"It looks like some sort of temple," said Nora, who remembered seeing pictures of stone temples in her history book. But this one was unusual, because it seemed to be built into the rock. There was a great half-broken archway, with roughly-carved pillars each side.

"Beowald! Do you know what this place is?" asked Jack. The goatherd came back and stood beside Jack's pony.

"It is old, very old," he said. "It is a bad place. I think bad men once lived there, and were turned into stone for their wickedness. They are still there, for I have felt them with my hands."

"What in the world does he mean?" said Peggy, quite frightened. "Stone men! He's making it up!"

"Let's go and see," said Jack, who was very seldom afraid of anything.

"No, thank you!" said the girls at once. But the boys badly wanted to see inside the queer, ruined old place. Beowald would not go with them. He stayed with the two girls.

"Come on. Let's see what these wicked stone men are!" said Jack, with a grin. He dismounted from his pony, and passed through the great broken archway. It was dark inside the queer temple. "Have you got a torch, Mike?" called Jack. Mike usually had a torch, a knife, string, and everything anyone could possibly want, somewhere about his person. Mike felt about and produced a torch.

He flashed it on – and the boys jumped in fright. Even Ranni and Pilescu jumped. For there, at the back of the

He flashed it on – and the boys jumped in fright

temple-like cave, was a big stone man, seated on a low, flat rock!

"Oooh!" said Paul, and found Ranni's hand at once.

"It's an old statue!" said Jack, laughing at himself, and feeling ashamed of his sudden fright. "Look – there are more, very broken and old. Aren't they odd? However did they get here?"

"Long, long ago the Baronians believed in strange gods," said Ranni. "These are probably stone images of them. This must be an ancient temple, forgotten and lost, known only to Beowald."

"That sitting statue is the only one not broken," said Jack. "It's got a great crack down the middle of its body though – look. I guess one day it will fall in half. What a horrid face the stone man has got – sort of sneering."

"They are very rough statues," said Pilescu, running his

hand over them. "I have seen the same kind in other places in Baronia. Always they were in mountain-side temples like this."

"Let's go home!" called Nora, who was beginning to be very tired. "What sort of stone men have you found? Come and tell us."

"Only statues, cowardy custard," said Jack, coming out of the ruined temple. "You might just as well have seen them. Gee-up, there! Off we go!"

Off they went again, on the downward path towards Killimooin Castle, which could be seen very plainly now in the distance. In a short while Beowald said goodbye and disappeared into the bushes that grew just there. His goats followed him. The children could hear him playing on his flute, a strange melody that went on and on like a brook bubbling down a hill.

"I like Beowald," said Nora. "I'd like him for a friend. I wish he wasn't blind. I think it's marvellous the way he finds the path and never falls."

The ponies trotted on and on, and at last came to the path that led straight down and round to the castle steps. Ranni took them to stable them, and Pilescu took the five tired children up the steps and into the castle.

They ate an enormous late tea, and then yawned so long and loud that Pilescu ordered them to bed.

"What, without supper!" said Paul.

"Your tea must be your supper," said Pilescu. "You are all nearly asleep. This strong mountain air is enough to send a grown man to sleep. Go to bed now, and wake refreshed in the morning."

The children went up to bed. "I'm glad we managed to see the Secret Forest," said Jack. "And that funny temple with those old stone statues. I'd like to see them again."

He did – and had a surprise that was most unexpected!

Robbers!

A few days went by, days of wandering in the lower slopes of the mountain, looking for wild raspberries and watching the swift shy little animals that lived on the mountain. Yamen and Tooku told the children more tales, and nodded their heads when Jack told them of the ruined temple and the queer statues.

"Ah yes – it is very old. People do not go near it now because it is said that the statues come alive and walk at night."

The children screamed with laughter at this. They thought some of the old superstitions were very funny. It seemed as if Yamen really believed in fairies and brownies, for always when she made butter, she put down a saucer of yellow cream by the kitchen door.

"It is for the brownie who lives in my kitchen!" she would say.

"But, Yamen, your big black cat drinks the cream, not the brownie," Nora would say. But Yamen would shake her grey head and refuse to believe it.

Yamen used to go to buy what was needed at the village near the foot of the mountain each week. She had a donkey of her own, and Tooku had two of these sturdy little creatures. Tooku used sometimes to go with Yamen, and the third donkey would trot along behind them, with big baskets slung each side of his plump body, to bring back the many things Yamen bought for the household.

One day Yamen and Tooku started out with the third donkey behind them as usual. They set off down the track, and the children shouted goodbye.

"We shall be back in time to give you a good tea!" called Yamen. "You shall have new-baked rusks with honey."

But when tea-time came there was no Yamen, no Tooku. Ranni and Pilescu looked out of the great doorway of the castle, puzzled. The two should be in sight, at least. It was possible to see down the track for a good way.

"I hope they haven't had an accident," said Nora.

An hour went by, and another. The children had had their tea, and were wandering round the castle, throwing stones down a steep place, watching them bounce and jump.

"Look!" said Ranni, suddenly. Everyone looked down the track. One lone donkey was coming slowly along, with someone on his back, and another person stumbling beside him. Ranni ran to get a pony and was soon galloping along the track to find out what had happened.

The children waited anxiously. They were fond of Tooku and Yamen. As soon as the three climbed the steps of the castle, the children surrounded them.

"What's the matter, Yamen? Where are the other donkeys, Tooku? What have you done to your arm?"

"Aie, aie!" wept Yamen. "The robbers came and took our goods and our donkeys! Tooku tried to stop them but they broke his arm for him. Aie-aie, what bad luck we have had this day! All the goods gone, and the two fine little donkeys!"

"They took all three," said Tooku, "But this one, my own good creature, must have escaped, for we heard him trotting after us as we hastened back home on foot."

"What were the robbers like?" asked Jack.

"Strange enough," answered Yamen. "Small and wiry, with strips of wolf-skin round their middles. Each had a wolf's tail, dyed red, hanging behind him. Aie-aie, they were strange enough and fierce enough!"

"We heard tales in the town," said Tooku, to Ranni and Pilescu. "Many travellers have been robbed. These robbers take goods but not money. They come down from the mountains like goats, and they go back, no man knows where!"

"Have the villagers searched for their hiding-place?"

asked Ranni. "Have they hunted all about the mountain-sides?"

"Everywhere!" said Yamen. "Yes, not a place, not a cave has been forgotten. But nowhere is there a sign of the fierce robbers with their red wolves' tails!"

"Poor Yamen!" said Nora. The frightened woman was sitting in a chair, trembling. Pilescu bound up Tooku's arm. It was not broken, but badly gashed. The children felt very sorry.

Paul's mother soon heard of the disturbance and she was angry and upset. "To think that such things should happen in Baronia!" she cried. "I will send word to the king, and he shall send soldiers to search the mountain-side."

"The mountain-folk themselves have already done that," said Ranni. "If they have found nothing, the soldiers will find even less! It is a mystery where these men come from!"

"Perhaps they come from the Secret Forest!" said Jack. The others laughed at him.

"Idiot! Come from a place where nobody can go to!" said Mike.

"You children will not stir from this place without Ranni or Pilescu!" said Paul's mother.

"Madam, they have already promised not to," said Ranni. "Do not be anxious. They are safe with us. We have always our revolvers with us."

"I wish we hadn't come here now," said the Queen, looking really worried. "I wonder if we ought to go back. But I hear that it is hotter than ever in the big palace."

The children had no wish to return when they heard that. "We shall be quite safe here," said Paul. "The robbers will not dare to come anywhere near this castle, mother!"

"Silly child!" said his mother. "Now that they know we are here, and that travellers will go to and fro, they will be all the more on the watch. They will haunt the road from

203

here to the high road, and from here to the next village. I must get some more servants from the big palace. We must only go about in small companies, not alone."

This was all very exciting. The boys talked about the robbers, and Mike felt three or four times an hour to see if his big scout-knife was safely in his broad belt. Paul thought of all the terrifying things he would do to the robbers if he caught them. Mike thought it would be marvellous to shut them all up in a cave somewhere. Jack pictured himself chasing the whole company down the mountain-side.

The girls were not so thrilled, and were not much impressed when the three boys promised to take care of them.

"What could you do against a company of robbers?" asked Nora.

"Well, this isn't the first time we've had adventures, and had to fight for safety," said Mike, grandly.

"No, it's true we've had some exciting times and very narrow escapes," said Peggy. "But I don't particularly want to be chased and caught by robbers, even if you boys rescue me in the end!"

"Perhaps it's the stone men in the cave that come alive and rob people!" said Paul, with a grin.

"I'd like to go and have a look at those statues again," said Jack. "Ranni, can we go tomorrow? It's only about an hour's ride."

"I don't want to go too far from the castle," said Ranni. "Well – we'll go as far as that old temple if you really want to. Though why you should want to see ancient statues, broken to pieces, when you've already seen them once is a puzzle to me!"

The children set off the next day to go to the old temple. They were on foot, as it really was not a great distance away, and Ranni said it would be good for them to walk. So up the mountain they trudged.

It was late afternoon when they started. They had their

tea with them. The sun shone down warmly and the children panted and puffed when they went up the hillside, so steep and stony.

"There's the old temple," said Jack, at last, pointing to the ruined archway, hewn out of the mountain rock. "It really is a funny place. It seems to be made out of a big cave, and the entrance is carved out of the mountain itself. Come on – let's go in and have another look. Nora, you come this time, and Peggy. You didn't come last time."

"All right," said Peggy. "We'll come."

They all went into the old temple, and switched on the torches they had brought. Once again they gazed on Beowald's "stone men," and smiled to think of his idea that the statues had once been wicked men, turned into stone.

The biggest statue of all, at the back of the cave, sat on his wide flat rock, gazing with blank eyes out of the entrance. He seemed to be in much better repair than the others, who had lost noses, hands and even heads in some cases. Jack flashed his torch around, and suddenly came to a stop as he wandered around.

"Look here!" he said.

The others came to him and looked down at the ground, where his torch made a round ring of bright light. In the light was the print of a small bare foot. Jack swung his torch here and there, and on the floor of the temple other footprints could be seen – all small and bare, the toes showing clearly.

"Someone comes here quite a lot!" said Jack.

"More than one person," said Mike, kneeling down and looking closely at a few prints with his torch. "These are not the prints of the same person's feet. Look at this print here – all the toes are straight – but this one has a crooked big toe-print. And that one is a little larger than the others."

"It couldn't be Beowald's prints, could it?" asked Nora, remembering the bare feet of the goatherd.

"No. His feet are much bigger than those shown in these prints," said Mike. "I remember thinking what big feet he had."

"Well – could it be the robbers' footprints?" cried Peggy, suddenly.

"It might be," said Jack. "But they are plainly not here – not living here, I mean! Anyway, they would be discovered easily enough if they did live here. Beowald would know."

Ranni called the children. "Come along. Tea is ready. We must hurry now, because it looks as if a mist is coming up."

The children hurried out of the dark temple into the bright sunshine. They sat down to have their tea, telling Ranni and Pilescu what they had seen. But the two big Baronians were not much impressed.

"The prints are probably made by the feet of the goatherds sent to search every nook and cranny of the mountain-side, to look for the robbers' hiding-place," said Ranni.

This was disappointing. The children had quite made up their minds that they must belong to the robbers! Mike pointed down the hillside.

"Look at the clouds down there below us," he said. "They seem to be creeping up towards us."

"They are," said Pilescu, beginning to gather up the tea things. "Come along. I don't want to get lost in a mountain mist!"

They all set off down the mountain-side. Jack suddenly spied some juicy wild raspberries, and slipped off the path to get them. Before he had eaten more than a dozen he found himself surrounded by a thick grey mist!

"Blow!" said Jack, making his way back to the path. "I can't even see the others now! Well, I know the path, that's one thing!"

He shouted, but could hear no answer. The others had gone round a bend, and could not hear him, though usually a shout in the mountains echoed round and round. But the thick mist muffled the sound, and Jack could hear no reply to his yell.

"I'll just go on and hope to catch the others up," thought the boy. He set off, but after a while he had no idea of the right direction at all. The mist became thicker and thicker and the boy felt cold. He pulled his fur-lined cloak round him, and wondered what to do.

Something familiar about the rocky face of the mountain caught his eye. "Well – look at that! I'm right back at the old temple!" said Jack, in astonishment. "I've doubled back on the path somehow, and reached the temple-cave again. Well, I can't do better than shelter inside till the mist clears. Maybe it won't be long. They come and go very quickly."

He went inside the cave where the old stone images were. He found a corner where he could sit, and he

Then one of the men went to the entrance of the cave

squatted down to wait. He yawned and shut his eyes. He hoped Ranni and Pilescu would not be very angry with him.

He dozed lightly, whilst the mist swirled round outside. He was awakened by the sound of voices, and sat up, expecting to see the other children coming into the temple to look for him. He half got up – and then sank back in the greatest astonishment.

The cave was full of strange, hoarse voices, speaking in the Baronian language, but using a broad country accent that Jack could not understand. It was dark there, and the boy could not see the people to whom the voices belonged. He dared not switch on his torch.

Then one of the men went to the entrance of the cave and looked out, calling back that the mist was still there, but was clearing rapidly. Jack looked at him in amazement. He was small and wiry, and wore no clothes at all except for a strip of skin round his middle. The boy crouched back in his corner, suddenly scared.

The mist thinned outsided the cave, and the man at the entrance was joined by others. They went out, and Jack saw that each man had a wolf's tail behind him, dyed red. They were the robbers!

There were many of them. Where had they come from? They had not been in the cave when the boy fell asleep, and if they had entered, he would have heard them. Where *had* they come from? There must be some secret entrance in the temple itself. But where could it be?

The Amazing Statue

The cave was now empty. Jack got up cautiously and crept to the entrance. The mist was almost gone. Not a sign of the strange men was to be seen.

"They must have gone off to rob someone again!" thought the boy. "I'll take a good look round the cave now I'm here and find out where those men came from. There *must* be some hidden entrance at the back. Possibly there's a big cave farther in, where they live. This is awfully exciting!"

But before he could put on his torch and look round he heard the sound of shouts outside.

"Jack! Jack! Where are you?"

It was Ranni's voice. Jack ran out of the old temple-cave. Ranni was some way down the mountain-path. The boy shouted loudly.

"Ranni! I'm here, quite safe! I got lost in the mist."

"Come along quickly, before the mist comes again!" ordered Ranni.

"But Ranni, wait! I've made a discovery!" yelled Jack.

"Come along at once," shouted Ranni, sternly. "Look at the mist coming up. It will be thicker this time. Come now, Jack."

There was nothing for it but to go to Ranni. Jack leapt down the path, and as soon as he reached the big Baronian, he began to tell him what he had seen. But Ranni, anxious about the returning mist, paid little heed to the boy's excited chatter, and hurried him along as fast as he could go. Jack had no breath left to talk after a while, and fell silent. He could see that Ranni was cross with him.

The others had reached the castle safely. Ranni hurried

Jack inside the door, just as the mist swirled up again, thick and grey.

"And now!" he said sternly, turning to Jack. "Will you kindly tell me why you left us all? I had to go back and find you, and I might have hunted the mountain-side for hours. I am not pleased with you, Jack."

"I'm sorry, Ranni," said Jack, humbly. "I just went to pick some raspberries, that's all. Ranni, I saw the robbers!"

"I do not want to talk to you," said Ranni. "You have displeased me." He went to his own room, leaving Jack behind.

Jack stared after the Baronian, rather hurt, and feeling decidedly small. He went to find the others.

"Jack! What happened to you?" cried Nora, rushing to him. "We lost you, and Ranni went back."

"I've some news," said Jack, and his eyes gleamed. "Strange news, too!"

"What?" cried everyone.

"I wandered about a bit, when the mist overtook me," said Jack, "and suddenly I found I was back at the old temple. So I went in out of the mist, and sat down to wait till it cleared. I dozed off for a bit – and suddenly I awoke and found the cave becoming full of voices! I heard more and more of them, and then a man went to the entrance of the cave and looked out – and it was one of the robbers!"

"Jack! Not really!" cried Peggy.

"Yes, really," said Jack. "When the mist cleared a bit, they all went out of the entrance, and I saw the wolves' tails they had, dyed red. They did look extraordinary."

"Did they come into the cave to shelter then?" asked Mike.

"No – that's the funny part," said Jack. "They didn't! I feel absolutely certain that they came into the cave by some secret way – perhaps at the back of the temple. I believe there must be a big cave further in, where they live."

"So those footprints we saw must be theirs, after all," said Paul. "Oh, Jack – this is awfully exciting, isn't it! What did Ranni say when you told him?"

"He wouldn't listen," said Jack. "He was angry with me."

"Well, he'll soon be all right again," said Paul, cheerfully. "Ranni's temper never lasts long. I know that."

Paul was right. Ranni forgot his anger in a very short time, and when he came into the children's room, he was his usual smiling self. The boys went to him at once.

"Ranni! We know where the robbers hide!"

"Ranni, do listen, please. Jack saw the robbers."

This time Ranni did listen, and what he heard made him call Pilescu at once. The two men were eager to hear every word that Jack had to tell.

"It looks as if we shall be able to round up the robbers quickly now," said Ranni. "Good! You must be right, Jack – there is probably a secret entrance somewhere in the cave, leading from a big cave farther in."

"We must make a search as quickly as possible," said Pilescu. "Ranni, the moon is full tonight. You and I will take our most powerful torches and will examine that temple from top to bottom tonight!"

"Oh, Pilescu, let me come too?" begged Jack.

"And me!" cried Mike and Paul together.

Pilescu shook his big head. "No – there may be danger. You must stay safely here in the castle."

Jack was angry. "Pilescu! It was *my* discovery! Don't be mean. You *must* take me with you. Please!"

"You will not come," said Pilescu, firmly. "We are responsible for your safety in Baronia, and you will not be allowed to run into any danger. Ranni and I will go tonight, and tomorrow you shall hear what we have found."

The two men went out of the room, talking together. Jack stared after them fiercely. The boy was almost in tears.

"It's too bad," he said. "It *was* my discovery! And they're going to leave me out of it. I didn't think Ranni and Pilescu would be so mean."

The boy was hurt and angry. The others tried to comfort him. Jack sat and brooded for a little while and then he suddenly made up his mind.

"I shall go, too!" he said to the others, in a low tone. "I shall follow them and see what they find. I won't miss this excitement."

"But you promised not to go out alone," said Mike, at once. All the children thought the world of their promises and never broke one.

"Well, I *shan't* be alone – I shall be with Ranni and Pilescu, and they won't know it!" grinned Jack, quite good-tempered again now that he had thought of a way to join in the adventure. For adventure it had become, there wasn't a doubt of that!

The others laughed. It was quite true. Jack would certainly not be alone!

So, that night, after they had gone to bed, Jack kept his ears pricked to listen to any sounds of Ranni and Pilescu leaving. The moon swam up into the sky and the mountain-side was as light as day. The boy suddenly heard the low voices of the two Baronians, and he knew they were going down the passage to make their way to the great front door.

He had not undressed, so he was ready to follow them. After them he went, as quietly as a cat. The others whispered to him:

"Good luck!"

"Don't let Ranni see you or you'll get a spanking!"

"Look after yourself, Jack!"

The big front door opened, and shut quietly. Jack waited for a moment, opened it, and crept after the two men. He had to be careful to keep well in the black shadows, for it was easy to see anyone in the moonlight.

Up the mountain track behind the castle went Ranni and Pilescu. They did not speak, and they made as little noise as they could. They kept a sharp look-out for any sign of the robbers, but there was none. Word had come

212

to the castle that evening that a company of local people, returning from market, had been set upon and robbed that afternoon, and the two Baronians had no doubt that the robbers were the men that Jack had seen in the cave.

"If we can find the entrance to their lair, we can get soldiers up here, and pen the whole company in, and catch them one by one as they come out," said Ranni, in a low tone. Pilescu nodded. He heard a sound, and stopped.

"What is it?" whispered Ranni.

"Nothing," answered Pilescu, after a pause. "I thought I heard something."

He had! He had heard the fall of a stone dislodged by Jack, who was following them as closely as he dared! The boy stopped when Pilescu stopped, and did not move again until the two men went forward.

In about an hour's time they were at the old temple. The moon shone in at the ruined entrance. Ranni gave a startled exclamation as he went in, for the moon shone full on the face of the old stone image at the back. It seemed very lifelike!

"Now," said Ranni, flashing his torch round the cave. "You take a look that side and I'll take this. Examine every inch of the rock."

The moon suddenly went behind a big cloud and the world went dark. Jack took the chance of slipping into the cave without the two men seeing him. He thought he could hide behind the images, as the men worked round the cave. He stood behind one near the entrance and watched Ranni and Pilescu examining the rocky wall, trying to find some hidden entrance to another cave beyond.

"I can find nothing," said Pilescu, in a low voice.

Jack stood behind the statue and watched, hoping that one of the men would discover something. How he wished he could help too – but he was afraid of showing himself in case Ranni was angry again.

He stared at the big squatting statue at the back of the

213

cave. The moon had come out again and was shining full on the image. As Jack watched, a very strange thing began to happen!

The statue's face began to widen! It began to split in half! Jack stared in astonishment and horror. What could be happening? Was it coming alive? Were those old tales true, then?

Then he saw that the whole statue was splitting slowly and silently in half. The two halves were moving apart. It all happened so smoothly and silently that Ranni and Pilescu heard no sound at all, and had no warning.

Jack was so amazed that he could not say a word. The statue split completely in half, the two halves moving right apart – and then, from the floor of the flat rock beneath, a man's shaggy head appeared, full in the moonlight – the head of one of the robbers!

Jack gave a yell. "Ranni! Pilescu! Look out! The robbers are coming! Look at the statue!"

Ranni and Pilescu, amazed at Jack's voice, and at what he said, swung round quickly. They stared in the utmost amazement at the split statue, and saw the head and shoulders of the robber below. With a wild yell the robber leapt up into the temple, calling to his friends below:

"Come! Come! Here are enemies!"

In half a minute the cave was full of robbers. Ranni and Pilescu, taken completely by surprise, had their hands bound. They fought and struggled fiercely, but the robbers were too many for them.

Ranni remembered Jack's voice, and knew that the boy must be somewhere about. He must have followed them! Ranni called out in English:

"Don't show yourself, Jack. Go and give warning to the others."

Jack did not answer, of course. He crouched down behind a statue, watching the fight, knowing that it would be useless to join in, and hoping that the robbers would not see him.

Before his astonished eyes, the boy saw the wolf-tailed men force the two Baronians down through the hole beneath the great statue. Every robber followed. Then the statue, smoothly and silently as before, began to move. The two halves joined together closely, and the image was whole once more, its cracked face shining in the moonlight.

"No wonder there was such a crack down the middle of it!" thought the boy. "It wasn't a crack – it was a split, where the two halves joined! Golly, this is awful. I wonder if it's safe to go."

He waited for a while and then stole quietly out of the cave, looking behind him fearfully as he went. But no robber was there to follow him. The boy sped swiftly down the track in the moonlight, anxious to get to the others.

They were all awake. Jack got them into his room and told them hurriedly all that had happened. Paul was shocked, and anxious to hear about Ranni and Pilescu, whom he loved with all his heart.

"I am going to rescue them," he announced, getting into his clothes at once.

"Don't be an idiot, Paul," said Mike. "You can't go after robbers."

"Yes, I can," said Paul, fiercely, and his big dark eyes gleamed. "I am a Baronian prince, and I will not leave my men in danger. I go now to find them!"

When Paul got ideas of this sort into his head, there was no stopping him. Jack groaned. He turned to the girls.

"We'd better go with Paul and keep the idiot out of danger. You go and wake Tooku and Yamen and tell them what has happened. They will think of the best thing to do. Don't frighten Paul's mother, will you?"

Paul was already out of the front door, running down the steps in the moonlight. Ranni and Pilescu were in danger! Then he, their little prince must rescue them. Mike and Jack tore after him. A big adventure had begun!

The Beginning Of The Adventure

Mike and Jack soon caught up with Paul. The boy was struggling up the steep track as fast as he could go. He had no clear idea as to exactly what he was going to do. All he knew was that he meant to find Ranni and Pilescu and rescue them from the robbers.

"Paul! You're going the wrong way," panted Jack, as he came up to Paul. "You really are an idiot. You'd be lost in the mountains if we hadn't come after you. Look – you go this way, not the one you're taking."

Paul was glad to have the others with him. He pulled his fur-lined cloak around him, for he was cold. The others were wearing theirs too. They climbed steadily up the mountain-side, the moon showing them the way quite clearly. Mike hoped that clouds would not blow up, for it would be impossible to find their way in the dark. He thought of Beowald, the blind goatherd. He did not mind the dark. It made no difference to him at all!

Up they went and up, and an hour went by. Paul did not seem to be at all tired, though Jack's legs ached badly. But then he had already been to the temple-cave and back once before that night!

They came near the cave, and trod softly, keeping to the shadows, in case any of the robbers should be about. Suddenly a figure showed itself from behind a rock! Quick as lightening Jack pulled the other two down beside him in a big shadow, and the three of them crouched there, their hearts beating painfully. Was it a robber, left on guard? Had he seen them?

The moon went behind a small cloud and the mountainside lay in darkness. Jack strained his eyes and ears to find out if the night-wanderer was anywhere near.

Then he heard the plaintive notes of the little flute that Beowald played! It must be the goatherd, wandering at night as he so often did.

"Beowald!" called Jack, softly. "Where are you?"

The moon sailed out from behind the cloud and the boys saw the goatherd seated on a nearby rock, his head turned towards them.

"I am here," he said. "I heard you. I knew you were friends. What are you doing up here at night?"

Jack came out from his hiding-place. He told Beowald in a few words all that had happened. The goatherd listened in amazement.

"Ah, so that is why I thought the stone men came to life at night!" he said. "It was robbers I heard coming forth from the temple, and not the stone men. There must be a deep cave below the floor of the temple. I will come with you to find it."

The goatherd led the way to the cave. The moon went in again behind a cloud, and the boys were glad to be with Beowald for the last piece of their climb. They could not have found their way otherwise. But darkness did not matter to the blind youth. He found his way as surely as if he were seeing the path in daylight!

They came near to the temple, treading very cautiously. Not a sound was to be heard. "We'd better creep into the cave whilst the moon is behind a cloud," whispered Jack. "Paul, ask Beowald if he thinks any robbers are about now. His ears are so sharp that surely he would know."

Paul whispered to Beowald in the Baronian language. The goatherd shook his head. "There is no one near," he said. "I have heard nothing at all, and my ears would tell me if a robber was in the cave. I should hear him breathing."

The boys crept silently into the dark cave. When they were in, the moon shone out and lighted up the strange stone face of the big statue at the back. It seemed to look sneeringly at the three boys.

Jack went up to the image, and ran his fingers down the crack that he had seen widen into a split when the statue divided into halves. He wondered how he could find out the working of the strange image. There must be some way of opening it, both from above and below. What was it? He must find it, or he would not be able to find the place where the robbers had taken Ranni and Pilescu.

But no matter how he felt and pushed and pulled, the crack remained a crack, and did not widen into a split. The other two boys tried as well, but they had no more success than Jack. They looked at one another in despair.

"Let my fingers try," said the voice of Beowald. "My eyes cannot see, but my fingers can. They can feel things that only the whiskers of a mouse could sense!"

This was perfectly true. The blind youth's fingers were so sensitive that they could tell him more than the eyes of others could tell them. The boys watched Beowald run his fingers down the crack in the middle of the statue. They watched him feel round the staring stone eyes. They followed his quivering fingers round the neck and head, touching, feeling, probing, almost like the feelers of an enquiring butterfly!

Suddenly Beowald's sensitive fingers found something and they stopped. The boys looked at him.

"What is it, Beowald?" whispered Prince Paul.

"The statue is not solid just here," answered the goatherd. "Everywhere else it is solid, made of stone – but just behind here, where its right ear is, it is hollow."

"Let me feel," said Jack eagerly, and pushed away the goatherd's fingers. He placed his own behind the right ear of the statue, but he could feel nothing at all. The stone felt just as solid to him there as anywhere else. The other boys felt as well, but to them, as to Jack, the stone was solid there. How could Beowald's fingers know whether stone was solid or hollow behind a certain spot? It seemed like magic.

Beowald put his fingers back again on the spot he had

found. He moved them about, pressed and probed. But nothing happened. Jack shone his torch on to the ear. He saw that it was cleaner than the rest of the head, as if it had been handled a good deal. It occurred to him that the ear itself might be the place containing a spring or lever that worked the statue so that it split in half.

The left ear was completely solid, Jack saw – but the right ear, on the contrary, had a hole in it, as have human ears! Beowald found the hole at the same time as Jack saw it, and placed his first finger inside it. The tip of his finger touched a rounded piece of metal set inside the ear. Beowald pushed against it – and a lever was set in motion that split the stone image silently into half!

Actually it was a very simple mechanism, but the boys did not know that. They stared open-mouthed as the statue split completely down the crack, and the two halves moved smoothly apart. Beowald knew what was happening, though he could not see it. He was afraid, and moved back quickly. He half-thought the statue was coming alive, when it moved!

"Look – there's a hole underneath the statue, in the middle of the low rock it sits on," said Jack, and he shone his torch down it. The hole was round in shape, and would take a man's body easily. A rope, made of strips of leather, hung down the hole from a staple at the top.

"That's the entrance to the robber's lair!" said Jack, in a low voice. "No doubt about that! I bet their cave is below this one, in the mountain itself."

"I'm going to see," said the little prince, who seemed that night to be more than a small boy. He was a prince, he was growing up to be a king, he was lord of Baronia, he was going to take command and give orders! Jack pulled him back as he was about to go down into the dark hole.

"Wait! We might all fall into a trap. Don't do anything silly. We shan't help Ranni and Pilescu by being foolish."

"I will go to rouse the local people and to bring help," said Beowald. "I would like to come with you, but I am no good in a strange place. My feet, my ears and my hands only help me when I am on my mountain-side. In a strange place I am lost."

"We will go down the hole and find out what we can," said Jack. "You get the others and follow us as soon as you are able to. The girls will have told Tooku and Yamen by now, and maybe·they will be on the way here with one or two of the servants. I expect Paul's mother will send for some soldiers, too."

Beowald did not understand all that Jack said, for the boy did not speak the Baronian language very well as yet. Paul quickly translated for him, and Beowald nodded his head.

"Do not fall into the hands of the robbers," he said. "Why do you not wait here until I come back?"

"I go to rescue my men," said Prince Paul haughtily. "Where they go, I follow."

"You must do as you wish," said the goatherd. Jack slid down into the hole, and took hold of the rope. He went down and down, whilst Mike shone his torch on to him. Beowald waited patiently, seeing nothing, but knowing by his ears all that was happening.

The hole went down for a long way. Jack swung on the rope, his arms getting tired. Then he found that there were rough ledges here and there on the sides of the hole, on which he could rest his feet now and again, to relieve his arms.

The hole came to an end at last. Jack felt his toes touching ground once more. He let go the rope and felt round with his hands. He could feel nothing. The hole must have come out into some kind of cave. The boy could hear no sound of any sort, and he thought it would be safe to switch on his torch.

He switched it on, and saw that, as he had imagined, he was in a cave, through the roof of which the hole showed, dark and round. "I wonder if this is the robbers' lair," thought the boy, flashing the torch around. But there was

He found rough ledges here and there

nothing at all in the rocky cave, whose rugged walls threw back the gleam of the torch.

Mike's feet appeared at the bottom of the hole and the boy jumped down beside Jack. Then came Paul. They all stood together, examining the cave.

"It doesn't look as if anyone lives here at all," said Mike. "There are no beds where you might expect the robbers to sleep, not a sign of any pot or pan. I don't believe this is their lair."

"Well, what is it, then?" demanded Jack. "I saw them go down here, didn't I? Goodness knows how Ranni and Pilescu were taken down, with their hands tied! Where can they be?"

"They're nowhere here at all," said Paul, flashing his torch into every corner. "It's odd. What can have become of them?"

It really was a puzzle. Jack began to go round the little cave, his footsteps echoing in a weird way. He flashed his torch up and down the walls, and suddenly came to a stop.

"Here's another way out!" he said. "Look! It's quite plain to see. I'm surprised we didn't see it before when we shone our torches round."

The boys looked. They saw that halfway up the opposite wall of the cave was a narrow opening. They jumped on to a ledge and peered through it. It was plain that it led out of the cave, and was a passage through the rock.

"Come on," said Jack. "This is the way the robbers must have gone. I'll go first!"

He was soon in the passage that led from the cave. He flashed his torch in front of him. The way was dark and rough, and the passage curved as it went, going downwards all the time. Where in the world did it lead to!

The River In The Mountain

As the boys crept down the rocky passage, they suddenly heard a curious noise in the distance. They stopped.

"What's that noise?" asked Jack. It was a kind of rumbling, gurgling sound, sometimes loud and sometimes soft. The boys listened.

"I don't know," said Mike, at last. "Come on. Maybe we shall find out."

On they went again, and very soon they discovered what the queer noise was. It was made by water! It was a waterfall in the mountain, a thing the children had not even thought of! They came out into a big cave, and at one end fell a great stream of water. The cave was damp and cold, and the boys shivered.

They went over to the curious waterfall. "I suppose the snow melts on the top of the mountain and the water finds its way down here," said Jack, thoughtfully. "It must run through a rocky passage, something like the one we have just been in, and then, when the passage ends, the water tumbles down with that rumbling noise. I'm quite wet with the spray!"

The water fell steadily from a hole in the roof of the cave, where, as Jack said, there must be a tunnel or passage down which the water ran before it fell into the cave.

"Where does the water go to, I wonder?" said Mike. "It rushes off into that tunnel, look – and becomes a kind of river going through the mountain. I think it's weird. I wonder if the robbers live in *this* cave – but there still seems to be no sign of them or their belongings. After all, if people live somewhere, even in a cave, they scatter a few belongings about!"

But there was nothing at all to be seen, and, as far as the boys could see, no way of getting out of the "waterfall cave," as they called it.

They wandered round, looking for some outlet – but the water seemed to have found the only outlet – the tunnel down which it rushed after falling on to the channelled floor of the cave.

The boys went back to the water and gazed at it. Jack saw that through hundreds of years the waterfall had worn itself a bed or channel on the floor of the cave, and that only the surface water overflowed on to the ground where the boys stood. The channel took the main water, and it rushed off down a tunnel, and then was lost to sight in the darkness.

"I suppose the robbers couldn't possibly have gone down that tunnel, could they?" said Paul suddenly. "There isn't a ledge or anything they could walk on, is there, going beside that heaving water?"

The boys tried to see through the spray that was flung up by the falling water. Jack gave a shout.

"Yes – there *is* a ledge, and I believe we could get on to it. For goodness' sake be careful not to fall into that churning water! We'd be carried away and drowned if so, it's going at such a pace!"

The boy bent down, ran through the flying spray, and leapt on to a wet ledge beside the water, just inside the tunnel into which it disappeared. He nearly slipped and fell, but managed to right himself.

He flashed his torch into the tunnel and saw the amazing sight of the heaving, rushing water tearing away down the dark vault of the mountain tunnel. It was very weird, and the noise inside the tunnel was frightening.

Paul and Mike were soon beside Jack. He shouted into their ears. "We'd better go along here and see if it leads anywhere. I think this is the way the robbers must have gone with Ranni and Pilescu. Keep as far from the water as you can and don't slip, whatever you do!"

The boys made their way with difficulty along the water-splashed tunnel. The water roared beside them in its hollowed-out channel. The noise was thunderous. Their feet were soon wet with the splashing of the strange river.

"The tunnel is widening out here," shouted back Jack, after about an hour. "Our ledge is becoming almost a platform!"

So it was. After another minute or two the boys found themselves standing on such a broad ledge that when they crouched against the back of it, the spray from the river no longer reached them.

They rested there for a while. Paul was terribly tired by now. Mike looked at his watch. It was four o'clock in the morning! The sun would be up outside the mountain – but here it was as dark as night.

"I feel so sleepy," said Paul, cuddling up against Mike. "I think we ought to have a good long rest."

Jack got up and looked around the broad platform for a more comfortable resting-place. He gave a shout that quickly brought the others to him.

"Look," said Jack, shining his torch on to a recess in the wall of the tunnel at the back of the platform. "This is where the robbers must sometimes rest before going on to wherever they live!"

In the recess, which was like a broad shelf of rock, lay some fur rugs. The boys cuddled into them, snuggled up to one another, closed their eyes and fell asleep at once. They were tired out with their night's travel.

They slept for some hours, and then Jack awoke with a start. He opened his eyes and remembered at once where he was – on the inside of the mountain! He sat up – and suddenly saw the platform outside the recess where the boys were, was lighted brightly. Voices came to him – and he saw a flaring torch held high. What could be happening now?

The other boys did not wake. They were too tired to

hear a sound! Jack leaned out of the rugs and tried to see who was holding the torch. He had a nasty shock – for it was held by one of the robbers! When Jack saw him turn round and his red wolf-tail swing out behind him, he knew without a doubt that the robbers were there within a few feet of him.

The boy tried to see what they were doing. They were at the edge of the river, at the end of the rocky platform. As Jack watched he saw two more men come up from the ledge that ran beside the river. It was plain that the broad platform they were on narrowed into the same sort of ledge that ran beside the upper part of the river. The men were coming up from lower down – and they were dragging something behind them, something that floated on the water. Jack could not see what it was, for the light from the torch flickered and shook, making shadows dance over everything.

The men called to one another hoarsely. They did something at the edge of the water, and then, without a glance toward the recess in which the boys were sleeping, they turned and made their way up the tunnel through which the boys had come, keeping along the ledge in single file. They were going up to the temple-cave, Jack was sure.

"Going to rob people again, I suppose!" thought the boy, excitedly. "They've taken Ranni and Pilescu somewhere further down, and tied them up, I expect – left them safe, as they thought. Golly, if only we could find out where they are, we could rescue them easily now that the robbers have left them for a while."

He looked at his watch. It showed ten minutes to nine! It was morning. Would Yamen and Tooku, Beowald and the villagers have arrived at the temple-cave yet, and meet the robbers on their way? Jack could not imagine what would happen. He woke the others and told them what he had seen.

"The thing to do now is to get along as quickly as we

can, and find out where Ranni and Pilescu are," he said. "The robbers have gone in the opposite direction. Come on, I saw where they came from. It's plain they follow the river."

The boys shook off the warm rugs. Jack flashed his torch round the comfortable recess to make sure they had left nothing behind. The light fell on a tiny shelf at the back. In it was something wrapped in a cloth. Jack unwrapped it in curiosity. Inside was a big Baronian loaf, crusty and stale.

"We'd better soak it in water and eat some," said Jack, pleased. "I'm hungry enough to enjoy bread and water, even if you two aren't! I suppose the robbers leave bread here to help themselves to when they rest in these rugs."

When they pulled off the crust of the big loaf they found that the bread was not too hard to eat after all. They did not even need to soak it in water. Paul, as usual, had a big packet of the honey-flavoured Baronian chocolate with him, and the three boys thoroughly enjoyed their strange meal beside the rushing mountain river.

There was a flattish sort of cup on the little shelf where they had found the bread, and the boys dipped this into the clear river water and drank. It was as cold as ice, and tasted delicious.

Jack bent down to fill the cup again and something caught his eye, as he flashed his torch round. He stopped and gave a surprised exclamation.

"Whatever's that? Look – that thing over there?"

The others looked. Tied by a leather thong to a jutting rock was what looked like a hollowed-out raft. It was broad and flat, with a hollow in the middle. The sides were strengthened with strip upon strip of leather, bound tightly over the edges.

"It's a raft-boat, or boat-raft, whatever you like to call it!" said Mike, surprised. "I've never seen anything like it before. Isn't it odd? What's it for?"

"To go down the river, I imagine!" said Jack, joyfully. "My word, we shall soon get along if we use that raft!"

"But how did the men get here on it?" said Paul, puzzled. "They couldn't float against the current, and it's very strong here."

"They probably crept up on the narrow rocky ledge that seems to run beside the river all the way," said Jack. "But behind them each time they come, they must drag a raft like this, which they use to get themselves back quickly. I say, this is getting awfully exciting! We can take the raft for ourselves, and that will mean that we leave the robbers I saw just now far behind us, for they will have to walk along the ledge as we did, instead of using their boat. Come on – let's try it!"

"I shouldn't be surprised if it takes us right to the place where Ranni and Pilescu are prisoners," said Paul. "Undo that leather thong, Mike, and let's get into the funny boat."

The boys untied the leather strip, and got into the

Down they went on the rushing mountain river

hollow centre of the solid raft. It was absolutely un-sinkable, made out of wood from a big tree, hollowed out carefully in the middle. The boys soon found out why the edges were bound so thickly and firmly with strips of leather!

They let the raft go free on the rushing stream. At once they floated into the dark tunnel from which Jack had seen the robbers come. The raft swung round and round as it went, and bumped hard against the rocky sides of the strange dark tunnel. The leather edges took off the worst jolts, but even so, the boys had to cling tightly to the raft to prevent themselves from being jerked overboard!

"This is the most exciting thing we've ever done!" shouted Jack, above the roar of the water. "Golly, aren't we going fast! I hope we don't come to a waterfall!"

Down they went on the rushing mountain river, down and down in the darkness. The raft rushed along as fast as a speed boat, and the three boys gasped for breath. Where did the river flow to?

In The Secret Forest

The raft rushed along, swinging and bobbing. Sometimes the water was smoother, and then the raft floated more slowly, but on the whole it rushed along at a terrific pace. Once the roof of the tunnel was so low that the boys had to crouch right down on the raft to prevent their heads being bumped hard against it.

"We're going down and down," said Jack. "The river must be running right through the mountain in a downward direction, and I suppose will come out at the other side."

"The other side! Do you mean where the Secret Forest is?" cried Mike.

Jack nodded his head and his eyes gleamed eagerly in the light of Mike's torch. "Yes! If the river *does* come out into the open, and I suppose it must at last, we shall be somewhere on the mountain-side overlooking the Secret Forest itself. So, you see, there *is* a way of getting there! And the robbers know it. I shouldn't be surprised if that really was smoke I saw that day we flew over it in the aeroplane."

The boys felt even more excited, if that was possible! They sat on the weird raft-boat and thought about their night's adventure. It was stranger than any they had ever had. This mountain river seemed never-ending. How long did it go and on and on?

After about two hours a startling thing happened. Jack saw a light, bright and golden, far ahead of them. "Look!" he said. "What's that?"

They floated rapidly nearer and nearer to the gleam, and soon they saw what it was. It was daylight, sunlight, bright and golden. They were soon coming out into the open air!

"We'll be able to get off the raft and stretch our legs a

bit!" said Jack, thankfully, for they were all beginning to feel very cramped indeed. But Jack was wrong. There was no getting off that raft yet!

It suddenly shot out into the open air, and the boys blinked their eyes, dazzled by the sudden bright sunshine. When they could see properly, they saw that they were indeed on the other side of the steep Killimooin mountains!

Below them, not very far away, was the Secret Forest! The mountain river, after having flowed for miles through the mountain tunnels, was now flowing down the slopes of the hill, taking the raft with it. It spread out into a wide river, and the raft sailed along in the middle, where the current was swift and strong. There appeared to be no dangerous waterfall to navigate! That was very fortunate, Jack thought.

"Do you suppose this river goes right down to the Secret Forest?" said Mike, trying to see where it flowed, far ahead of them. He caught glimpses of silver here and there, near the forest. It really did look as if the river flowed to it!

"I believe it does," said Jack, as the raft floated swiftly down the current. "We are getting nearer and nearer!"

After some time the river was very near to the great forest. The boys could see how wide and thick and dark it was. Now it no longer looked merely a great stretch of green; they could see the trees themselves, tall and close-set together. The river flowed on and on towards it.

The raft reached the outermost fringe of trees, and the river then disappeared into the forest. The boys were swept along on the raft, and as soon as they entered the forest, the sunshine disappeared, and a dim green light was all they had to see by.

"How dark and thick the trees are!" said Jack, awed. "The river must go right through this forest."

"I wonder where it goes to," said Mike. "Rivers all go to the sea. How can this one get out of this closed-in valley? You would think it would make a big lake – all this water flowing down the mountain-side like this, with nowhere to escape to!"

This was a puzzle, too. The boys thought about it as the raft swung along beneath the arching trees. Then, quite suddenly, they were in a big, wide pool, like a small lake, completely surrounded by trees. The river flowed through the pool, and out at the opposite side.

The raft swung to the side of the pool, and Jack gave a cry of surprise.

"This is where the robbers live! Look at those strange houses, or whatever you like to call them!"

The boys saw that round the lake-side were strange, bee-hive shaped houses, made of branches of trees and dried mud. From a hole at the top smoke appeared. Then Jack knew that he had been right when he thought he had seen a spiral of smoke from the aeroplane! The smoke from the bee-hive houses joined together as it rose into the air, and made a straight streak of blue smoke that hung almost motionless, for no wind came into that still valley.

No one was to be seen. If there was anyone in the huts, they must be sleeping, Jack thought! Their raft swung silently to the bank and the three boys leapt off at once. They crouched down in the bushes watching to see if anyone had noticed them. But nobody had. Not a soul appeared from the curious huts.

The boys were very hungry indeed, but they dared not go to ask for food. They whispered together, wondering what to do. Behind them was the deep, dark forest. In front was the great pool, out of which flowed the river, disappearing into the depths of the Secret Forest.

"Do you suppose all the robbers have gone up to the temple-cave?" whispered Mike. Jack shook his head. "No," he said. "I only saw five or six. Hundreds must live here. Sh! Look, there are some children!"

The boys saw four or five children coming from the forest, going towards the huts. They had nothing on at all, except for a strip of skin round their waists. They were dirty, and their bright hair was tangled and long. They wore bright bird-feathers behind their ears, and looked real little ruffians.

A woman appeared at the door of one hut, and the children shouted to her. Paul turned to the others.

"Did you understand what those children said? They said they had been to see the big men who were prisoners! So Ranni and Pilescu must be here somewhere. Shall we try going along that path where the children came from?"

"We should get completely lost in the Secret Forest," said Mike, feeling scared. "There are probably wolves here too. I almost wish we hadn't come. We should have waited and come with the others!"

"We will go down the forest path," said Paul, suddenly becoming the Prince of Baronia again. "Stay here if you do not wish to follow me. I, myself, will find Ranni and Pilescu!"

There was nothing for it but to follow Paul. He skirted the pool carefully and then found the narrow path down which the robber-children had come. It ran between the thickly-growing trees, and was evidently much used. Here and there the trees were curiously marked as if with an axe.

"Perhaps it's the way the robbers have of marking their way through the forest," said Paul.

"Yes – sort of signposts," answered Jack, who had thought the same thing. "Well, as long as I see those marks, I shan't feel lost!"

They went on down the narrow, twisting path. It curved round trees, wandered between the thick trunks, and seemed never-ending. Now and again the children saw the axe-marks on a tree-trunk again. The forest was very quiet and still. No wind moved the branches of the trees. No bird sang. It was very mysterious and silent.

Jack's sharp ears heard the sound of voices. "Someone's coming!" he said. "Shin up a tree, quick!"

233

The three chose trees that did not seem too difficult to climb quickly. They were up them in a trice. A squirrel-like animal bounded away in alarm from Jack. The boy peered down between the branches.

He saw three more children going along, fortunately towards the pool they had left. They shouted to one another, and seemed to be playing some sort of hopping game. They soon passed, and did not guess that there were three pairs of anxious eyes following their movements from the branches above them.

As soon as the robber-children were out of sight the boys jumped down and went on again. "I hope that they haven't hidden Ranni and Pilescu too far away!" said Jack, with a groan. "I'm getting tired again and awfully hungry!"

"So am I," said Mike. Paul said nothing. He meant to go on until he found his men. He did not seem to be tired, though he looked it. Jack thought he was a very plucky boy indeed, for he was younger and smaller than the other two, and yet managed to keep up with them very well.

Jack stopped again and motioned to the others to listen. They stood still, and heard voices once more. Up a tree they went at once, but this time the voices did not come any nearer. Paul suddenly went red with excitement. He leaned towards Jack, who was on the branch next to him.

"Jack! I think that is Pilescu's deep voice. Listen!"

They all listened, and through the forest came the deep tones of Pilescu's voice, without a doubt. In a trice the boys had shinned down the tree again and were running down the path towards the voices.

They came out into a small clearing. In the middle of this there was a hole, or what looked like a hole from where the boys stood. Across the top of the hole were laid heavy beams of wood, separated each from the other by a few inches, to allow air to penetrate into the hole.

It was from this hole or pit that the voices came. Mike took a quick look round the clearing to see if anyone was there. But it seemed to be completely empty. He ran across to the pit.

"Ranni! Pilescu?" he cried, and Paul tried to force apart the heavy logs of wood.

"Ranni! Are you there? Pilescu, are you hurt?" cried Paul, in a low voice.

There was an astonished silence, and then came Ranni's voice, mingled with Pilescu's.

"Paul! Little lord! What are you doing here? Paul, can it be you?"

"Yes – I'm here and Mike and Jack," said Paul. "We have come to rescue you."

"But how did you get here?" cried Ranni, in amazement. "Did you come through the mountain and down the river into the depths of the Secret Forest?"

"Yes," said Mike. "It has been a tremendous adventure, I can tell you."

"Are you all all right?" asked Pilescu.

"Yes, except that we're awfully hungry," said Jack, with a laugh.

"If you can move those logs, with our help, we will give you food," said Ranni. "We have some here in this pit. The robbers put bread and water here, and we have plenty. Goodness knows what they meant to do with us. I suppose they captured us because they knew we had found the secret of their coming and going, and did not want us to tell anyone."

The boys began to try and move the heavy logs. Ranni and Pilescu helped them. They shifted little by little, though it was as much as the whole five of them could do to move them even an inch! At last, however, there was enough space for Ranni and Pilescu to squeeze out of the pit, and haul themselves up on to the level ground.

They sat there panting. "Not a nice prison at all," said Ranni, jokingly, as he saw tears in Paul's eyes. The boy had been very anxious about his two friends, and now that he had Ranni's arm about him again, he was so relieved he felt almost like crying.

"Funny boy, isn't he!" whispered Mike to Jack. "So awfully brave, and yet he cries like a girl sometimes."

"We'd better hide quickly," said Ranni. "The robbers may come back at any moment and we don't want them to find us all here. They would have five prisoners then, instead of two! Let's push the logs back exactly as they were, Mike. It will puzzle the robbers to know how we escaped, when they see that the logs have apparently not been moved!"

Back To The Robber Camp

It was easy to shift the logs back into position for now Ranni and Pilescu were able to use the whole of their strength, instead of being hindered by being in a deep pit. They finished their task and then went to discuss their next move under some thick bushes at the edge of the clearing.

They had a good view of the path from there and could see anyone coming, though they themselves could not be seen. They sat down and talked earnestly. Jack told the two Baronians all that had happened, and they were amazed.

"Shall we try and get back home the way we came?" asked Mike. "Perhaps that would be best."

"I don't know about that," said Ranni. "Once the robbers discover that we are gone, they will be on the look-out for us, and probably men will be guarding the way back, ready to take us again."

"Well, what else is there to do?" asked Paul, impatiently.

"Let us think carefully, little lord," said Ranni. "Can there be any other way out of this Secret Forest, so well-hidden within the great Killimooin mountains?"

Everyone was silent. It was quite impossible to climb the surrounding mountains, even if they could make their way through the depths of the forest towards them.

Jack spoke at last. "Ranni, where do you suppose this river goes to? It must go somewhere. If it was penned up in this valley, it would make a simply enormous lake, and it doesn't do that, or we should have seen it from the air, when we flew over."

Ranni sat and thought. "It must go somewhere, of

course," he said. "Maybe it finds its way underground, as it did in the mountain. You think perhaps it would be a good idea to follow the river, Jack, and see if we can float away on it, maybe through a tunnel in one of the mountains, to the other side."

"We could try," said Jack, doubtfully. "We could go back to the queer beehive-like houses tonight and see if our raft is still there. If it is, we could board it and go off on the river. The river won't take us backwards, that is certain, so we shall have to go forwards with it!"

"Well, we will try that," said Ranni, though he did not sound very hopeful. "Let us eat now, shall we? You must, as you said, be very hungry."

The Baronians had brought the bread with them from the pit. All five began to eat, thinking of the adventure that lay ahead. Pilescu looked at the three boys. He saw that they were worn out.

"We will find a good hiding-place and rest there," he said to Ranni. "We shall need to be fresh for tonight. Come, then. I will carry Paul. He is already half asleep!"

But before they could creep away, they heard the sound of voices, and saw three or four robber-women coming down the path, carrying pitchers of water and more bread! They had evidently come to bring food to the prisoners. Very silently the five vanished into the trees.

The women went to the pit and placed the food and water beside it. They had apparently been told to take it there and leave it, so that the men could hand it down to the prisoners when they came later, and could move the logs a little apart. It was beyond the women's strength to move them.

The women peered curiously between the logs, and were amazed when they could not see the prisoners. They chattered together excitedly and then peered down again. It was dark in the pit, but even so, they should have been able to catch sight of the two men. Had not the children been to see them that morning and come back with tales of their fierce shouts and cries, their fiery red hair and beards? Then why could not these things be seen and heard now?

The women became certain that the prisoners were not there. Yet how could they have escaped? The logs were still across the mouth of the pit, and no men could move those without help from outside! It was a mystery to them. Chattering loudly, they fled away back to the robber encampment to tell the news. They left the food and water beside the empty pit.

As soon as the women had gone, Ranni slipped out of his hiding-place and went to the pit. He took the bread and ran back to the others.

"This may be useful!" he said. He tied a leather thong around it, and hung it at his back. It was a flat, round loaf, easy to carry.

"Now we will find a good hiding-place," said the big Baronian. Pilescu picked up Paul in his arms and the two men strode away into the forest to find a safe hiding-place to rest until night came.

Presently they found one. A great rock jutted up between the thickly-growing trees, and underneath it was a well-hidden hole, draped by greenery. Once in the shelter of that rock, no one would see them.

"Do you know the way back to the clearing, Pilescu?" asked Paul, sleepily, as the big man arranged him comfortably on the ground, on the fur-lined cloaks that he and Ranni had taken off for the time being. They made good rugs for the three tired boys.

"I know it, little lord. Do not worry your head," said Pilescu. "Now sleep. You must be wide-awake tonight, for you may need all your wits about you!"

The boys soon slept. They had had so little sleep the night before, and were so exhausted with all their adventures, that it was impossible to keep awake. The men kept a watch. They had been very touched to know that the boys had followed them to rescue them. Now it

239

was their turn to watch over the boys, and save them from the robbers!

The sun began to slide down towards the west. The day was going. Ranni dozed, and Pilescu kept watch. Then Pilescu dozed whilst Ranni kept eyes and ears open. He heard excited cries towards the evening, coming from the clearing, and guessed that the robbers had discovered their escape. Then all was silence again. The Secret Forest was the most silent place that Ranni had ever been in. He wondered if the wind ever blew down in that valley, and if birds ever sang. It made him jump when a mouse-like creature scurried over his foot.

Twilight came creeping into the forest. It was always dim there, and difficult to see the sunshine. Twilight came there before the outer world had lost its daylight. Ranni looked at his watch. Half-past seven. The boys still slept. Let them sleep for another hour or two, and then they would creep through the darkness of the forest, back to the clearing where they had left the raft.

Jack awoke first. He stretched himself and opened his eyes, looking into complete darkness. He wondered where he was. Then he heard Ranni speaking in a low voice to Pilescu, and everything came back to him. He was in the Secret Forest, of course – hidden under that rock! He sat up at once.

"Ranni! Pilescu! What time is it? Is everything all right?"

"Yes," said Ranni. "Soon we will go to get the raft. We will wake the others now, and eat. Paul! Mike! It is time to wake!"

Soon all five of them were eating the hard bread. Ranni had some water in his flask, and everyone drank a little. Then they were ready to go.

By the light of his torch Ranni made his way back to the clearing where the pit was. He flashed his light around. There was no one there at all. The logs had been dragged away from the pit, when the robbers had come to see if what their women had said was true.

"We will take the path back," said Ranni. "It is over there. Take hands and go in single file. We must not lose hold of one another. I go first. You next, Paul. Then Mike and Jack, and Pilescu last. Now – are you ready?"

They found the path and went along it quietly in single file. The boys felt excited, but perfectly safe now that they had Ranni and Pilescu.

Ranni halted after a while. He flashed his torch here and there. He had gone from the path!

"We are not very far from it," he said. "I saw the axe-marks in a tree only a little way back. We must look for them."

It was anxious work looking for the axe-marks which would tell them they were once more on the right path. Mike felt very uncomfortable as he wondered what would happen if they really got lost in that enormous forest! He thought he saw two gleaming eyes looking at him from between the trees and he jumped.

"Is that a wolf?" he whispered to Jack. But it was only his imagination! There was no wolf, merely a couple of shining leaves caught in the light of Ranni's brilliant torch!

"Ah!" said Ranni, at last, in a glad voice. "Here is the path again. And look, there are axe-marks on that tree. Now we can go forward again. Keep a look-out, all of you, for the axe-marks that tell us we are on the right path."

Everyone watched anxiously for the marks after that. It was impossible to stray far from the path if they followed the marks. They were made at regular intervals, and the little company soon made steady progress.

"We must be near the encampment!" said Ranni at last, in a low voice. "Can you hear the lapping of water? I think we are nearing that big pool."

In another minute his torch shone on to the glittering waters of the pool. They had reached the cluster of huts. If only the robbers did not see or hear them!

A Way Of Escape?

Everything was quiet. There were only a few small night-sounds – the lapping of the water, the squeal of some small animal, the splash of a fish jumping. There was nothing else to be heard at all.

The five stood quite still beside the big pool, listening. A curious sound came on the air, and the boys clutched one another.

"It's all right," whispered Ranni, a laugh in his voice. It's only one of the robbers snoring in the nearest hut!"

So it was. The sound came again, and then died away. Ranni, who had switched off his torch, switched it on again. He wanted to find the raft that Paul had told him about. Luckily it was quite near him, about ten yards away, tied to a tree.

"Did you come down the mountain river on a raft like that?" whispered Paul to Ranni. The big man answered in a low voice.

"We came on a raft only as far as the outlet of the river, just where it leaves the mountain. The men steered the raft to the bank there, and we all jumped off. They tied up the raft and we walked the rest of the way to the Secret Forest. Apparently, whenever the robbers go up to the Temple Cave they walk along the ledge beside the mountain river, and drag a raft up with them, floating it on the rushing water. It must be hard work!"

"Oh! Then that's why there are no rafts to be seen on this pool," said Jack, who had been puzzling about this. "They only use them inside the mountain, to bring them down quickly."

"Sh!" said Pilescu, warningly. "We had better not talk any more. Hold your torch higher, Ranni, so that I can see to untie the raft."

It did not take long to free the raft. Ranni found a broken branch to use as a paddle. He did not want to be completely at the mercy of the river. With the branch to use, he could steer a little, and, if necessary, bring the raft to the bank.

"Get on the raft," whispered Ranni. They all got into the hollowed-out piece in the centre. it was a tight fit! Ranni pushed the raft into the centre of the big pool, where it was caught in the current that flowed through it. The raft swung along at once, very slowly but surely. Soon it was out of the pool and on the river, which ran through the Secret Forest for miles.

It was very weird and mysterious, swinging along on the swift river, through the heart of the dark forest. Sometimes branches of trees swept down low and bumped the heads of the travellers, scraping their faces. It was impossible to prevent them. Ranni tried shining his torch so that they might have warning of overhanging boughs but the river was swift, and the down-sweeping branches were on them before they knew.

The boys huddled against one another, stiff and uncomfortable. When a big branch nearly took Paul overboard and gave him a great bruise on his forehead, Ranni decided to moor the raft till the night was over. He did not expect the robbers to pursue them down the river, because they had no boats.

So he tied the raft to a tree, and the five of them nibbled bread and talked in low voices. Ranni fell off to sleep after a while, but the boys were wide-awake now. Pilescu kept watch. It seemed a long long time till dawn, but at last it came. The trees were so thick just there that the boys could see no sunlight, only a gradual lightening around them, as the tree trunks began to show, and the leaves to take on colour.

"We'll go on now," said Ranni. He untied the raft and on they went again, caught by the strong current. Now they could see when branches of trees would scrape over the raft, and Ranni steered to avoid them.

243

The river wound in and out, and suddenly took a great curve, almost doubling back on itself.

"I hope it doesn't flow back very far!" said Pilescu. "We don't want to land back near the robber camp!"

The river did wind back a good way, and at one part, although the little company did not know it, it was only about a mile from the robbers! It had a strange course in the Secret Forest. It flowed half-way through, doubled back, and finally flowed out of the trees about six miles from where it first flowed in. The travellers did not know this, though Ranni could tell, by the position of the sun, that they were now travelling almost in the opposite direction.

The trees suddenly thinned, and sunshine flooded down here and there, almost dazzling the two men and the three boys. The river flowed more rapidly, and the raft bobbed about.

"We are coming out of the Secret Forest!" said Jack, shading his eyes and looking forward. "The trees are getting thinner and thinner. Where does this river go. I wonder? I do wish it would take us right through the mountains somewhere and out at the other side. Then we could just walk round them till we come to Killimooin Castle."

"Not so easily done!" said Pilescu.

A shout made them turn their heads. To their horror, between the trees, they saw one of the robbers! He called out something, and then ran off to tell his comrades, his red wolf-tail swinging behind him.

Six or seven more came running with him after a few minutes, and they stood watching the raft as it swung along in the distance.

One robber yelled something after them. "What did he say?" asked Jack. Ranni looked a little solemn.

"He speaks a curious dialect," he said, "But I think I understood him to say, "Soon, soon, you will be in the middle of the earth!" I wonder what he meant."

Everyone thought about it. "Do you think it means that the river goes down underground?" asked Jack. "Well if it does, it's what we want, isn't it?"

"It depends on whether there is room for the raft or not," said Ranni. "We must keep a sharp look-out."

The river ran on. The boys saw the mountains of Killimooin around them. In front of them, slightly to the left, was the one they knew, on the other side of which Killimooin Castle was built. It looked very different from this side, but the summit was the same shape.

Suddenly they heard a terrific roaring sound ahead of them. Quick as thought Ranni plunged the tree-branch into the water and tried to steer the raft out of the current. But it was very swift and the raft kept on its course.

Jack saw that the big Baronian looked pale and anxious as he tried in vain to swing the raft from its steady course. "What's the matter?" he asked.

"Can you hear that noise?" said Ranni. "I think the river makes a fall somewhere ahead – maybe a big waterfall. We don't want to be caught in it. I can't get this raft out of the current.

Pilescu suddenly slipped overboard, and, taking the raft with one hand, tried to swim to the shore with it. But he could not move it from the swift current.

"Jump!" he cried to the others. "Jump, and swim. It is our only hope. We are getting near the fall."

Everyone jumped into the water. Paul was the weakest swimmer and big Ranni took him on his back. The raft went bobbing off by itself.

Pilescu helped Mike and Jack, but it was a stiff struggle to get to the bank of the swiftly-running river. They sat there, exhausted, hoping that no robber would come by, for they had no strength to resist anyone!

They recovered after a while. The hot sun dried their clothes, and steam began to rise from them.

"I wonder what happened to the raft," said Jack.

"We'll go and see!" said Ranni. "The noise is so

245

tremendous here that the waterfall, or whatever it is, can't be very far ahead. I think it must be where that fine mist hangs in the air over there, like smoke."

They walked on beside the river, over rough ground. The noise became louder and louder. Then they suddenly saw what happened to the mountain river!

They rounded a big rock and came to the place where fine spray flew. The great silver river rushed by them – and then disappeared completely!

No river flowed ahead. The whole of the water vanished somewhere in that little place. Ranni went forward cautiously. He called to the others:

"It's a good thing we got off the raft when we did! The river goes right down into the earth here!"

All the others joined Ranni. The spray soaked them as they stood there, trying to see where the volume of water went to.

It really was most extraordinary. There appeared to be a great cavern or chasm in the ground into which the river emptied itself with a terrific roar. The water fell into the enormous hole and completely disappeared.

"So that's what the robber meant when he shouted that we should soon be in the middle of the earth," said Jack. "That water must go deep down into enormous holes and crevices among the rocks. I suppose it goes right under the surrounding mountains and comes out somewhere else as a river again. How amazing!

"What a mercy we leapt off the raft!" said Mike, feeling scared at the thought of what might have happened if they and the raft together had plunged down into the heart of the earth. "Golly! This river has an exciting course! Through the mountain, down the slope, into the Secret Forest, out again, and down this chasm. Well – there's no way out for us here, that's certain."

The five travellers left the curious place, and went to sit by a sun-warmed rock to dry their spray-wet clothes once more.

246

Everyone jumped into the water

"The robbers must think we are all lost in the depths of the earth now," said Pilescu. "They will not be on the watch for us any more. That is something to the good, at any rate."

"What are we going to do?" asked Paul

"There is only one thing to do, my little lord," said Pilescu. "We must go back the way we came!"

"What! Up into the mountain, beside the river all the way, and back to the temple-cave?" cried Paul. "Oh, we shall never do that!"

"We must," said Ranni. "It is the only way out. I am going to climb a high tree so that I may see where the river flows out of the mountain."

He climbed up the biggest tree nearby, and shaded his eyes for a long time. Then he came down.

"I cannot see where the river comes forth from

247

Killimooin," he said. "It is too far away. But I can see where the water enters the Secret Forest – or I think I can. We must go the east, and walk until we come to the river. We cannot miss it, for it will lie right across our path!"

"Let us have something to eat first," said Paul. "Where is the bread? There is plenty left, isn't there?"

There was not plenty, but there was enough. They sat and ate hungrily. Then Ranni rose, and everyone got up too.

"Now to find the river again," said Ranni. "We will skirt the Secret Forest until we come to the rushing water. Then we will follow it upwards to the mountain!"

The Terrible Storm

Meanwhile, what had happened to the two girls? They had done as the boys had suggested, and had awakened Tooku and Yamen at once. The couple sat up in their bed, bewildered at the children's extraordinary story. Ranni and Pilescu captured by the robbers! The statue that split into two! All the boys gone! It seemed like an unbelievable nightmare to Yamen and Tooku.

"We can do nothing tonight," said Tooku, nursing his injured arm. "The servants would be of no use to hunt for the boys and the others. They would be too afraid. Tomorrow, early, we must send the servants to gather together the villagers of the mountain-side."

The girls did not want to wait so long, but there was nothing else to be done. They went back to bed, but not to sleep. They cuddled together on a small couch, covered with a warm fur rug, and talked together, worried about the boys. At last, just before dawn, they dozed off, and were awakened by Yamen.

Soon everyone in the castle knew what had happened the night before. The servants went about with scared faces. Paul's mother heard the girls' story again and again, tears in her eyes as she thought of how Paul had marched off to rescue his men.

"He is a true little Baronian!" she said. "How glad I am that Mike and Jack are with him! Oh, why didn't they wait until we could send soldiers or armed villagers to find Ranni and Pilescu?"

A band of people came climbing up on mountain ponies, fetched by servants of the castle and by the goatherd, Beowald. They had been amazed at the tale told to them, but all of them were determined to rescue their "little lord" as they called Paul.

Beowald was with them. He led them up the hill to the old temple-cave. The villagers shrank back in fear when they saw the queer stone images. The statue of the sitting man, at the back, was now whole again. The robbers that the boys had seen the night before had come up to the cave, found the statue in half, and, fearing that their secret had been discovered, had closed the two halves together once more and gone back into the cave below.

Peggy and Nora watched Blind Beowald put his finger into the right ear of the statue. The villagers cried out in wonder when they saw the stone man split in half, and divide slowly. Beowald pointed down to the hole that the statue hid so well.

"That is the way," he said.

The villagers went to the hole and looked down. They shivered. They did not want to go down at all. Thoughts of mysterious magic, of mountain-spirits, filled their heads.

But one bolder than the rest slid down the rope, calling to the others to follow. One by one they went down. The girls wanted to go too, but Tooku and Yamen forbade them sternly. "This is men's work," they said. "You would only get in the way." So the girls had to go back to the castle, where Paul's mother sat waiting for news, white and anxious.

Nora and Peggy tried to comfort her by telling her of the adventures they and the boys had had before, and how they had always won through in the end. The Queen smiled at them, and sighed.

"You are adventurous children!" she said. "Wherever you go, you have adventures. I shall be glad when this adventure is over!"

There was no news at all that day. The search party did not return. Beowald came down from the temple to say that although he had listened well by the hole, he had heard nothing. For the first time he was angry with his blindness, for he badly wanted to follow his friends into the mountain. But he did not dare to, because he would be completely lost in a place he did not know.

Towards tea-time the sky suddenly darkened. The girls went to the window. Yamen was with them, and she looked out too.

"A storm is coming," she said, pointing to the west. "A great storm. You must not be frightened, little ones. Sometimes, when the weather has been hot, the big clouds blow up, and the lighning tears the sky in two, whilst the thunder roars and echoes round."

"We are not afraid of storms, Yamen," said Nora. "It ought to be a wonderful sight, a storm in the Killimooin mountains!"

The sky grew so black that the girls could not see to read. Great clouds began to roll round the mountain itself, and soon the castle was completely swallowed up in the thick, swirling mists. Thunder rumbled in the distance. The little children in the nurseries of the castle began to cry.

"There's the lighning!" said Nora, as a vivid flash appeared, and everything was lighted up clearly for an instant. "Oh – what thunder! I've never heard anything like it!"

Killimooin seemed to be in the midst of the storm. Thunder cracked round the castle, and the lightning shivered the sky to pieces. It was as dark as night between the flashes.

"Although the two girls were not afraid of storms, they were awed by this one. The noise was so terrific and the lightning was so grand.

Then the rain came. Rain? It sounded more like a waterfall pouring down on the castle, lashing against the windows, forming itself into rivulets that rushed down the hillside at top speed. Never in their lives had the two girls seen or heard such rain. It almost drowned the thunder that still rolled around!

"Well, it's a mercy the boys are not out in this, but are somewhere in a cave," said Nora, trying to be cheerful.

251

But the boys were not in a cave! No, they were making their way towards the river where it entered the Secret Forest! They were almost there, and could see its shining waters. They were glad, because now they felt that they knew their way. They had only to follow the river's course backwards to the mountain, and climb up beside it as it flowed down through the heart of the hill!

Then the sky darkened, and the storm blew up. First, it was very still, and Ranni glanced uneasily at the sky. He knew the Baronian storms! They were as grand as the mountains themselves!

The storm broke, just as the little party reached the river and began to follow its swift course backwards to the mountain. Thunder cracked above their heads, and lightning split the darkened sky.

"We had better shelter," said Ranni, and looked about for somewhere to go. He did not want to stand under the trees in case they were struck by lightning. There were some thickly-growing bushes nearby with enormous flat leaves. The rain fell off the leaves as if they were umbrellas.

"We'll crawl under these bushes," said Ranni. "We can draw our cloaks over our heads. The rain will not soak through the fur lining."

But it did! It soaked through everything, and once again the company were wet! The boys hated the fierceness of this rainstorm. The drops pelted down, stinging them, slashing them, soaking through the bushes, their fur-lined cloaks, their clothes, and everything.

"What a storm!" said Paul. "It is the worst I ever remember in Baronia. I don't like it, Pilescu."

Pilescu pulled the small boy to him and covered him with his great arms. "You are safe with Pilescu," he said. "Not even the worst storm can harm you now!"

For two hours the rain poured down, never-ending. Jack was astonished to think that so much water could be held by clouds! It was as if someone up in the sky was emptying whole seas of water down on to the earth.

252

At last a break came in the clouds and a bit of brilliant blue sky showed through. The thunder died away. The lightning no longer flashed. The clouds thinned rapidly, and the rain stopped. The boys heaved sighs of relief. They were wet, cold and hungry. Ranni felt about in his big pockets and brought out some chocolate. It was very welcome.

"Now we must get on," he said. "If the sun comes out strongly, before it sets, we shall soon be dry again. We have a long climb ahead before we reach the place where the river gushes forth from the mountain. Shall I carry you for a while, little lord?"

"Certainly not," said Paul. "I can walk as well as Mike and Jack!"

But after three hours of hard walking the little prince was only too glad to be hoisted on to Pilescu's broad back! They made their way slowly on and up, the noise of the water always in their ears. They saw no sign of the robbers at all, though they kept a sharp look-out for them.

When evening began to fall they reached the place where the river flowed out of the mountain-side, rushing and roaring as if in pleasure to see the sun. They sat by the water and rested. They were all tired now.

"Well, we must begin our watery climb now," said Ranni, at last. "It will take us some hours to follow the river up to where it falls into the cave above. The way will be steep and often dangerous. Paul, I am going to tie you to me, for if you fall into the river, I cannot save you. You will be whirled away from me in an instant."

"Well, tie Mike and Jack to Pilescu, then," said Paul. "I don't want to be the only one."

In the end, all five were roped together, so that if one fell, the others might pull him up again to safety. Then the five of them entered the cavernous hole in Killimooin mountain, and prepared to climb up beside the rushing torrent.

There was a narrow ledge, as Ranni had guessed. It was

wet and slippery, and sometimes so narrow that it seemed impossible to walk on it. But by finding firm hand-holds in the rocky wall of the tunnel, the climbers managed to make their way steadily upwards.

Once Paul slipped and fell. He almost jerked Ranni off his feet, too. The boy half fell into the rushing water, but Ranni caught hold of the rope and tightened it quickly. The boy was pulled back to the ledge, and knelt there, gasping with fright.

"You are safe, little Paul. Do not be afraid," said Ranni, comfortingly, shouting above the rushing of the water.

"I'm not afraid!" yelled Paul, and got to his feet at once. He had had a bad scare, but he would not show it. Ranni felt proud of the little prince.

The toiled upwards, not saying a word, because it was soon too much effort to shout to make themselves heard above the noise of the river. It seemed as if they had been climbing up the narrow ledge for hours, with Ranni's torch showing the way at the front, and Pilescu's at the back, when the five saw something that startled them exceedingly.

The light from Ranni's torch fell on something swirling down the torrent! In surprise Ranni kept his torch pointed towards it – and the little company saw that it was a raft, on which were five or six of the small, wiry robbers, bobbing rapidly downwards to the Secret Forest!

The robbers saw them too, and uttered loud cries of amazement. In half a minute they were swept away down the river, out of sight, lost in the long black tunnel through which the water rushed downwards.

"They saw us!" yelled Jack. "Does it matter, do you think? Will they come after us?"

Ranni and Pilescu stopped to consider the matter. They thought it was possible that the robbers *would* turn back and pursue them. It would be easy to swing their raft against the side and leap out. They could drag their raft up

254

behind them, as they apparently did each time they climbed up to the temple-cave.

"Ranni!" yelled Jack, again. "Do you think they'll come after us?"

"We think it is likely," replied Ranni. "We must push on quickly. Come, there is no time to be lost."

The five of them set off again. It was a hard and tiring journey. They were splashed continually by the river, which also overflowed time and again on to the ledge so that their legs were always wet. Sometimes the tunnel was very low, and once the company had to go down on hands and knees and crawl like that round a bend of the ledge, their heads touching the roof of the tunnel!

Ranni's torch gave out and Mike was glad he had one with him to lend to Ranni, for it was necessary to have two, one at the back of the line and one at the front.

"How much further have we to go?" groaned Paul. "How much further, Ranni?"

A Journey Up The Mountain River

It was a long, long climb. Ranni shone his torch on to his watch, and saw that it was nearly midnight! No wonder poor Paul was groaning, and wondering how much further they had to go. Even the two men were tired.

"Ranni, there's a sort of platform place somewhere," said Jack, remembering the broadening out of the ledge, where he and the others had slept in a recess at the back two nights before.

Ranni and Pilescu did not know about this. Jack shouted into their ears, telling them about it, and the two Baronians hoped that they would soon come to it. Then they would all have a rest. One or other could be on watch in case the robbers came!

Up they went again, stumbling over the rough, rocky ledge that ran beside the river. Once Mike slipped and fell headlong into the water. He pulled Jack right off his feet, and both boys disappeared. Paul gave a scream of fright.

But Pilescu stood steady, and gripped the rope. He pulled Jack and Mike firmly back to the side and helped the soaking boys out. The were shivering as much with fright as with cold! It was not at all a nice feeling to take a plunge unexpectedly into the icy mountain water. They were glad that Ranni had had the idea of roping everyone together. Jack hoped that neither of the big Baronians would fall into the river, for he was sure that if they did they would jerk the boys in after them! But Ranni and Pilescu were sure-footed, having been used to climbing hills and mountains all their lives, and neither of them slipped!

Paul was getting so tired that he could hardly stumble along. It was impossible for Ranni to carry him, for he needed both his hands, one to hold the torch, and the other to find hand-holds for himself. His heart ached for the tired boy stumbling along just behind him.

It was a long time before they came to the platform. Ranni did not even know he had come to it. He went along the ledge, feeling the wall, not noticing at first that he was getting further from the river. Mike gave a shout.

"I believe it's the platform! Oh good! This ledge is widening out tremendously!"

Ranni and Pilescu stopped and flashed their torches around. It *was* the platform, as the boys called it! Thank goodness for that.

"There's the recess where we slept, look!" shouted Mike. The men saw the hollowed-out recess in the wall at the back, lined with fur rugs. They saw something else, too. On the little shelf above was more bread, placed there by the robbers the company had seen swinging down on their raft two or three hours before!

"Now this is really good," said Ranni. He set Paul on his knee, took the bread, and broke it into pieces. Mike and Jack took some and began to eat hungrily. But Paul was too exhausted. He could eat nothing. His head fell forward on Ranni's broad chest, and he was asleep at once.

"You boys must rest on those rugs on that rocky couch there," said Ranni, speaking to Mike and Jack. "I will hold Paul in my arms to warm him. Pilescu will keep watch for the robbers in case they come back."

Mike and Jack flung themselves on to the strange resting-place at the back of the platform, and pulled the fur rugs over them. They were asleep in half a second. The two Baronians were sleepy too, but Pilescu was on guard and did not dare even to close his eyes.

Ranni fell asleep holding Paul. Only big Pilescu was awake. He felt his eyes closing. He had switched off his torch, for he did not want the robbers to see any light, if they came back. It was difficult to keep awake in the dark, when he was so tired!

His head nodded. He stood up at once. He knew it would be impossible not to sleep if he remained seated. He began to walk up and down the platform, like a lion in a cage. That kept him awake. He was not likely to fall asleep on his feet.

He paced steadily for two hours. Then he stiffened and listened. He could hear voices! They echoed up from the tunnel below. It must be the returning robbers!

"They have managed to get their raft to the side and land, and have turned back to come after us!" thought Pilescu. "What are we to do? They will be on us before we can escape. How I wish I had a gun with me!"

But the robbers had taken away all the weapons carried by the Baronians. Neither Ranni nor Pilescu had anything to defend themselves with, except their bare hands. Well, they could make good use of those!

The voices came nearer. Pilescu woke Ranni and whispered the news to him. Ranni put the sleeping Paul into the recess at the back, with the other boys. He did not wake.

"We will cover ourselves with our cloaks and sit with our backs to the wall, on either side of the recess," whispered Ranni. "It is just possible that the robbers may not see us, and may not guess that we are resting here. They would think that we were going ahead as fast as we could."

They could not hear any voices now. They guessed that the robbers were very near. They carried no torch but were coming along the ledge they knew so well, in complete darkness.

Ranni's sharp ears caught the sound of panting. A robber was on the platform! The two Baronians sat perfectly still, hoping that the three sleeping boys would make no sound. They had covered them completely with the rugs so that any snoring might not be heard. It was amazing that Ranni had been able to hear the robbers, because the river made almost as much noise there as anywhere else.

There came the sound of a loud voice and it was clear that all the robbers were now on the platform. Ranni and

Pilescu strained their ears for any signs that the wolf-tailed men were going to explore the wide ledge.

There appeared to be no more sounds at all. Neither Ranni nor Pilescu could hear panting or voices. They sat like statues, hardly breathing, trying to hear any unusual sound above the noise of the water.

They sat like that for ten minutes without hearing a sound. Then, very silently, Ranni rose to his feet. He felt for his torch, and pressed down the switch suddenly. The light flashed out over the platform. It was quite empty!

"They've gone," whispered Ranni. "I thought they must have, for I have heard nothing for the last ten minutes. They did not think of searching this platform. They have gone higher up, probably hoping to catch us in the cave where the great waterfall is."

"That's not so good," said Pilescu, switching off his torch. "If they wait for us there, they will catch us easily. Jack said that Beowald was going to fetch the villagers to hurry after us – it is possible that they might have got as far as the waterfall cave, and might help us. But we can depend on nothing!"

"We will let the boys rest a little longer," said Ranni. "There is no need to rush on, now that the robbers are in front of us, and not at the back! I will watch now, Pilescu, whilst you sleep."

Pilescu was thankful to be able to allow himself to close his eyes. He leaned his big head against the wall at the back, and fell into a deep sleep at once. Ranni was keeping guard, his eyes and ears on the look-out for anything unusual. It was a strange night for him, sitting quietly with his sleeping companions, hearing the racing of the mountain river, watching for wolf-tailed robbers to return!

But they did not return. There was no sound to make Ranni alert. The others slept peacefully, and the boys did not stir. Ranni glanced at his watch after a long time had passed. Six o'clock already! It was sunrise outside the mountain. The world would be flooded with light. Here it was as dark as midnight, and cold. Ranni was glad of his warm cloak.

Pilescu awoke a little while later. He spoke to Ranni.

"Have you heard anything, Ranni?"

"Nothing," said Ranni. "It is nearly seven o'clock, Pilescu. Shall we wake the boys and go on? There is no use in staying here. Even if the robbers are lying in wait for us above, we must push on!"

"Yes," said Pilescu, yawning. "I feel better now. I think I could tackle four or five of those ruffians at once. I will wake the boys."

He awoke them all. They did not want to open their eyes! But at last they did, and soon sat munching some of the bread they had found on the little shelf nearby the night before.

Ranni told them how the robbers had gone by in the night without discovering them.

"It's not very nice to think they're somewhere further up, waiting for us!" said Mike, feeling uncomfortable. "I suppose they'll be in one of the caves. "We'll have to look out!"

"We'll look out all right!" said Jack, who, like Pilescu, felt all the better for his night's sleep. "I'm not standing any nonsense from wolf-tailed robbers!"

They left the platform, and made their way to the ledge that ran beside the river, beyond the platform. As usual Ranni went first, having tied them all together firmly.

"It's not so very far up to the waterfall cave from here, as far as I remember," said Jack. "About two hours or so."

They began to stumble along the rocky ledge again, the water splashing over their feet. The boys were surprised to find that the ledge was now ankle-deep in water.

"It wasn't when we came down this way," said Mike. "Was it as deep as this when you and Pilescu were brought down by the robbers, Ranni?"

"No," said Ranni, puzzled. "It barely ran over the ledge. Look out – it's quite deep here – the river is overflowing its channel by about a foot. We shall be up to our knees!"

So they were. It was very puzzling and rather disturbing. Why was the river swelling like that?

In The Cave Of The Waterfall

The higher they went, the deeper the water became that overflowed the ledge. The river roared more loudly, too. Ranni puzzled over it and then suddenly realized the reason.

"It is the terrific rainstorm that has caused the river to swell!" he called back, his voice rising over the roar of the water. "The rain has soaked deep into the mountain, and has made its way to the river. You know what a rainstorm we had yesterday – it seemed as if whole seas of water had been emptied down on the earth. The river is swelling rapidly. I hope it doesn't swell much more, or we shall find it impossible to get along."

This was a very frightening thought. It would be dreadful to be trapped in the mountain tunnel, with the rushing river rising higher and higher. The three boys put their best feet forward and went as quickly as they could.

When nearly two hours had gone by, they began to hope they were nearing the waterfall cave. The river by now had risen above their knees and it was difficult to stagger along, because the water pulled against them the whole time. Ranni and Pilescu began to feel very anxious.

But, quite suddenly, they heard the sound of the waterfall that fell down into the big cave! It could only be the waterfall they heard, for the noise was so tremendous. "We are nearly there!" yelled Ranni.

"Look out for the robbers!" shouted back Jack.

They rounded the last bit of the ledge, and, by the light of Ranni's torch, saw that at last they were in the big cave, from which led the passage that would take them to the cave below the temple. They all felt very thankful indeed.

There was no sign of the robbers. The five of them went

cautiously into the cave and looked round. By the light of Ranni's torch the waterfall seemed to be much bigger than they had remembered. It fell from a great hole in the roof of the cave, and then ran down the channel to the tunnel, where it disappeared.

"It is greater now," said Ranni. "It must be much swollen by all the rain that fell yesterday. It already fills the hole through which it falls."

"What will happen if the hole can't take all the extra water?" asked Jack, curiously.

"I don't know," said Ranni. "Now, what shall we do next? Where are those robbers? Are they lying in wait for us somewhere? Are they up in the cave below the temple – or have they gone out on the mountain-side to rob again?"

"Well there's nothing for it but to go and see," said Pilescu. You boys stay down here, whilst Ranni and I go through the passage to the other cave."

"No – we'll go with you," said Paul, at once.

"That would be foolish," said Pilescu. "There is no need for all of us to put ourselves in danger. You will stay here until I or Ranni come back to tell you that it is safe for us all to go back down the mountain-side to the castle."

The boys watched the two big Baronians disappear into the narrow passage at the end of the cave opposite the great waterfall. It was difficult to stay behind and wait in patience. They sat in a corner and watched the tremendous fall of water at the other end of the cave.

"It's roaring as if it was angry!" said Jack. "I don't believe that hole is big enough now for all the volume of water to pour through. It will burst it bigger. I'm sure of it!"

"Well, the hole's made through the solid rock," said Mike. "It will have to burst the rock!"

Even as they spoke, a frightening thing happened. The water falling from the roof seemed suddenly to become bigger in volume and noise – and the boys saw a great mass of rock fall slowly from the roof! As Jack had said, the hole was no longer big enough to take the rush of water, and the force of its rush had burst away part of the solid, rocky roof!

Water at once flowed over the floor of the cave, almost to the feet of the astonished boys. They leapt up at once, staring at the water falling from the roof at the other end of the cave.

"I say! I hope the whole roof doesn't give way!" said Jack. "There must be a terrific rush of water to burst through the rock like that."

Nothing more happened, except that the extra volume of water made more noise and flooded the floor of the cave almost up to where the boys stood.

"Well, anyway, we're safe," said Mike. "We are just at the opening of the passage that leads upwards to the other cave. The water comes from the other direction. If it gets deep in here we'll have to go up the passage, that's all, away from it."

It got no deeper, however, so the boys waited patiently. Twenty minutes went by, and there was no sign of the return of Ranni or Pilescu. Mike began to feel worried.

"I wish they'd come back," he said. "I feel as if I can't stay here doing nothing much longer!"

"Whatever are Ranni and Pilescu doing?" said Jack, impatiently. "They must be right out on the mountain-side by now!"

"Let's go up the passage and find out," said Paul, at last. "I simply can't sit here any longer."

"All right," said Mike. "Come on. We can easily rush back if we hear Ranni and Pilescu coming."

They made their way up the narrow, curving passage, leaving behind them the noise of the great waterfall. But before they were half-way up, they heard the sound of someone else coming down!

"That must be Ranni and Pilescu coming back!" said

Mike, in a low voice. "Come on – we'll get back. We don't want to get into trouble for not waiting, as we were told."

They stumbled back down the rocky passage, and came out once more into the cave of the waterfall. It was still falling at the other end, with a mightier roar than ever.

"Here they come!" said Mike, as a light shone out of the passage. He flashed his own torch upwards to welcome Ranni and Pilescu.

And then he and the other two boys stared in horror. Certainly it was Ranni and Pilescu returning – but returning as prisoners! Once again they were captives, angry, but completely helpless! Six or seven robbers were behind them, kicking them and pushing them, holding sharp-pointed knives behind their backs to urge them on.

"Ranni! What's happened?" cried Paul, springing forward.

But before anything could be explained, the robbers, with cries of satisfaction, leapt at the three boys and forced their arms behind them. Mike tried his hardest to get out his scout-knife but it was impossible!

The robbers bound the boys' arms and legs together with thongs of supple leather. No matter how they struggled, they could not free themselves. They were placed on the floor of the cave, like trussed chickens. Ranni and Pilescu stood roaring like angry bulls, trying to free their own hands, which had been tightly tied behind them as before. The robbers tripped them defly to the ground and tied their legs together, too.

Small as they were, the Secret Forest robbers were very strong. Ranni and Pilescu were big giants of men, but the robbers swarmed over them like ants, and by their very smallness and deftness they overcame the two big men.

The robbers chattered together exultantly. Now they had all five prisoners to take back. But suddenly one of them pointed to the water that flowed over the floor of the cave.

They all looked at it in surprise. Clearly they had never

seen water flowing over the floor of the cave before. They looked at the water falling from the now bigger hole in the roof of the cave, at the other end. They saw what had happened, and ran fearfully to the ledge that ran beside the roaring river.

The water was now above their knees. They had left their raft behind them, below the platform-ledge. They gazed in panic at the water. They could not hear themselves speak, so near the waterfall, and ran back to where the five prisoners were, shouting to one another in terror.

The noise of the water grew louder. Everyone gazed fearfully at the hole through which it poured from the roof. And then more of the rocky roof gave way and fell to the floor of the cave with a crash. Water followed it at once, forcing its way out, pouring down into the cave with a noise like thunder.

The robbers gave a scream of terror. They knew that never would they be able to get back to the Secret Forest if they did not go at once, for now that more and more water was pouring down, the river in the mountain tunnel would rise so high that no one would be able to walk beside it on the rocky ledge.

They disappeared in the spray. Jack raised his head and saw them dimly in the distance, trying to force their way on to the ledge beside the river where it entered the tunnel. It was above their waists!

"They'll all be drowned," said Jack. "The water will sweep them off the ledge. It's getting deeper and deeper."

"Don't worry about the robbers!" said Ranni, sitting up with a jerk. "It's ourselves we must worry about! Look at the water – it's right up to us now!"

So it was. It lapped round them. The five captives managed to get themselves upright, though it was difficult, with both hands and feet tied. They struggled with their bonds, but the robbers were too clever at knots for them to be undone or broken.

"We'd better try to get up the passage," said Ranni,

trying to hop towards it with his tied-up legs. But he fell at once. He cracked his head against a rock, for he could not save himself with his hands. He lay quite still, and Paul looked at him in terror.

"He's just knocked out for a minute or two, that's all," said Pilescu, comfortingly. But really, the big Baronian was as frightened now as little Paul. They were all in a terrible plight. At any moment more of the roof might fall in and the cave would be completely flooded with water. They could not help themselves to escape because they were so tightly bound.

"Ranni! Open your eyes!" begged Paul. One of the robbers had left a torch shining on a ledge nearby, and its light shone on to Ranni's face as he lay with his eyes shut, half-leaning against the rocky wall. "Pilescu! How did you get caught like this?"

"We went up into the cave below the temple," said Pilescu. "We found the statue was divided into half, and we climbed up. We could not see a robber anywhere. We went to the mouth of the cave and looked out. We could see nothing at all, because there is a thick mist on the mountain-side this morning. We went back into the cave to return to you, when into the cave rushed all the robbers and flung themselves on us. They must have seen us standing at the entrance. They were waiting for us there! We could not see them in the mist.

"Oh, Pilescu – just as we had got to the end of our journey!" cried Prince Paul. "What are we going to do now? Is Ranni badly hurt? He hit his head so hard on the rock!"

Ranni opened his eyes at that moment and groaned. His head ached badly. He tried to sit upright, and then remembered everything with a rush.

"More of the roof is falling!" cried Jack. He was right. With another tremendous roar a great mass of rock again fell down at the other end of the cave, and a still greater volume of water poured out. It was now all round their legs. The five captives struggled to get up on ledges out of the way of it.

"It is rising higher now," said Mike, watching the water swirling in the cave. The bright light of the torch glittered on the blackness of the icy-cold water. It looked very threatening.

"Pilescu, what *are* we going to do?" said Jack, desperately. "We shall all be drowned soon if we don't do something! Oh, why didn't someone come after us – some of the servants, or villagers. Beowald said he would fetch some!"

Beowald, of course, *had* fetched the villagers, and they had gone down as far as the cave of the waterfall. But they had not been able to guess that the way the boys had gone was along the narrow, rocky ledge beside the rushing river. They had left the cave and gone back to the mountain-side, telling Beowald that he must be mistaken. No one had gone down into those caves below! The robbers and their prisoners must be somewhere on the mountain-side!

They had searched the mountains well, hallooing and shouting for hours. When the thick mist had come up, they had had to leave their search, for, good mountaineers as they were, they could lose themselves in the mist as easily as any child.

Beowald alone had not stopped searching. The mist did not hinder him, for neither darkness nor mists made any difference to him. He wandered about all night long, looking for his friends, the big mountain goat keeping him company.

When the sun was high in the sky Beowald made his way back to the temple-cave. He listened outside. There was no sound. He went to the big stone image at the back. It was still split in half. Beowald stood thinking. Should he go down himself, and seek for the others? The villagers had already said there was nothing below but empty caves, with rushing water in one. Beowald would be lost in a strange place. But something made him decide to try.

The blind goatherd slipped down into the hole, hanging

deftly on to the rope. Down he went, and down, and came at last to the little cave below. He explored it carefully with his hands stretched out in front of him, going round the rocky, irregular walls.

He soon found the opening that led into the narrow, rocky passage. He went down it, feeling before him and beside him with his hands. Down and down went the passage, curving as it descended.

Beowald came out into the cave of the waterfall, and stood there, deafened by the roar. Water swirled over his feet. At first he was so deafened by the terrific noise that he heard nothing more.

And then, to his extreme astonishment, he heard his name called.

"Beowald! Beowald!"

"Look – it's Beowald! Beowald, help us, quickly!"

Beowald the goatherd stood at the entrance of the waterfall cave, his blind eyes seeing nothing, his ears hearing voices he could hardly believe in!

But even more astonished were the five captives! Beowald had appeared before them, like a wizard, just as they had given up all hope of being saved!

Beowald To The Rescue!

'Beowald! Quick! Set us free!" shouted Ranni. The water was already high, and more and more was flooding into the cave. It had increased a great deal in the last few minutes. Ranni was afraid that the whole roof might give way beneath the terrific weight of water – and then there would be no hope for the little company at all.

"What is it? Where are you? What is this water?" cried Beowald, lost in this strange new world of roaring and wetness.

"Beowald! Listen to me!" shouted Ranni, urgently. "Listen carefully. You are standing at the entrance to a cave, where I and the others are, all bound tightly, so that we cannot walk, or free ourselves. Water is pouring into our cave, and we shall be drowned if you do not hurry. Step down, Beowald, walk towards my voice. Do not be afraid."

"I will come," said the blind goatherd. He stepped further into the water, and then stopped, afraid. He was never afraid in his own mountain world. He knew every inch, every rock, every tree. But this was all new to him and strange to him, and it frightened him.

"Hurry, Beowald, hurry!" cried Ranni. "Come to me, quickly. Get our your knife. Cut my bonds."

Beowald stumbled through the water and felt about for Ranni. His hands brushed the big Baronians face. Ranni was half-lying, half-sitting. On his head was an enormous bump where he had struck it against a rock. Beowald's fingers felt the bump, and he wondered what had caused it. His hands ran down Ranni's body and he felt that the man had his arms tied behind his back.

He took out his knife and, with a careful stroke, cut the

leather thongs that bound Ranni's hands together. The big man stretched out his arms gladly, trying to get some strength back into them for they were stiff and swollen with being bound so tightly.

He snatched Beowald's knife from him and cut the thongs that bound his ankles together. He stood up, and at once over-balanced, for the thongs had cut into his legs, and for the moment he could not stand on them. He rose again, and went to Paul.

In a trice the small boy was free, and was trying to get to the entrance of the passage. "Quick, quick!" he cried. "Set the others free, Ranni. They will be drowned!"

As quickly as he could Ranni cut the thongs that bound the others, and set them free. They tried to stagger out of the water that now swirled above their knees. The cave was rapidly filling.

Ranni picked up the torch that was still lying on the rocky ledge, shining brightly into the cave. He held it so that everyone could see how to get into the narrow passage that led upwards to the other cave, away from the water. Beowald had already gone into the passage, anxious to get back to the mountain-side he knew. He felt so strange and so lost underground.

Ranni swung his torch round the cave of the waterfall for the last time – and then he saw that what he had feared might happen, was about to happen! The whole roof of the big cave was giving way! The pressure and weight of the water above it, trying to find its way out of the already enlarged hole, was too much for it. It had to give way. The rain that had fallen in torrents on the mountain-top, had to get away somewhere, and it had found the ordinary channels in the mountain too small for it. It was forcing and pressing everything in its way – and now the roof of the cave had to give in to its enormous pressure.

With a terrific roar the roof fell in, and after it poured the biggest volume of water that Ranni had ever seen. He gave a shout of terror and rushed up the narrow passage after the others. He was afraid that the water might flood even that passage, and trap them before they could get into the other cave!

"What's the matter, Ranni, what's the matter?" cried Paul, hearing the terrified shout.

"Hurry! Hurry! The roof has fallen in and the cave is nothing but swirling water!" panted Ranni. "It will find its way up this passage, before it can get its own level and drain away downwards. Hurry, Paul; hurry, Mike!"

The five in front of him, frightened by the fear in his voice, hurried on as swiftly as they could, stumbling over the rough, rocky way. Beowald was terrified. He was afraid of falling, afraid of the unknown, afraid of the roaring of the water behind him.

The water had found the narrow passage and was making its way up there too. Ranni felt sure he could hear it lapping behind him! He pushed the others on, shouting and yelling, and they, full of panic, went staggering through the dark and winding passage.

"Thank goodness the passage goes upwards all the way," thought Ranni, thankfully, as he came to a steep piece. "Now we are safe! The water cannot reach us here. We are too high. Never will anyone be able to get down into the cave of the waterfall again. There will always be water there now that the roof has fallen in."

They came out into the cave below the temple at last. All of them sank down on the floor, trembling in every limb. Surely there had never been such a narrow escape.

"If Beowald had not come when he did, we should all have been drowned by now," said Paul, in a choking voice. "Oh, Beowald – however was it you came down there just at that moment?"

Far away, down the passage, the muffled roar of the water could still be heard. Beowald's voice rose clearly above it:

"The search party went down to this cave and to the waterfall cave, but they could not find you. They are

272

seeking for you still out on the mountain. I was anxious, and when I came into the temple-cave, I felt that I must come down by myself, though I was afraid. That is how I found you."

"We have had such adventures!" said Mike, beginning to feel quite a hero. "We've been to the Secret Forest, Beowald!"

"That is marvellous," said the blind goatherd. "Surely no man has even set foot there before!"

"Oh, yes!" said Paul. "The robbers live there, Beowald. They must have lived there for years and years. Ranni, will the robbers ever be able to come up the mountain river now, climbing along that ledge, to get to Killimooin this side?"

"Never," said Ranni. "We are well rid of them!"

Little by little the boys stopped trembling from their exertions, and their hearts beat less fast. They began to feel able to stand. Mike got up and found that he was quite all right again.

"I want to get back to the castle," he said. "I want to see the girls and tell them all that has happened to us. My word, won't they be jealous of our adventures!"

"I want something to eat," said Paul. "I'm terribly hungry. I shall ask Yamen to give me the very nicest, most delicious food she's got."

The thought of food made everyone eager to set out again. Ranni got up and pulled Paul to his feet. "Well, come along then," he said. "We shall soon be home now!"

One by one they hauled themselves up the rope that led to the temple-cave. Their feet found the rough places to help them, as they went up, and at last all six of them were standing in the big temple-cave.

It seemed dark there, darker than it should have been. Ranni looked towards the entrance.

"We can't go home!" he said in disappointment. "Look at that mist! It is like a thick fog. We could not see our hands in front of our faces if we went out in that. We should be completely lost in two minutes."

273

"Well, we must stay here till the mist clears," said Pilescu. "I am afraid it will not clear for some hours. When the mountain mists are as thick as this one, they last a long time."

"Oh, Pilescu! We *must* get back now we're so near home!" said Paul, almost in tears. "We must! I'm so hungry I can't stay here one more minute."

Jack looked at the blind goatherd, who was standing, quietly listening.

"Beowald can guide us back," said Jack. "You know your way by night, or in the thickest mist, don't you, Beowald?"

Beowald nodded. "It is all the same to me," he said. "If you wish, I will take you back to Killimooin Castle. My feet know the way! Is the mist very thick? I can feel that there is one, but I do not know how thick."

"It's the thickest one I've ever seen," said Pilescu, peering out. "I'm not at all sure I like to trust myself even to you, Beowald!"

"You are safe with me on the mountain-side," said the goatherd. He took out his little flute and played one of his queer tunes on it. An enormous horned head suddenly appeared at the entrance of the cave, and everyone jumped in fright.

"Ha, old one, you are there!" cried Beowald, as he heard the patter of the big goat's hooves. "Keep by me, old one, and together we will lead these friends of ours safely down our mountain-side!"

"Take hands," ordered Ranni. "Don't let go, whatever you do. If anything happens, and you have to let go, shout and keep on shouting so that we keep in touch with one another. We have had enough narrow escapes for one day!"

Everyone took hands. Beowald went out of the cave, playing his flute, his left hand firmly clasped in Ranni's big one. Behind Ranni came Paul, then Mike, then Jack, then Pilescu, all firmly holding hands.

"I feel as if we're going to play 'Ring-a-ring-of-roses'!" said Jack, with a laugh.

"Well, don't let's play the 'all-fall-down' part," said Mike at once. "It wouldn't be at all a good thing to do on a steep mountain-side like this."

They felt light-hearted at the idea of going home at last. With Beowald's music sounding plaintively through the mist, they stumbled along down the steep mountain-path. Two or three times one or other of the boys fell, and broke hands. They shouted at once, and the party stopped and joined together again.

It was slow work walking in the thick mist. They could barely see the person in front. Only Beowald walked steadily and surely. He could see with his feet!

"Don't go too fast, Beowald," said Ranni, as he felt the little prince dragging behind him. "Remember, we cannot see anything – not even our own feet."

"Neither can Beowald!" thought Mike. "How marvellous he is! Whatever should we have done without him?"

They stumbled downwards slowly for more than an hour and a half. Then Ranni gave a shout.

"We're almost there! I can hear the hens clucking at the back of the castle, and a dog barking. Bear up, Paul, we are nearly home!"

They came to the flight of steps, and stumbled up them, tired out. Beowald slipped away with the big goat. The others hardly saw him go. They were so excited at getting back in safety. Killimooin Castle at last! They hammered on the big iron-studded door impatiently.

The End Of The Adventure

The door flew open – and there stood Yamen with Nora and Peggy close behind her. With screams of excitement and delight the two girls flung themselves on the boys. Yamen beamed in joy. The lost ones were home again! They were dragged indoors, and Yamen ran up the big stone staircase, shouting at the top of her voice:

"Majesty! They're back! The little prince is safe! He is safe!"

The whole household gathered to hear the story of the returned wanderers. Servants peered round the door. The smaller children, clinging to the hands of their nurses, gazed open-eyed at the untidy, dirty boys and the two big Baronians. Tooku, his arm still bound up, came running up from the kitchen. What an excitement there was!

"We've been to the Secret Forest!" announced Paul, grandly. He had forgotten his tiredness and his hunger. He was the Prince of Baronia, back from rescuing his men.

"The Secret Forest!" repeated Yamen, with awe in her voice, and all the servants sighed and nodded to one another. Truly their prince was a prince!

"No, Paul, no – you cannot have been there!" said his mother. She glanced at Ranni and Pilescu, who nodded, smiling.

"It's true, mother," said Paul. "We found that Ranni and Pilescu had been captured by the robbers, and taken down below the temple-cave. There's a mountain river flowing underground there, and it's the only way there is to the Secret Forest!"

Bit by bit the whole story came out. Everyone listened, entranced.

276

When Paul came to the part where the roof had fallen in and they had almost been drowned, his mother caught him up into her arms, and wept tears over him. Paul was very indignant.

"Mother! Let me go! I'm not a baby, to be cried over!"

"No – you're a hero, little lord!" said Yamen, admiringly. "I go to get you a meal fit for the greatest little prince that Baronia has ever had!"

She turned and went down to her kitchen, planning a really royal meal. Ah, that little Paul – what a prince he was! Yamen marvelled at him, and at the two English boys, as she quickly rolled out pastry on her kitchen table. She would give them such a meal. Never would they forget it!

"Where is Beowald?" asked the Queen, when she had listened again and again to the thrilling tale of how Beowald had appeared just in time to free them before the cave filled with water. "I must thank Beowald and reward him."

"Didn't he come in with us?" said Jack. But no, Beowald was not there. He was far away on his mountain-side, playing to his goats, hidden by the mist.

"Mother, I want Beowald to come and live with me," said Paul. "I like him, and he plays the flute beautifully. That shall be his reward, mother."

"If he wants to, he shall," promised the Queen, though she did not think that the blind goatherd would want such a reward. "Now, you must get yourselves clean, and then a good meal will be ready. Oh, how thankful I am that you are all back in safety!"

Half an hour later the whole party looked quite different. They were clean again, and had on spotless clothes. How tired they looked, thought the girls. But perhaps they were only hungry!

Yamen had prepared a marvellous meal. The smell of cooking came up from the big kitchen, and the five travellers could hardly wait for the first dish to appear – a thick, delicious soup, almost a meal in itself!

The boys had never eaten so much before. Ranni and

Pilescu put away enormous quantities, too. Paul had to stop first. He put down his spoon with a sigh, leaving some of his pudding on his plate.

"I can't eat any more," he said, and his eyelids began to close. Pilescu gathered him up in his arms to carry him to bed. Paul struggled feebly, half asleep.

"Put me down, Pilescu! I don't want to be carried! How could you treat me like a weakling?"

"You are no weakling, little lord!" said Pilescu. "Did you not rescue me and Ranni by your own strength and wisdom? You are a lion!"

Paul liked hearing all this. "Oh, well, Mike and Jack are lions too," he said, and gave an enormous yawn. He was asleep before he reached his bedroom, and Pilescu undressed him and laid him on the bed, fast asleep!

The girls hung on to Mike and Jack, asking questions and making them tell their story time and again.

"We were so worried about you!" said Nora. "When the villagers came and said they couldn't find any of you, it was dreadful. And oh, that terrible storm! We hoped and hoped you were not caught in it."

"Well, we were," said Jack, remembering. "And it was all because of that storm, and the torrents of rain that came with it, that the waterfall in the cave became so tremendous and swelled up the river that ran from it. I wonder if the robbers got down safely! My word, if they got down to where they left their raft, and got on to it, they'd go down that river at about sixty miles an hour!"

"Now Mike and Jack, you must go to bed, too," said big Ranni, coming up. "Paul is fast asleep. You have had a very hard time, and you need rest, too. Come."

The children themselves could hardly believe that all their adventures really had happened, when they awoke next day. The boys lay and blinked at the ceiling. They felt stiff, but happy. They had rescued Rannie and Pilescu. They had found the robbers. They had been in the Secret Forest. They couldn't help feeling very pleased with themselves.

"Mother, I'm going up on the mountain-side to find Beowald," said Paul at breakfast time. "I'm going to tell him he must leave his goats and come to live with me. When we go back to the palace he must come too. I shall never forget all he did for us."

"Take Ranni and Pilescu with you," said his mother. "I'm afraid of those robbers still."

"You needn't be," said Paul. "You will never see them again! Ranni! Will you come with me, and find Beowald?"

Ranni nodded. He and Pilescu looked none the worse for their adventure, except that Ranni had a great bump on his head.

The mist had entirely gone. The mountains shone clear all around, their summits sharp against the sky. The five children, with Ranni and Pilescu, mounted their ponies, and turned their shaggy heads up the mountain-side.

They came to the temple-cave after about an hour. Beowald was not anywhere there. Ranni lifted his great voice and shouted down the mountain-side:

"BEOWALD! BEOWALD!"

They heard an answering cry, musical and clear, coming from a distance. They sat down to wait for the blind goatherd. Paul was already planning a uniform for him. He would show Beowald what princely gratitude was!

Soon the children heard the playing of the little flute Beowald always carried with him. Then, rounding a curve nearby came a flock of capering goats. At the head of them marched the old goat with his big curling horns.

"Here he comes!" said the little prince, and he ran to meet the goatherd. Beowald came to sit down with the company, asking them how they felt after their adventure.

"Oh, Beowald – it was a thrilling time," said Paul. "I don't know what would have happened to us if it hadn't been for you. I want to reward you, Beowald. We are all grateful to you – but I, most of all."

"Do not speak to me of rewards, little lord," said the goatherd, and he played a little tune on his flute.

"Beowald, I want you to come and live with me," said Paul. "You shall come back to the big palace, and I will give you a uniform. You shall no longer herd goats on the mountain-side! You shall be my man and my friend!"

Beowald looked towards the little prince with his dark, empty eyes. He shook his head and smiled.

"Would you make me unhappy, little prince? I would break my heart in a strange place, under a roof. The mountains are my home. They know me and I know them. They know the feel of my feet, and I know the song of their winds and streams. And my goats would miss me, especially this old one."

The big horned goat had been standing by Beowald all the time, listening as if he understood every word. He stamped with his forefoot, and came close to the goatherd, as if to say, "Master, I agree with you! You belong here! Do not go away!"

"I did so want to reward you," said Paul disappointed.

"You *can* reward me, little lord," said Beowald, smiling. "Come to see me sometimes, and let me play my tunes to you. That will be enough reward for me. And I will make you a flute of your own, so that you too may learn the mountain songs and take them back to the big palace with you."

"Oh, I'd like that," said Paul, picturing himself at once playing a flute, and making all the boys at school stare at him in admiration. "You must teach me all the tunes you know, Beowald!"

"Let's go into the cave and have a look round," said Jack. They all went in, but Ranni and Pilescu forbade the children to slip down the hole to the cave below.

"No," he said. "No more adventures whilst we are here! We have had enough to last us for a lifetime – or, at any rate, for two months!"

"Now the Secret Forest will never again be visited by

anyone!" said Mike. "The only way to it is gone. The water will always keep people from travelling through the mountain to get to it."

"And the robber-people will never be able to leave the Secret Forest!" said Jack. "How strange! They will have to live there, year after year, a people lost and forgotten."

This was a strange thought. "But perhaps it is a good punishment for robbers," said Nora, thoughtfully. "It will be like keeping them in a great prison, which they can never escape from to rob other people!"

"We shall never see the Secret Forest again," said Mike, sadly. "It is such an exciting place!"

But he was wrong. They did see it again, for when, towards the end of a lovely holiday, their mother and father flew over in the White Swallow to fetch the children. Ranni took the whole company, Captain and Mrs Arnold as well, in the blue and silver aeroplane, right over the Killimooin mountains, and over the Secret Forest!

"There it is, Daddy!" cried Mike. "Look! You can see where the river flows out of the mountain. Go down lower, Ranni. Look, there's where it goes into the Secret Forest – and where it comes out again, after doubling back on itself. Oh, and there's where it disappears into a chasm, falling right down into the heart of the earth!"

The aeroplane was now so low that it almost seemed as if it was skimming the tops of the trees! The robbers heard the great noise, and some of them ran out from the forest in wonder.

"There's one of the robbers – and another – and another!" shouted Paul. "Goodbye, robber-people! You'll have to live in the Secret Forest for ever and ever and ever."

The aeroplane swept upwards and left the Secret Forest behind. Over Killimooin it went, and the children heaved a sigh.

"It's been the loveliest holiday we've ever had!" said Nora. "I wonder what adventures we'll have *next* time?"

"You've had quite enough," said Ranni.

But they are sure to have plenty more. They are that kind of children!